LITTLE OCCULT AFFAIRS

UNTOLD MYSTERIES UNFOLD

Edited & Compiled by

Yash Runwal

Inkfeathers Publishing

First Published in India in 2020
Inkfeathers Publishing
New Delhi 110095

www.inkfeathers.com

Co-Authored By

Tanishk Patil ~ Snigdhaa Ghai & Bhavey Wadhwa ~ Kuldeep
Cariappa ~ Manoj Vaz ~ Akshara Bruno ~ Midhun Harilal ~
Vishvak ~ Spandan Nath ~ Soumya Srivastava ~ Nena Patel ~
Sachin Shanbhag ~ Krishna Anap ~ Ranjitha Ravindran ~ Guduru
Sai Bhuvan ~ Nayanika Chatterjee ~ Veddansh Kapoor ~ Karvi
Gupta ~ Hari Pudipeddi ~ Aastha Gupta ~ Ranjana Reghunath ~
Tirtha Mutha ~ Khushi Thakare

CONTENTS

ABOUT THE EDITOR

YASH RUNWAL
∞ ♥

An arts student by day, a reader, poet and sometimes a stargazer by night, Yash is the archetypal teen following his heart's desire to the edge in every possible aspect of his life - be it mental, physical or metaphysical altogether. Ambivert and massively influenced by dark humour, he spends most of his nights planning to kill the world with kindness and some people in it without it. If he wishes he simply doesn't just want but as he quotes is "destined to attain it."

EDITOR'S NOTE

Little Occult Affairs and its journey is a brainchild, a shower thought, a creation and redemption of my love of writing, craving of mystery and odium of my writer's block. Being an avid reader myself, I had always wanted to pay forward something to the world of words that has given me so much. Compiling amazing hand-picked stories of 23 mystical minds was just it.

My inclination towards elements like death, darkness, space, poison, disruptions, murder, cataclysm, mystery, love, infinities and much more which are equally found in my speech, thoughts and writing has led me to hunting down like-minded authors with a calibre enough to satisfy and feed these elements in the mind of the reader through the stories in this anthology, giving them a thought-chain pulling them towards the depths of abyss and also to give reader the vision to picturize the mystery of life altogether.

In this journey my close friends have been nothing less than my backbone, my family and the writers in this anthology have been extremely cooperative throughout the process. The anthology is nothing but my very soul on white pages which will give the reader an insight in to all the lives that I have lived or the ones that I want to.

LITTLE OCCULT AFFAIRS

STORY ONE

HOURS OF GREEN

---

by Tanishk Patil

Five O'clock

Deep's Apartment

Getting out of the cab, Parth called Omkar, informing him that he had arrived near Deep's apartment, and that he would stop by a bakery first to buy a cake. A soft 'meow' made him turn his head towards the curb to find a golden-haired tiny kitten staring right up at him.

"Oh, well hello there, little meow," said Parth.

The cat replied with another meow.

Like any typical cat person, Parth moved forward to pet her, only to find that she, too, was a typical cat, to run away to a distance, and meow back. Being used to this, Parth followed her quietly, not making her do anything impulsive. She kept walking away, and he kept following her until they reached the corner of the main street, at the crossroads by a traffic signal.

After a moment of silence between both of them, there was a sudden noise, loud and screeching. Parth looked to his right, and saw that the signal had tuned green. Loads of two-wheelers, cars and a couple of trucks honked their way through the traffic, making dust fly all over. Like a wave hitting the seacoast, a green sedan came to a stop in front of Parth and the kitten. The doors of the passenger seat opened and a slender woman, probably twenty-three, four years elder to Parth, bent down and picked the cat up between her ringed fingers. Her sunglasses, tight enough on her eyes so as to conceal them completely, gave him a blank look, perhaps telling him to turn around and not walk, but run away.

A few seconds later, a sudden surge of pain shook Parth. It was a bullet shot at his leg, just missing his hip. The blood had flown quick and in a large amount, making him both scared and confused, confusion being the more prominent state of being. He looked at his thigh feeling dazed. The blood loss made him feel weak and not having control over his mind made him feel weaker. As he started falling to the ground a while later, he felt his hand grab onto something. It was hard; but felt warm in the November evening breeze. It was strong; feeling like it had some strength of its own. Then he felt fingers, which were not his. In his last long second of consciousness, all he saw was an arm, covered in a full green sleeve, pulling him up. After a whiplash to his neck, Parth was surrounded with darkness.

△▼

Thirty Past Five

Deep's Apartment

Omkar: He's not answering.

Deep raised his head from his palms, his hair dishevelled.

"Now what do we do? We've tried calling him thrice from my phone and twice from yours. Where is he?" Omkar's voice sounded frustrated, which was as rare as rare can be.

Deep: Well, we've already tried all the cake shops in the vicinity. I don't think he'll be wandering off somewhere far only to buy a cake or even a gift. Ugh, my birthdays always suck."

"Maybe we should try calling Purva. Maybe he..."

"Don't even finish your sentence. I don't want to think about how my ex 'lured' my best friend into dating her. At least not on my birthday."

"Okay, how about we take a stroll outside, see if something rings."

And something did ring. It was Omkar's phone.

Deep: Please tell me it's Parth.

Omkar shot Deep a sad look with his dry brown eyes.

"It's Purva."

△▼

Thirty Past Six

Purva's Apartment

Deep: Are you kidding me!

Purva: Do you think I am?

"You better not be."

"Well I am not! Parth is as important to me as he is to you guys, if not more."

"Oh please, you're just going to ditch him in a few weeks and find some other guy to pay for your stuff."

"Don't you da…"

Omkar: Guys, please, it's been four minutes since we've been in this apartment, and it's been a long time since Parth is missing. You guys have to co-operate."

"Tell her that," screamed Deep.

"I'm telling this to everyone here! Stop yelling and think!"

"I'm sorry, okay?"

Purva: We can't do anything. Those guys are going to come in this apartment in another… sixteen minutes, that's what they said on the call. They told me that they'll be informing me about Parth, where and how he his, and what they are going to do with him. But I'm sure nothing that sort is going to happen. They'll just take all of us, too.

Deep: That's real hopeful of you.

"I think we've all watched enough movies to know what these kind of things lead to."

Omkar: Well, this isn't a movie. We won't let it be a movie. And even if it is a movie, we'll make sure that the good guys win.

△▼

Fifty-Nine Past Six

Purva's Apartment

The next sixteen minutes passed by quickly. Then Purva saw a green sedan pull up by the sidewalk. A man got out from the back seat followed by a woman, who though slender, seemed strong and hard, both mentally and physically. The man looked dumb, according to the stereotype of heavy men. He looked like the only thing he ate was meat, eggs and steroids. His bald head did not shine. The weight in his abdomen made his green blazer look small. Purva told the boys what she saw, and they all took positions. The studio apartment was small for three people to fit in, but it was big enough to hide.

Entering from the door, there was a kitchen counter to the right, and to its right was a sink, and to its right, a refrigerator. Straight ahead was what could be called a living room, with a couch on the right and a TV set on the left wall. Straighter still was a balcony overlooking a street, some buildings, cafes, a theatre, and a train station. Before the TV set, on the left, was a door which led to the only bedroom, on whose left was the bathroom. It was a place to which Deep had gotten used to, and to which Omkar didn't want to. The doorbell rang, and the boys in the bedroom clenched the knives in their hands, stretched and loosened up. Purva opened the door followed by a short three-sentence conversation. Heels clicked on the floor. Four heels, two of them smooth, two of them slow. The woman had entered first. Following the sound, the boys figured that the woman was sitting on the couch, the man wasn't. A light rattle in the kitchen. Sound of water poured in glass. Omkar looked at Deep who had his eyes closed. He figured it was to keep himself calm, something he might've learned from his yoga training.

The boys tried to listen through the door. They couldn't hear much, but they figured that Purva was talking in a voice louder than usual to let them hear and know where the conversation was heading to. It seemed normal for the first five minutes. Normal again for another five minutes. Then they heard Purva gasp. Omkar tried to fight off all the thoughts coming to his head. Is Parth hurt? Is he dead? What might've they done to him? Omkar wanted to slap himself for such thoughts, but he couldn't.

They heard Purva's voice, then the woman's, Purva's voice, the woman's.

Purva's voice trembled. The woman got up and started moving with the man following her. Purva seemed too dazed to move. While leaving, the woman said something which made Purva scream, "But why?"

Deep opened the door slightly, only enough to let a few mosquitoes go through.

The woman: Because we value paper more than people.

Her voice was as blank as the evening air.

When they left, the two boys abandoned their hiding post and rushed to the living room. They saw Purva sitting on the couch, her head in her hands. Visibly dismayed, she was taking short breaths in, probably crying. Deep hesitated to do anything. Omkar wasn't sure if he should do anything. A moment later, Deep sat beside her, put his arm around her, pulled her closer, and rested her head on his shoulder. She let out a cry - soft but painful, and buried her head in his chest as they hugged.

Omkar got a glass of water for both of them. She wiped her eyes on the sleeve of her pullover. Several minutes passed. The only sound they heard was of the vehicles on the streets and the clock above the TV.

Purva broke the silence: They kidnapped him. They have him held in a house. They said they're taking care of him, because they are going to sell him.

Her chin trembled. "They are going to sell him to the highest bidder. They earn a lot of money that way. And that's the only reason they're doing this for - money and power. They said they're going to build an organization so powerful that the next name the World Order will know will be theirs."

Silence.

She continued, "The woman said the last time she will see him will be in The Royale on Saturday, one hour after noon."

△▼

Eight O'clock

Purva's Apartment

Seventeen hours. Fourteen kilometres. No idea how to get in. No idea how to get out. The first thing that came to their mind was to imitate those people. What would set them apart from others? Green blazers? Green cars?

Green?

They had but one car, Deep's. It was white. Not really his colour, but it was a gift from his dad.

Deep: Now what do we do? Colour it?

Omkar: Can we really do that? We don't have much time.

Purva: Wait a second. I'll call someone.

"Okay we've got an appointment for our car."

Deep: Who was it?

"An old friend," she said, getting in the back seat.

△▼

Ten O'clock

Purva's Apartment

Fifteen Hours

The car now looked green, dark and shiny. They ate dinner with whatever they had in the kitchen- instant noodles, instant pasta, bread and leftover gravy from last night.

Omkar: Okay, what next?

Purva: We call the police and assist them. We tell them that we have a decoy vehicle. We get their back up. When we get in the hotel, we signal them. They storm the place and we secure Parth. We win. Then we celebrate like there isn't no tomorrow.

Deep called the cops: Hello. Yeah we are reporting about a kidnapping.

△▼

Fifteen Past Eleven

Purva's Apartment

Thirteen Hours Forty-Five Minutes

Omkar screamed: What in hell was that? The cops can't do anything?

Purva stared into blankness. She thought if the police failed to respond to other people, too, in such times. She wondered how many times people might've disappeared and their families might've called the police and they would've been let down.

Omkar: Ugh man, Parth. What have you gotten yourself into?

After six minutes of total silence, the doorbell rang. They shot each other confused looks.

"It's the green guys. The cops told them that we had called. Now we're successfully going to the auction if we don't die here."

Deep: You aren't going to die on my watch.

Omkar looked at him, nodded and picked up the knife. So did Deep.

Purva waited for the approval and opened the door. She moved parallel to the door's trajectory resulting in being hidden behind the door. Deep pounced forward and shoved the knife straight. He felt his hand go left then up. Then he felt a blow in his armpit, then his abdomen, then the floor slipped from his shoes, and the whole world seemed to go down, as he went up and collided straight on the floor on his back, only mindful enough to stop his head from banging on the floor. He looked up; the man looked down. He wasn't the fat, bald and dumb man and neither was he wearing green.

"I'm Tanmay, Counter Terrorism Operatives Organization. We happened to overhear your call to the police."

"Uh, okay, what?" asked Omkar

Tanmay: I work with a group of people. We track calls to the police and keep up with the happenings. And then, as it mostly happens, if the police fail to act on time, or fail to act at all, we move in.

Purva: So, you're like, vigilante guys.

"You can say that."

Omkar: So, you're here to help us? Where are the rest of your friends?

"Nah, you just have me."

Sitting on the floor, Deep: Ah man, are you serious? You tell us you're one of the people who do stuff to keep the place safe, and now you're saying we aren't getting help from you guys?

"You are getting help. I am the help."

"Who are you, John Wick?"

"No, I'm the guy you sent to kill John Wick."

"Classic," Omkar said, having nostalgia of watching the movie with Parth.

Purva: I like you already.

Deep: Of course, you do. Look, Tanmay or whatever it is, if you pull off anything stupid, and if I get the faintest hint that you're not what you're saying you are, you are a dead man.

"I'd like to see you try."

"Yes, you would."

△▼

One O'clock

Purva's Apartment

Twelve Hours

Tanmay: Get some sleep. You might need it.

Purva: You're welcome to stay here if you want.

Deep: Of course, you are.

"Would you shut up for a minute? He's helping us out; can't we be a bit generous?"

"Actually, no thank you. I have a reservation at The Royale."

They all exchanged looks. After a brief talk, they figured that his organization already knows what is going on.

When Tanmay left, Purva went in her bedroom and Deep and Omkar made themselves comfortable on the couch. They turned the TV on but couldn't find any cricket except for highlights, so they turned it back off, and slept.

△▼

Seven O'clock

Purva's Apartment

Six Hours

A short six hours later, their doorbell rang. Omkar was the first to wake up, then Purva, and then they woke Deep up. The bell rang again.

Tanmay: Hey, it's me.

They recognized the sound from earlier that night. Deep let out a disgusted sigh and fell back on the couch, hoping to continue whatever dream he was having. Purva opened the door.

"Good morning," Purva said.

Omkar: Did you even sleep?

He filled a glass of water and handed it to Tanmay.

Tanmay: Yes, I had enough. Thank you.

"Chai?"

Deep raised his hand and said yes, his voice muffled by a pillow. Tanmay agreed to have a cup too.

Purva: I want coffee.

Omkar smirked and said, "Make that yourself."

He poured some milk in a pot for his chai.

Tanmay: Everybody, hurry. We have to reach the hotel in an hour.

After a lot of confusion, disagreement, discussion and planning, Tanmay told them that the only way they were going to get in the auction was being inside the hotel before it starts. He said he had plotted plans, places and exits while he was in the hotel.

As per the plan, Tanmay would secure the cameras facing backstage, where the people who were being sold at the auction would be kept. When he would spot Parth, he would signal Deep, who would be in a bellboy's clothes. Omkar would wait at the back exit of the auditorium, in a waiter's clothes, with a table, covered with cloth. Deep would escort Parth outside, secure him under Omkar's table and both of them would flee the scene. With the table, Omkar would enter the kitchen and take his table to the back entrance, where Parth would get in Tanmay's car and he would take him to Deep's apartment as Purva's apartment's location is already known to the 'ReCyclists.'

Purva: ReCyclists? That's what those people call themselves?

"Yes. Apparently, they're very proud of recycling people."

"Well, where do I come in?"

"You will be the deviator. Wherever you see those guys, you tell them 'Madam needs a drink."

"Explain," said Purva, instantly

"Whenever the Madam wants something done, she says that she needs a drink. Whoever does that work for her gets rewarded, and after finishing the work, they say, 'Your drink has been served.'"

Omkar: Big Drama.

Tanmay: You bet.

△▼

Eight O'clock

Street 74

Five Hours

Cruising in Tanmay's car, which was already green, Deep felt pumped. He felt good picturing Parth's smile. This crisis, though big, seemed achievable now. As much as he hated Tanmay, partly for his physical strengths and partly because he was flirting back and forth with Purva, he also felt confident around him. Deep's faith in Omkar, and now in Tanmay, made him feel more awake than he had been in the past two days.

Omkar was doing what he did best. He was sitting quietly, revising the scenes through his head.

In the front seat, Purva sipped her coffee and exchanged a few glances with Tanmay.

At thirty past eight, they could see The Royale around the corner, in its grandeur, now filled with horror. Tanmay turned right, to the opposite side of the hotel, into an alley. He got out, opened the trunk and handed them the decoy clothes. He did it as quickly as possible as he was starting to get nauseous by holding his breath. He closed the car's doors again and breathed hard. Then he looked inside the car from the back and saw confusion, irritation, anger, fear, and struggle to open the doors. He wanted to enjoy, smile and laugh and cherish the moment. But his loyalty got the better of him. He dialled the number he liked to dial the most.

After a short second, the call was answered. After another second, when he saw Omkar, Purva and Deep fall unconscious, he said, "Madam, your drink has been served."

HALLUCINATIONS

by Snigdhaa Ghai and Bhavey Wadhwa

He was ready to walk in, his head swamped with a million questions. It had been a while that he had been struggling, and it was time to face the truth, confront his feelings or whatever haunted his thoughts. With a deep long sigh, he countered his escapist thoughts with determined ones and walked in. The office was cosy, it had a warm aura and comforting interiors. It was not as unnerving as he had expected a therapist's office to be. He asked himself again - why was he really there - and the answer came to him like a soft murmur from inside that said he was there because the world had started saying that he had bouts of hallucinations.

He was aware that stepping inside meant more than just blabbering about what had really happened. It was a secret he hadn't shared with anyone, ever...till now. It wasn't going to be easy; he knew it. He would have to search inside him and open up layer by layer to unearth the secrets he had so consciously buried inside himself. He just hoped it wouldn't be as tough as he imagined it would be. No one who really knew could keep it with them, it had to end when it began. It was like a disease where he was the patient zero, and it had to end. No one could live and survive with it.

His eyes landed on the calm and still figure seated on a chair and he thought, "How unearthly it is for someone to be so still." The therapist really did possess some level of calmness, and collectedness. He felt like he was at a lack of words, how did these things usually start?

"Umm, hello. Is this Dr. Sethi?"

"Yes. Please come in. Mr. Sehra, I assume?"

The therapist's voice was deep and contained. He was a young-looking man, presumably in his mid-30s. He was attractive in a nonchalant manner and his confidence radiated from his posture. There was something soothing in his demeanour that made him seem like the right person for the job. He gestured for him to take a seat, and so he did.

"So, tell me Mr. Sehra, what brings you here?"

"Please call me Abhishek. And I don't really know why I am here. People say that something is off about me. I don't know what it is, but I can guess when it happened. I want to share that with you, it should help me fix myself."

"Okay Abhishek, I'm here to help you. Share your story with me. Here, help yourself to a cup of coffee, settle in. We can start slower, by sharing some basic things about yourself. Help me get to know you better."

"Okay, makes sense. So, I am Abhishek Sehra, oh wait I already mentioned that." He chuckled, embarrassed. "Well, I am a historian, I am 20 years old, and I am passionate about my work. I love going to old sites, digging up stuff, just finding cool facts. I look into old myths and legends to find the reality behind them, if any. I specialise in studying the proofs of folklore in smaller regions and studying the regional tales."

"That sounds interesting. Anything in specific, anything you remember or comes to the top of your mind? Something you'd like to share with me."

"Actually, there is. It is about the time when I was visiting a small village in Himachal Pradesh to study the local myths about a ghost that wandered in an old mansion. As the story goes, there was a young couple in love who was going to get married soon. One day, a lady accused the girl of not having a shadow and saying that she was a witch who had lured the young man into her trap. The boy knew that it wasn't true, he was a man of reason. The villagers, however, burned her alive. Soon after, the lovesick boy killed himself too. He had been telling people that he couldn't live without her. Her voice echoed in his head, he could hear her calling out to him, addressing him with love and writing poems for him. He needed to be next to her. His soul is said to hold the mansion, and that he had resolved to get his revenge. It is believed that the ghost recites poetry to capture the attention of people inside the mansion and when they are drawn to the sad and beautiful poetry, he kills them. No one dared to venture in, fearing their demise. The few who did trespass, never came out alive." "Okay, and did you go to that village then? Were you successful in finding the origins of the story?"

He was prepared to open up now. As he entered the realm of truth all over again, reality and instances turned into perspiration, rolling down his forehead. The only comfort he felt was the hotness that his coffee radiated. He got up from the couch and walked his way to the window slowly. Standing there, he shut his eyes to focus and face his past with all his might.

Closely observing his body language, the psychiatrist sat, trying to look into his eyes and read his mind but all he could get was a glimpse of a mysterious smile that gave way to his words. He was a mystery, a closed one, that was clear. The psychiatrist knew that he was going to have a tough time with this patient, but that was the high point of his career - to meet mysterious people once in a while, with different stories that don't begin with them crying or end in the same.

By the time his story was ready to evolve from the depths of his deepest nightmares, the aura had changed into something that none of them ever felt before. The small noises like the ticking of the clock became prominent because of the eerie silence that resounded within those four walls. The room was stinking with the curiosity upheld, the tension in the air thick enough to be cut with a knife.

With a sigh of fear and relief, he began, "Ominous was the word I would choose to describe that house.

The floors so well furnished, the wallpapers efficiently selected.

Like an intoxicating beauty and temple of aesthetic luring, it stood.

But who knew the play of captivity, the devoid veiled inside?"

He ended his monologue with a small sigh, his words heavy and poetic, as if he had taken a lot of time to carefully choose all his words, so that they fit together perfectly.

A well thought of account - that was a new thing for a therapist. Usually people come and rant, they divert, they sob, they work on extremes between facts and emotions, but never before had he seen someone give such a detailed account of a house.

He continued, "Somewhere guarded by the shallow hills and eerie valleys, was built the very farmhouse.

Having billions at valuation, drowned in natural beauty it stood. The clouds thundered as loud as they could,

The lighting so silvery made my heart thump more emphatically the moment I stepped in for the first time.

I was there for the first time, and hopefully the last.

Nothing scared me, yet something about that place pulled you into it yet shunned you away."

The psychiatrist sat glancing at the puzzling incident that his patient narrated. He hadn't mentioned what he did, but he must have been a writer because he did have a certain way with words. Not reading too much into the beauty of the words, and the depth with which he spoke, he tried to dwell on the meaning of the words that were spoken. His thoughts seemed as if they had seen the light of the day, been liberated in a way. There was an odd stillness in his voice, yet it was shaky in some ways, like a permanent tiredness had seeped into it.

"Suddenly, silence surrounded me.

When I was outside, there was nature's voice all around me, and in here, everything grew still as if this was a different world in itself.

The silence was broken with the falling of my keys on the ground, and it resounded and echoed as if there was a ripple effect.

The sound so loud, a menace it became and pierced through my ears.

Keys had fallen before, the ghastly effect of the noise they made was new. Oh, the impending disaster!

Windows began to rattle, winds blew cyclonically. The night was the darkest ever, the rattling the most terrifying that I had ever seen.

Heartbeat getting faster, I rushed to the room. It was the first-time thing that actually added up to seem like a disaster.

All the hangings crashed on the floor due to the vibration, even though it was a logical explanation, but it still seemed rather odd.

I was least bothered or so I told myself, I was safe inside the four walls of the room."

He rested his elbows on the windowsill, shifting his weight from one foot to the other. He still hadn't faced the therapist. A lot of people did that, they did not look at him while talking so it is easier to confess the embarrassing accounts they had to share.

The psychiatrist, still enough, now listened unmistakably, "Instantaneously, I ran to bolt the windows. There I sighed!

The tale of the ghost began to strain my mind.

I could hear poetry echoing in my mind. Maybe I was reading too much into it, maybe I wasn't.

As the chill of the weather caught up with me, the storm that raged outside gave way to a growing calamity inside me.

To distract my mind from the ruthlessness of nature, I decided to visit the ancient library and see what it withheld.

There was a charm in the old books, the looks and the scent of them.

As if it were a force, a pull dragged me to the end of the room, to what seemed like a treasure chest.

I knew it was a farfetched idea, maybe it was just an ancient looking box covered in dust.

An old book caught my eye, its pages looked as strong as thunder and lightning, its shady look an incentive enough to give it a look.

As I flipped through the pages, I saw images and old ink shabbily scribbling words, words of what seemed like a love story, perhaps a tragic one.

The end, however, wasn't talked about as the guy had given up on his life and death engulfed him with open arms.

There were a lot of poems in the book, poems which recited themselves in my mind.

As if, I did not have to read them, they just played in my mind while I held the book.

It left a curiosity in me, a gripping desire to know what happened to the lovers.

The story had ended with the man claiming that he would stay there till the day their souls met again or if not, then no other soul shall ever breathe freely. He would create havoc in the world of the living and make them all pay for the pain they had caused them.

This, I assumed, was the story of what the world called the ghost of the mansion and ran away from.

This was the legend they talked about, the one I was there to investigate.

Her eyes so bright
They shone under the moon
My eyes so desperate
To catch a glimpse of her face
That was my moon

The night was dark
Stars couldn't suffice
Nothing could brighten the skies
like the moon
And mine, was she ·
The one who brightened my life

As shock seeped into my skin, my blood inside me turned cold and a chill crawled up my spine.

I shut the book and decided to retreat to my safe haven.

Even though it was merely a story, there was something about the heartfelt words of the lover, a reality that I had refused to believe in.

Now it lay in front of me, a proof that there was indeed something which the people believed in and not just a myth.

Maybe, there are no ghosts, and just like every other lover, this was an exaggeration.

Yet something about that made me feel uneasy and unsettled."

The cosiness hatched by the coffee had now ceased as he gulped the last sip, still next to the window. The warmth that the liquid once provided was lost now.

Secretly catching the therapist's expressions, he continued, "As I turned back, I saw that the lights started flickering. The werewolves collectively started to roar outside, around the periphery of the house, this time more threateningly.

I rushed and as I reached the door, it shut. I had hardly reached the window when my mind began to collapse, the feeling of unease grew and spread throughout my body and I began to lose the coolness I had in my head.

In front of me stood a body, a mass that could barely be called human.

I had been backed into a corner, and stood back paralysed with fear, forced to look at my oppressor.

The creature had yellow teeth with strains of crimson in them, his face was wrinkled, and his skin folded in multiple layers hanging loosely over the bony structure of his face.

If wrinkles were to give away age, his birth wouldn't be dated in this century. His large silvery blue eyes had a streak of void in them and they trembled with anger while his lips stretched wide, his muscles loosened over time.

I was awestruck and fascinated yet paralysed, I stood.

This was something new, some element of the sublime that stood close and near to me.

My eyes whirled around the room, desperately looking for a way to escape as my survival instinct kicked in.

Trapped in a remarkably anomalous volume, swallowing my trepidation I asked who he was.

I think, it was in the moment the obvious became so hard to accept and I made the mistake of actually seeking answers.

Curiosity kills the cat, doesn't it?

My first mistake was asking him who he was, I knew it the minute I asked him that question.

Maybe, in retrospect, things would have taken a different turn if I had just let it go.

Laughing his ghoulish laughter, he tautly replied, 'The devilish majesty of the place where you stand.'

His words were laced with a sense of superiority and sarcasm. He was aware of the effect he had on me.

The scribbled words now began to prove their phantasm, as if they had become personified somehow.

His words echoed in my mind, the idea of death too foreign to me, yet like a known stranger it loomed over me.

As my mind twisted and turned, shuffled through my memory for any warnings that would help me live through this night, just to get out somehow, my senses seemed to have given up.

Here he was, my fate written on his weapon and my pain in his devilish smile.

As I forced my mind to calm down, to look for another way out, I shut my eyes.

I needed a distraction, to somehow escape the clutches that death seemed to have on me now.

I thought about it, what could captivate and divert an old man, what was the deepest desire of his heart with which I could play.

And when they opened again, they shone with a new vigour, a passion for life.

I had my way out, soon it would all be a memory I could bury somewhere deep in my mind, "So, you did not find her?" I asked, the answer to which came as a disappointed nod.

"And now you want to take down this world." His response now was an affirmative nod, and his weary eyes shone with determination and passion.

"Why not do it with me then?" I asked with a matching devilish smile.

That was the moment where it all began. You see, we had a deal.

As the air turned thicker and the night cold, my soul fled my body and he accepted me as his partner in crime."

He turned around to gauge the expressions on the face of the therapist. There was a paleness on his face, masked with a sense of professionalism just like he was supposed to. In the moment, he related to him, he saw the same desperation in his eyes that he had before he came up with this devious plan. He too, was fishing for an escape but he was betrayed by his mind. There was no escape. He could try and convince himself that it was a hallucination. It was almost fun to be able to read his mind, the trivial thoughts of the human mind.

As he finished his monologue, his smile radiated enough confidence. "Scared? You should be, doctor. Hallucinations you had said? Oh wait, you haven't said it out loud yet. Doesn't seem like I am hallucinating now, does it? Why don't we, together, make you hallucinate your death?"

He said as his brown orbs shone with a green light, his fair skin gave way to a dusky one with wrinkles and freckles like the one he had mentioned in his account. Now it was crystal clear, he wasn't scared, the details weren't scars to his memory. He looked up to and admired the ghost. He memorised them out of dedication, passion. As the lights of the room flickered, like the heartbeat of the psychiatrist, no one in that room dared to see the morning sun after the hallucination arose.

STORY THREE

THE NEW BRIDE

by Kuldeep C

ONE

Crowded buses are an extremely rare phenomenon in the route between Mudigere to Byrapura, the towns in the foothills of Western Ghats deep inside Karnataka. As the bus that shuttles once in two days swayed in the curves and turns in the lush green estate roads that were curtained regularly by fog, people drowned themselves in conversations about two very important happenings- the miracle of the thing that carried them all, called a motor bus and the beautiful new bride in the house of Hegdes.

Hegde Eerappa got off the bus dusting his silk wraparound dhoti and towel, a dear gift by his in-laws, while the anticipating crowd at the bus stop looked at the door of the bus in wait for his newly wedded wife. Once done with his dusting ritual, Eerappa looked around as the citizens of Byrapura looked at him with a wide, meaningless smile, irritating the man inside him.

15-year-old Meenakshi's shoulders trembled at the command in his stern voice to get down. Her jhumka earrings rocked at the dear welcome of her husband of a few hours. Tears rushed out of her eyes anxiously and stood on her lashes, trying to look at her husband for the first time, blurring her view. One such drop jumped out in a hurry landing on her cheek, followed by more such hasty water droplets, gushing them on to her silk saree, making it greener wherever it touched.

△▼

Meenakshi was busy taking out jackfruit seeds from her secret place in the backyard shed, well hidden from her younger brother. She ran back inside her house in hope of dodging the rain but in vain. "Mahatma Gandhi in his address in New Delhi yesterday has said that if Indian independence was assured, he would cease to function as Congress Party adviser. He further stated that he had no intention of promoting further civil disobedience and announced that he had a solution for the problem of India." A female voice in the huge radio set spoke in the living area with static noise in between. Soon the radio voice deadened.

"Appa must be around," the thief inside her thought. As she approached the fireplace in the kitchen to roast the seeds, she overheard voices laughing in the verandah. She pressed her ears closer to recognize the reason behind the unknown laughter. Voices grew louder as her toes crept further in quest for answers. Her father jumped between "Good," "Very good," "We just trust you," "Hahaha" and "Hmm hmmm hmm" in no particular order. However, the unknown voice spoke information. "Treated like a queen," "Clerk,"

"No need to do any work," "Haa haa. 24 years" and so on. She also heard her mother's chuckles in between, who also praised a new God every time she spoke. Her investigation was brought to a halt when she stumbled upon her sister-in-law. Startled, Meenakshi dropped the seeds on the ground which bounced haphazardly before disappearing into the seen and unseen corners. Sister-in-law, with a wide smile on her lips and Meenakshi's face in her hands, whispered, "They just fixed your marriage. It's a great family, you're really lucky."

Meenakshi took a deep breath as her eyes moistened up and face turned red. Her mother walked in beaming, "Groom is a gem they say. He will take good care of you. You will live like a queen." Meenakshi freed herself from both and stormed out through the backdoor she had just entered from. Her sister-in-law stood at the door and shouted, "He will gift you silk sarees from Mysore."

Meenakshi held her saree up from her ankle while kicking off the cup filled with rice topped with jaggery off the sill of the main door, a symbol of welcoming prosperity along with the new bride. Her eyes brightened up as the plate of arathi was swayed in front of the newlyweds' faces. The couple prayed to different Hindu deities in the small prayer room, stood in front of photo frames of Eerappa's grandparents and his father with folded hands and then touched the feet of the elders present, trying to be blessed by as many as possible.

Eerappa's mother blessed them and hugged Meenakshi. Her eyes watered again; it was her mother-in-law's saree's chance to turn dark as her tears spread. She sat down with her daughter Gopamma in the kitchen to comfort Meenakshi with talks about the greatness of the Hegde family, Eerappa's routine and hence her routine that was about to shape up around his. She was told that the mother-in-law stayed with her elder son in his estate in a nearby village, 27kms away from Byrapura. Sister-in-law Gopamma was married with three kids to a school teacher in a far-off town called Hassan. A city she vividly remembered visiting in her childhood, about a year ago.

Meenakshi spent the rest of her afternoon being lost amongst her new family. She was introduced to her future companions in the house for years to come- the kitchen, the store room attached to it, an attic on the first level, a prayer room with photo frames of Hindu deities, two cows and three calves that lived in their shed in the backyard and an open well beyond that. Bath house was a shed built a couple of hundred meters away inside the dense coffee estates that extended till 44 acres.

Soon dusk dissolved into darkness and three kerosene lamps were lit inside the house of the Hegdes. Meenakshi sat on the edge of the cot in her room expecting her husband anytime soon. Her palms drenched in sweat as she remembered her mother instructing her two days ago to oblige to whatever her husband does and not to resist. Chills passed her skin as cold air crept into the dark room that was barely lit by a kerosene lamp.

Meenakshi sat up straight with a jolt as she heard the metal chains of the wooden door rattle. Her hands clung to her saree while her eyes looked down into darkness. Eerappa closed the door and hung his black coat, black cap and white shirt to the nails on the wall. Meenakshi's toes curled and gripped the mud flooring. He slowly walked to the window and closed the shutters, stabilizing the lamp flame.

Eerappa then stood majestically in front of Meenakshi as her breathing increased. Sweat oozed out of her body. She gasped when Eerappa cleared his throat and in a blunt, dead voice said "Eyy…!!" He touched her shoulders with two fingers and pushed gently. Terrified Meenakshi looked up with moist eyes. "Move aside and sleep on that side of the bed," said the voice again. She stared blankly at him, for even she did not know what she expected him to do, but definitely not to 'move aside and sleep'. His grunt brought her back to senses from nowhere and she jumped to sleep in the corner. Eerappa put off the lamp and laid down next to her with one hand resting on his face. In no time he turned around and Meenakshi could recognize him sleeping with his back facing her as her eyes adjusted to the new darkness. She looked at him in amusement for a few seconds and slowly crept to sleep, with wide eyes looking at the emptiness that was supposedly her husband's back.

The crescent moon glided through the clouds in the sky as wolves howled. Crickets chirped to fill the emptiness in the air whenever the wolves took a break. The cold breeze still made its way inside through the cracks in the window shutters and as the breeze roamed around the room, Eerappa slept facing the wooden ceiling. His snore reminded the forests around about human existence amongst them in that dark night. Meenakshi slept next to him facing the wall. Her face reminded the breeze of a feather it had been carrying around the whole day with pride.

Her eyes opened abruptly and she spent the next couple of minutes staring at the void blankly. She got off her bed, opened the door, and walked out of the room while Eerappa still roared his lungs out. She walked all the way to the kitchen in pitch darkness, opened a huge copper vessel and drank water out of a copper cup.

As she closed the vessel a gust of light air touched her sweaty forehead and exited from the open window in the kitchen. Meenakshi stood looking outside the window. She felt weightless as she stood there losing track of the non-existent time. Cold wind fondled with her delicate skin erecting minute mountains of goosebumps on her body.

She breathed heavily watching the nothingness while a hand from behind grabbed her shoulder and rocked it mildly. Meenakshi gasped and came back to her senses. Eerappa stood confused looking at his panting wife. "What are you looking at?" he asked holding the kerosene lamp higher to her face.

"I...Tha...I was... Thirsty. I couldn't sleep and I was thirsty and I... I came to drink some water. Was just getting some air. You had..."

"It's okay!" Eerappa cut her off in between, looked into her eyes for the first time, in anticipation of answers for the questions he didn't know. "Get back to sleep. Go."

She briskly walked out of the gloomy kitchen. Eerappa walked behind her, ready to roar again.

△▼

TWO

Meenakshi woke up to the first crow of the rooster. She sneaked out of the bed and tiptoed her way out of the room. Gopamma was already folding the beds with few other women she couldn't recognize. "Why are you up so early? It is really okay if you want to sleep more," Gopamma said caringly. Meenakshi lowered her head and said that she had slept early last night and couldn't sleep anymore. She suddenly heard a burst of laughter from her sister-in-law and others which made her turn red. Her mother-in-law who had walked in a minute ago silenced the laughing women and asked Meenakshi to take a nap in the afternoon. "Take her with you. Show her where to sit," she said to one of the women.

Meenakshi soon bathed in the ice-cold water while dawn tried to throw some orange into the misty mornings of Western Ghats. She drew rangoli in the front yard, stepped back to have a clear view and smiled with pride at her art work. She ran inside the kitchen where all the women she had encountered in the morning were busy cooking breakfast. She was asked by one of them on her cooking knowledge to which she listed out all the delicacies she was taught by her mother. She felt a slight pinch of guilt when she included some of the dishes she had never ever tried her hands on. But soon felt delighted at the surprise and appreciation of her audience. The mother-in-law was praised by all for finding such a worthy bride for her son.

Meenakshi tried to look at Eerappa's face when she served him breakfast. Fair, grumpy with a big and neat moustache- her sister-in-law was correct, she was lucky indeed. She scuttled into the kitchen and came out only half an hour later when her mother-in-law asked her to hand over his lunch box. She stood behind the door looking at Eerappa as he hopped on his bicycle and rode away. She waited until he disappeared from her sight beyond the bougainvillea bushes, hoping him to look back at her once, in vain.

When the sun had crossed his halfway mark of the day, Meenakshi had just finished her lunch and was busy doing the dishes of the entire household when a bunch of relatives visited her in the backyard to bid goodbye. She smiled forcibly at the unknown faces, rubbed her hands to her saree and touched their feet. She got back to her work and finished it soon. She took them to the store room and began arranging the washed utensils. A copper plate stumbled from her hands when she heard someone behind her. "Nap for some time dear," mother-in-law stood there with a smile.

She kept the last few vessels in haste and stood up. "I am not tired really. Can I go round the estate for a while?"

"Of course, of course. Just take care. Don't get lost in there. Take our Bheema with you."

Bheema, a brown, lean dog, trained to hunt stood at the doorway in the backyard. Meenakshi smiled deliberately. "I… Can I go alone? I am scared of dogs. I can manage. We have a huge estate too. Had I mean…"

Mother-in-law looked at her curiously. "Yes, but you do have to get used to him. He has to be taken care of or Eera will be furious." She chuckled and then moved to exercise her nap.

Meenakshi walked into the estate amongst the well grown coffee plants, orange, teak, wild jack and other trees. She stopped and looked up at the sun who had been trying to catch a glimpse of her. She held her hand to her face, seeing the sun lonely up in the clear blue sky without a single patch of cloud to accompany him. Moist soil soothed her bare feet and lusty thorns tried to get a touch of her soft skin when she passed by them. Her eyes widened as she spotted a jungle fowl and she began chasing it. After an eternal day in Byrapura she finally felt at home. She ran to collect a wild mango she had just hunted from a tree, cleaned it by rubbing off the dirt on her silk saree. The wild mango smiled back at her when she took it near her lips. Her eyes closed and lips widened as the sour tinge touched her tongue. She opened her eyes, still smiling, and froze!

Her face dropped. So did the mango. Meenakshi was as blank as the sky above her.

△▼

Eerappa moved back-and-forth vigorously with his muscular arms gripped firmly against the bed. A pair of slender, yet rigid hands cupped his bare back and moved to his face, wiping his sweat off. The other bare body tried to bend forward towards Eerappa's face; he pushed the body down and increased his pace. The two panting breaths tried to be careful not to let the sound leave the room. Two neat fingers reached Eerappa's mouth as he closed his eyes and looked up. He flinched suddenly and left a groan which resonated and ended with a long sigh. Eerappa rolled over, laid down on the bed facing the ceiling. Sheela remained panting, her sweat moved from her forehead to touch her smile on her lips. Her Adam's apple moved up and down when she gulped her saliva in thirst. She moved her hand on Eerappa's chest and fondled the sweaty hair as she planted a delicate kiss there. She looked up at his face and pushed her body up to kiss his face. Eerappa pushed her aside and got up.

"I'll take a quick bath. Is the water hot?" he asked, tying his wraparound dhoti.

"Why can't you stay for some more time?" Sheela sat up; legs spread wide. Her thick eyebrows frowned; mouth stayed open anticipating an answer. Her voice reminded Eerappa of his uncle, by whom he was touched first under a coffee plant as tender as him, when he was merely 12.

"I must go soon. I am expecting guests at home. Is the water hot?" he repeated his question while walking to the bathroom.

"It is," said Sheela under her breath, lowering her head in shame. She got up and pulled her petticoat up. She tried hard to look at her face amongst the stickers of three Hindu deities of different powers and sizes pasted randomly in the small mirror that was nailed to the wall. A huge red Kumkum dot made her proud of her manly face. A crow cawed outside her window, disturbing her act of self-admiration. She touched her face with her fingers and wondered if her pride was justified.

Chain of thoughts dragged her to her life in Mangalore. The bustling port city, her home: a small shed behind a mosque in the main street, a decent family of 25, her neighbours, her school: Government Boys Model Primary School, her classmates laughing at her, her father and uncles hitting her boy body, her running away and spending days on streets, her meeting Eerappa, a new life and now this home. Life had brought her a long way.

"Is this all in the same life?" she wondered as her fingers still creased her face. The cawing crow intensified its rant, dragging her out of her thoughts. Irritated, she opened the window to shoo it away.

Meenakshi sat on the sludge with legs spread wide. Her eyelids didn't bat. Breathing slowly, to the fullest of her lungs, she sat there with her eyeballs focused on a crow that stayed motionless on the ground in front of her. The thick red fluid made the black feathers stick to each other with soil grains garnished on them. She stood up and walked away with a smirk, hands not swinging.

△▼

Eerappa washed his legs outside his house before entering. His mother greeted him by taking his lunch box. "Where is she?" asked his stern voice.

"She went to stroll around the estates in the afternoon. She will be back soon. You go freshen up. I will get you something to eat"

"So, she stays roaming around after I come home? What is this?"

"It has just been a day since she's here. She will understand things gradually. You go freshen up," his mother said to calm her soon-to-be-angry son.

His eyes soon set on Meenakshi who had just walked in through the backyard and then on her saree which was crumpled and soiled on the lower part. Meenakshi twitched at the sudden roar of "You dirty whore!" Eerappa raged towards her but was stopped by his mother who hugged him sideways with all her might.

"You go inside. And change soon," she said still holding her son. "She is just a child, Eera. What are you doing?" it was mother's turn to yell. She loosened her grip when her son's fury subdued. Eerappa stood there, unknowing where to channelize his anger. He grabbed a towel that hung on a wooden chair in the living room and stormed out by jerking it on to his shoulder. "She can go back to her father's to do all the whoring if she wants to. I don't want her!"

Meenakshi cried on Gopamma's shoulders knowing that her mother-in-law's pride that was beaming that morning was now left shattered.

AN ETERNAL MISTRESS

by Kuldeep C

THREE

Meenakshi spent the next eight days with the same routine of waking up to the first rooster call, bathing, applying turmeric to her body, blackening her eyes with kohl, decorating her hair with jasmines along with other self-care exercises in anticipation to be touched by her husband any day soon.

Her mother-in-law remained a pained mute witness to this loveless marriage where Meenakshi waited behind the door every day in hope of Eerappa turning back to bid his lovely wife a goodbye. But he never even looked into Meenakshi's eyes.

On the ninth day, Meenakshi's chest felt heavy with the lump in her throat that was choking her breath since morning. She finally broke down when her mother-in-law hugged her. Gopamma hugged her next and held her face in her hands. "Remember everything I said, will you?" she asked. Tears sprung out of Meenakshi's eyes when she nodded in assertion and began her crying streak, easily irritating the ever-irritated husband.

Eerappa carried their bags out. Gopamma, her children and her mother - the last few guests at the house of Hegdes were on their way back to their homes.

"Don't cry my dear. You both visit us next week. You can write or send the servant Ambu to me whenever you need me in between. Okay?" Although her mother-in-law's kind words soothed her, they had little effect on her emotions. Meenakshi stood behind the door crying, looking at them. To her surprise all of the leaving guests looked back and waved at her. She ran inside the house wiping her tears as Eerappa burst in.

"I am late to work. Serve me the breakfast soon," he said.

Meenakshi listened to his instructions and continued to turn the cooked paddus into a vessel. She waited in the kitchen for him to be seated and served hot paddus and chutney on to his plate; soon went back into the kitchen to attend to the ones baking on the stove. She jogged out of the kitchen with a lunch box when she heard Eerappa walk out of their room. He tried to look at her face but couldn't see more than her bent head, red cheeks, swollen eyes, partitioned hair and a red line in between. He hung the lunch box to the handle of his bicycle and looked back after walking a few steps at the abandoned door that was left wide open. Eerappa sighed, looked up at the sunny sky, hopped on to his bicycle and rode off to work.

△▼

Rain droplets showered on the bicycle that leaned on the walls outside Sheela's house. A lady in the new radio set that Eerappa had gifted Sheela spoke. "Mahatma Gandhi in his address in New Delhi yesterday has said that if Indian independence was assured, he would cease to function as Congress Party adviser. He further stated…" The All India Radio broadcasted news that was irrelevant to the audience in that house. But Sheela enjoyed the luxury in the air.

Eerappa washed his hands in the plate he had just eaten from and wiped his hands-on Sheela's saree. She placed a gentle pat on his shoulder and turned towards the kitchen with a curry pot in her hand. Eerappa pulled her saree further dragging her towards him and kissed gently on her belly. Sheela closed her eyes, keeping the pot back on the table and pulled him up towards her face, his lips traced her skin throughout the journey. Her manly fingers ran through his hair as he tugged softly on her earlobes. Eerappa paused suddenly and looked at her face with a smile.

"What?" asked Sheela, looking into his eyes, surprisingly.

"I… have to go," he said.

Sheela adjusted her saree in reflex, picked up the vessels she had orphaned minutes ago and stormed into the kitchen.

"I told you I have guests over. Please understand!" Eerappa followed her with his explanation.

Vessels rattled in Sheela's kitchen in anger. Eerappa walked in slowly with caution and hugged Sheela from behind. The kisses on her cheeks that followed made Sheela close her eyes again and her lips bloom with a smile. "I will stay back tomorrow," Eerappa hissed into her ears.

"Promise?"

"Mmm hmmm," he moaned and bit her ears. Sheela moved her back closer to his crotch in affirmation.

"Is the water hot?" he asked, panting. Sheela turned around, looked into his eyes and kneeled down.

"Severe monsoon rains have forced the British forces to practically cease their operations in Burma..." the lady on the radio continued to speak alone.

△▼

Meenakshi sat alone in her veranda peeling off beans and recalling Gopamma's advice on wife's duties to attract, satisfy and hence keep the husband happy. She mentally prepared herself with a detailed plan to seduce her beloved man. She jumped on to her feet when she heard the bells of a bicycle ring. She looked towards the bougainvillea bushes, rushed inside before she could see the shadows of the bicycle of her husband and came out with a bucket of warm water and a towel. Eerappa washed his feet after she took his empty lunch box. He wiped his hands on the towel and walked inside his home.

"I have heated the water. Take a bath soon. I will serve something to eat," Meenakshi spoke to his back as he walked away.

"I am not hungry. I will take a bath and sleep," came his short reply.

Meenakshi froze. Eyelids unbatted, eyeballs focused on his direction, breathing slowly as she stood amongst the carved wooden pillars. Bheema ran inside, skidded in the front yard and started barking aimlessly. Meenakshi stood unmoved. As Bheema's barks intensified, she turned back and walked towards it, hands intact without swings. The ferocious dog trained to hunt began to squeal and stepped back. Meenakshi stepped out of the house and Bheema ran back into the estate. She stood there looking at the water patch where her husband had washed his legs a while ago.

△▼

FOUR

Meenakshi's next morning wasn't any different. First rooster call, bathing, turmeric on skin, kohl on eyes, jasmine flowers, chopping vegetables, fresh dosa steamed on the pan, her hands rotated the grinding stone, chutney paste splashed on to a vessel, breakfast served to her already waiting husband, his lunch box filled and packed. Spontaneous and mechanical - that was what her actions looked like.

"Did you eat your breakfast?" Meenakshi's eyes widened hearing her husband enquire about her. Eerappa saw her eyes moisten and spoke further, unable to bear the awkwardness. "Breakfast is delicious. Eat soon." Meenakshi lowered her head, tear droplets bulleted towards the ground near her feet. Uncomfortable Eerappa patted her shoulder, "I will be back early today" and exited his house. Lunch box swayed on the handle of his bicycle when he hopped on and rode off as the sun shone brighter and hotter above him.

Meenakshi didn't remember what chores she happened to do that day, neither did she remember what she thought about. Her stomach and chest tickled with every thought of seeing her husband again in the evening. She only realized the time while involuntarily milking the cows. The sun had turned the clear sky crimson, painted with strokes of clouds. She mumbled cursing herself and sprang into action. She ran into the kitchen, adjusted the firewood inside the stove, blew into the cinder, boiled the milk, and burned her fingers while keeping it aside. The pain didn't seem to bother her as she sucked her finger once and started preparing kesaribath instantly, a sweet her mother-in-law said he loved. She went out and put more firewood into the fireplace in the bath shed. She took a bath and finished her body care procedures. She then sat in the veranda looking at the bougainvillea bushes with a smile she carried since Eerappa touched her shoulders that morning; she realized her jaws hurt.

△▼

Eerappa looked drenched in sweat. Sheela admired her proud possession that stood naked at the window and looked outside at the raining streets. She sensed his anxiety when he wiped his sweat and lit a beedi. She walked up to him and hugged him gently from behind, rubbing her bare body to his, her penis touching his butt crack. Eerappa moved closer to the window, hence away from her, holding his face to the rain droplets that splashed inside. "Are you alright?" she asked.

"Yes. Yes. I just need to leave"

Sheela moved closer and gripped him tightly. "You said you would stay back today! Why do you have to go now?" Eerappa smoked from his nostrils when he sighed and pushed her gently. She tried to look into his eyes as he looked away, in shame. Eerappa took his fallen dhoti from the ground and wrapped it around his waist. "Is the water ready? I will freshen up and leave soon." Sheela snatched his dhoti making him naked again. "But you promised me yesterday!"

△▼

The darkness made Meenakshi ease her skin. Her smile disappeared gradually and wrinkles formed on her forehead when her husband who had promised to be back early hadn't been home yet. Her face glowed bright when she struck the matchstick and lit up a kerosene lamp. She headed towards the kitchen to cook dinner for her husband who might come home hungry. She stopped on her way and held the lamp ahead towards their bedroom that awaited them with her. She stared at it, not knowing what she wanted to see. Eventually she moved to the kitchen, placed the lamp on a slab, blew into the cinder again using a metal pipe and ignited the stove. Just as Meenakshi placed the vessel on the stove she felt a light and cold air touch her neck. She turned back slowly and tried to concentrate towards the darkness. She got hold of her lamp and held it towards the direction she was looking at.

△▼

"I... not just today... I wo... won't be able to..." Eerappa stammered as he tried to find the right words to break the news to Sheela.

"You what? Dear? Look at me please?" Sheela held his face in her hands forcibly.

"I won't be seeing you," Eerappa spoke at once, freeing himself from her clutch. Sheela stood shocked, breathing with her mouth open. "I am getting married soon. In three months," Eerappa spoke before she could argue. "They have looked for a bride. I didn't know about it until today morning. Look, I am sorry. But I cannot come see you again."

△▼

Meenakshi got up and walked slowly towards the unknown in her house. She entered the living area and tried looking in all directions. She walked towards the backyard door, checked the chained locks, and walked back towards the kitchen. Her eyes froze when she re-entered the living room on her way back. Her jaw dropped and hand shivered. She stared at a window for a long time and gathered enough courage to walk towards it. Every step felt heavier for she had to drag herself searching for darkness, in darkness. A shadow that caught her attention when she walked in grew bigger as she approached closer. Her body trembled and began sweating profusely. Her shaky hands reached the curtain that stood between her and the shadow. The dark image remained still. She took a deep, shaky breath, gripped the curtain and moved in a jolt. She breathed out slowly through her mouth finding nothing in her adventure. She fluttered the curtain hysterically with one hand and lamp in the other. She felt a cold breeze behind her and turned back at once. Tear drops stood on her lashes blocking her view again from seeing what still looked like a dark figure.

Sheela pressed her back to the wall tightly and collapsed to sit on the ground. "Look, I won't ask you for anything. I won't obviously tell anyone. But please don't do this to me. Please don't abandon me. I will do whatever you want me to do. Please don't leave me!" she cried. Her grip on Eerappa's hand tightened and scratched him when he tried to release himself.

"Are you out of your mind? Leave me you filth!" he roared.

Sheela froze in shock. Mucus from her nose dripped on towards her open mouth. "What did you say? I am filth? Now that you have used me for years I have turned into filth?" Sheela held him with both her hands and began shaking him. The look of a crying manly face with a huge red dot on her forehead, sweaty face and mucus drooling frightened Eerappa. He picked his dhoti again and turned to walk out. Sheela jumped and grabbed his shoulder with a huge groan. Eerappa freed himself by pushing her back.

△▼

A shadow walked on the opposite wall in the darkness. Meenakshi hugged her knees tightly. The shadow stopped in front of her. Goosebumps arose on her skin for the breeze touching her turned colder. She sensed the smile of the dark patch and shook vigorously. Her grinding teeth clattered. She sobbed trying not to make any sound of her breath. Her breathing paused when the shadow glided towards her gradually. Meenakshi closed her eyes tightly and hid her face in her knees.

△▼

Eerappa put his shirt and dhoti on. The air seemed to get colder. Eerappa pulled out a few notes from his pocket and turned back to give it to Sheela. Notes dropped from his hands, landed on a pool of blood that had almost reached his feet. Eerappa's eyes traced the path of blood to Sheela's head that laid with her eyes wide open looking at him. Teardrops and mucus now dipped into the bloodstream on the ground. His legs moved a few steps backwards.

Eerappa hopped on to his bicycle and sped in the rain. It had been nearly five hours since he had moved Sheela out and cleaned her house. It had begun to get dark. A digging rod with a lump of soil sticking to the edges sat firmly in the back carrier of his bicycle. He stopped on a bridge that crossed his path. Rain splashed on his face washing off the dirt from his feet. Eerappa unbuttoned his blood and mud stained shirt and flung it off the bridge. Hemavathi river flowed under him carrying his shirt and sins as one.

Eerappa pedalled his bicycle again, his mind flooded with images of Sheela, her bleeding head, open eyes, rigid hands, her voice, his uncle, his home, the new girl his mother had arranged his marriage with. He realized he was speeding when his bicycle wobbled and lost control for a split second. "I cannot let any of this affect the honour of my family," he thought. He tried to recall his conversation with his mother that morning. "They are a very good family. The girl is very beautiful and well behaved. You will like her Eera. Meenakshi is her name."

△▼

Meenakshi hid herself between her knees and chest and tried not to shake. She held herself tightly in an attempt to make her arms and brain go numb. Suddenly she felt the withdrawal of the cold breeze and loosened her hands. She opened her eyes and looked up. The shadow slowly descended to sit in front of her. The kerosene lamp swayed like a snake and threw some light on to the shadow. Meenakshi blinked vigorously to shed tears and gain back her clear vision. A man! A man dressed in saree, with neatly made eyebrows, a big round blood red Kumkum dot in between them, eyes blackened with kohl. Meenakshi looked petrified at the sight of what she found to be inhuman. Her lips shivered; breath choked. A lump of mucus glided from the man's nose like a snail. The man smiled at Meenakshi who closed her eyes suddenly. She felt the breeze again. Colder and stronger this time. She tightened her closed eyes and trembled. Breeze engulfed her as she felt chills on her back. Meenakshi inhaled a long breath and held it in her lungs. She pierced her skin with her nails in an attempt to grip harder. She felt blood droplets on her fingertips. Her ears felt blocked. She slowly let go off her breath and opened her eyes. The room felt empty.

Meenakshi sat there spreading her legs wide, a lump of mucus glided out of her nose. Eerappa entered his house, "I am sorry I got late. Had to wind up some work at the office," he spoke as he kept the lunch box on a wooden teapoy, unbuttoned his shirt and grabbed the towel from the chair. Meenakshi sat breathing easily with a smile invisible to him in the darkness of the night. "Ah, it's so hot. I'll take a quick bath and rest. Did you eat?" he said while opening the backyard door. "I have heated the water," said Meenakshi in a feeble voice, a sustained smile, mucus dripping from her chin. She sat there while Eerappa bathed joyously and dried himself up.

Meenakshi got up slowly and walked into the kitchen, hands intact. Eerappa hung the towel on the chair and went into his room. She walked into the store room, stared at a digging rod, smiling. She dragged it out and walked through the kitchen and then into their bedroom. She stood near the bed where Eerappa laid facing his left. Bheema ran from inside the forest to the front yard and began barking, waking him up. "Why are you standing dear? Come sleep," said Eerappa with a welcoming smile. Meenakshi gripped the rod and widened her smile.

THE MAN-EATER

by Manoj Vaz

"Until the beast learns to write, every story will glorify man."
~African Proverb

Her name was Rani. She had killed two young men in the vicinity - able-bodied, strong men who could take care of themselves. He read about her in the news. Her story aroused him the way only danger can.

"Let me get a piece of action, life in the city is getting claustrophobic," he said to himself as he dumped his basic belongings and his old Winchester rifle and two dozen rounds in his army discarded Willy's jeep as he embarked to Gosaba, the little known village near Sundarbans Tiger Reserve.

It was a four-hour drive from Kolkata so he reached Gosaba in the evening. He preferred driving in the day on non-lit roads. The village was desolate, mourning the loss of the two good men. Everywhere, there were talks of the man-eating tigress. Rani, the Royal Bengal Tigress had pervaded their mind and catalysed their sweat glands.

The villagers had gathered at the local temple, praying fervently to the forest Goddess Bonbibi to keep them safe.

He camped at the Government Circuit House, a Bungalow on the outskirts of the tiger reserve that was built by the British. On knowing that he was a hunter, the village chieftain and a few elders visited him that night. They even offered him Rs. 5000/-, a princely sum for them, to kill the tigress. He smiled and told them it was not necessary.

The next morning, he set out stalking his prey. In his backpack was water and food to last him a couple of days and his trusted rifle and rounds. Ramu, the young guide from the village travelled with him to the spot where Rani was sighted last. The jeep was not of much use once the marshy land began but fortunately in January, the land was harder but so was the cold weather.

All day he stalked her. From her pugmarks, he realized that she was not putting much weight on her right front leg. "So, you are carrying an injury sweetheart," he said to himself.

The injury meant that Rani would not be too far away. It also meant that she would be twice as dangerous. By evening he knew that he was quite close to her. Something also told him that she had sensed him.

He took refuge on a tree for the night. His eyes peering into the darkness, his ears perked for any unusual sound till he drifted into a light sleep even as the eerie glow of the full moon lit up the forest.

A sudden sound of fluttering wings woke him up. In a second, he was ready, clutching his trusty rifle. He knew she was near, the forest noises told him that. Then he heard her soft cough like chuffing that reverberated in the quietness.

"She's in pain," he reasoned.

Then he saw her limping away at a distance. Full grown, majestic, and beautiful.

He cocked up his rifle but he did not have a clear shot and she was a fair distance away. Slowly he climbed down the tree and followed her. For more than half an hour he followed her, waiting for her to rest so that he could get a clear shot.

Suddenly, it was all stillness in the moonlit night. He could not hear or see her. He stood still, "You are playing games with me..." he murmured, "come on, show yourself sweetheart."

Then she exploded, charging towards him, regardless of her injured leg.

He was smart. He had not walked into her trap. He had kept enough distance between him and the bushes to allow him a couple of clear shots as she charged.

His rifle was ready and he could clearly see her in his sights. But her beauty mesmerized him.

"The trigger... squeeze it!!!" the voice inside him urged. But he was so captivated by her raw beauty that his finger froze.

"I cannot kill you sweetheart. You are too beautiful." He said to himself.

It seemed like an eternity by the time she was on to him. As she pounced on him, he threw away the rifle and embraced death with a smile.

Then he woke up, sweating despite the air conditioner. The majestic image of the tiger remained in his wide-open eyes. He looked around him.

There she was, sleeping blissfully. Her beauty, almost angelic, in the first light.

He got up and walked to his bureau, switched on the table lamp and opened the top draw. Inside was a brown paper envelope. He opened it and went through the contents again.

△▼

In there were photographs and irrefutable proof that she was having an affair with her boss, her gym instructor, and a colleague.

He had always suspected her of infidelity so he had commissioned a private investigator to find out. Now he had the proof.

She was now in his sights. He had the gun and the ammunition to take her down.

Just then the light woke her up. She stretched and purred softly, "What are you doing honey?"

"Introspecting," he replied truthfully as he dressed up to leave, "I am going for a run."

When he did not return all day, she rummaged through his draw. The images of her infidelity that lay in front of her stopped her heart momentarily.

"I am sorry for everything," she picked up her phone and texted him, "I will die if you leave me!"

The silence from his end was deafening to her.

She willed herself to not check her phone to see if he had replied. It had been about three days now. She hated that she was constantly checking his 'last seen at' status and yes, he was online just five minutes ago. Yet she couldn't stop herself. This sinking feeling to find absolutely no communication from him was becoming unbearable, almost torturous.

And then, just as she sat down in her chair, her phone vibrated. With her heart thudding in her ear, she unlocked her phone and stared at the screen. Finally! It was a message from him.

But when she opened it and read it, she nearly stopped breathing. She didn't know if he was joking or not.

"What was this?" she wondered.

It read, "I am sorry. I cannot live without you either." She didn't know what he meant.

Did it mean that he was coming back to her? Or was it a suicide note?

THE BEGINNING OF THE END

MIKE

by Akshara Bruno

I'm very sorry for your loss, Mrs. Roberts," apologized the doctor. Darcy sobbed onto her husband's shoulder letting the entire hallway of the hospital know of the sad news. Her only child was now dead.

Michael was his name but he was popularly known as lil' Mike. A little over 6 years old, he was loved by everyone in the neighbourhood. And why wouldn't they? He was a charming, adorable young boy who greeted every other living being walking past him and never missed a beat to be kind. "Good morning Mr. Whiskers!" was his morning ritual. Mr. Whiskers was his fluffy Persian cat.

Just a week ago, I saw him playing by himself in his home's front yard. Mrs. Whittaker, the oldest caretaker in this vicinity, was walking close by with two huge brown paper bags of groceries on her either hands. At her sight, Mike immediately dropped his ball, ran up to her and asked in a sing-song manner, "Do you need help Mrs. Whittaker?" Anyone at that moment would leap with joy at the sight of his face. Believe me, that's what she did too. Of course, she didn't need any help and hence kindly turned down his humble offer. Ah, good behaviour - that was Darcy's highest priority.

I had just entered their home to hear any improvements to the missing case when I heard Darcy wailing at the top of her lungs and the police officers expressing their condolences. Matt, Mike's father met me at the door with a dead face, stricken with a baggage of unforsaken news that he was lost in thoughts of his son. I walked over to the living room to find a brown file on the coffee table. I picked it up to read its contents. With the conversation fading away from my ears, I read through. Cause of death: drowning. Apparently, he was found by a fisherman in a lake which is half a mile away from our present residence.

"Mrs. Roberts, we understand this is a hard time. But you must know Michael's case is rather unusual for us. His bike was found near the ice cream stall down the avenue. Whatever happened, must've begun there. So, we should know if you have any particular person in your mind who would want to hurt you or your son, frequent to this location perhaps," said officer Burns.

I excused myself from their abode and sat outside facing the lawn. Grief overtook me. I moved into this lane only a year ago. As soon as I found out about Darcy, I approached her to catch up on our lives for we were long-lost friends. Her family was just as beautiful as her.

Greatly fond of Michael, we got along very quick too. Sometimes, I even took him for ice cream. Since Darcy didn't encourage junk, it was our little secret. With the warming memories rushing my mind, my heart sunk with the heaviness. I wished it was only a dream hoping to wake up soon enough.

The officers came out through the red door to leave. They knew who I was as they got to know me through the questioning for the then missing case, now with a dead end. They were sorry for the parents' loss. The other officer asked me if I had any piece of information to update their evidence. Unfortunately, I didn't. That was a lost cause.

I knew Darcy well. We go way back to Malcom Public High School. Their brochure states that they only graduate the best of best and they have 100% graduation without fail every year. The bonkers that vile marketing teams come up with.

△▼

First day of sophomore year. Me and my supposed buddy, Alan, walked down the hall. That's when I saw her for the very first time. Darcy, in her yellow polka dotted white dress with red ballet flats. Not the most flattering style among the girls but it was her fashion statement. Polka dots and glaring flats.

Through the window, I could see both of them in pain. Deciding not to intervene in such a pressing moment, I treaded back to my house, right across the street. Went into the living room and lit up a cigarette, but remembering that Darcy had a 'No smoking' rule in front of Mike, I put it out. With such distaste, I laid on my back on the couch, to attain some peace because the fact that Darcy was suffering from such a tragedy only made things worse for me. Who would've thought events would lead up to this? With a raging country out there and imbeciles out in the street as expressed by the concerned newspapers, the law was not accustoming to the needed pressure. Every other day, you see multiple death reports and toss the paper away because they mean nothing to you. And suddenly the victim is a piece of you and who can be blamed?

△▼

1998. The year I met Darcy. The year of resurgence, for me at least. Just from a distance I could see that she was that one girl who can help you get to your light at the end of the tunnel. After being completely awestruck by her charisma, I decided to befriend her. She was about to grab her bike from the parking lot. I took the chance, went over and shot my hand towards her for a handshake saying, "Name's Richard. Nice to meet you, Darcy." Yes, I was eccentric that way. "Aye there matey. Pleasure's not mine. How dare you speak up to Captain Darcius?!" she responded with a pirate rudeness. Completely confused, the next 10 seconds of my silence seemed the longest in my series of awkwardness. She burst out laughing saying, "I'm obviously kidding, silly. Although, your expression was priceless." Rest assured, we proceeded to hang out for the first time to grab a few churros and two cups of soda. We attended parties, went to flea markets, and had fun in yearly fairs, just enjoying each other's company. Soon after, I learnt that Darcy had a knack for impressions which made our first meet, a funny story. And till this date, it remains my favourite memory.

△▼

I wanted to help Darcy. So, the next morning when they were going to hospital to see their son for one last time, I went along. We reached St. John's hospital within 15 minutes. A nurse directed us to a room upon enquiry where we met Dr. John. He was Mike's paediatrician. He heard of the news and rushed to talk to Matt and Darcy. He narrated how sorry he was and how he and his colleagues tried their best to bring his life back whereas I only found his slick back hair and 'profound' sympathy as a religious act done to aid any helpless relative of the deceased. I have never been a fan of any medical attendee and this guy made no difference. Irony huh? Look where I ended up.

When we returned, I tried to have a normal conversation with Darcy but in vain. She wouldn't go inside her home but sat out on the porch, teary-eyed, murmuring a prayer under her breath, desperately looking to the left and right of the road thinking Michael might come running home to her. I tried to remind her of our glorious past, trying to give her some rest from the thought of her son. "Hey, remember the time when we went trekking?" She said, "hmm." "I stood on top of a table on the camping offsite, yelling 'I am on top of the world'. Right when I was being a prude, I slipped and fell and tore my knee. You wouldn't stop telling that story to every other climber on that trip," I told her this and definitely made her smile but had no new words. "Darcy, I can't imagine how hard this is. But you were there in my times of need. Back in high school when I had multiple episodes of psychosis, you were there for me. Every moment was frustrating and confusing, and you helped me through it. Likewise, I'll be here, for you, no matter what. Remember what you used to tell me. 'This too, shall pass'." She nodded but I knew she wasn't ready to let go. I bid her goodnight and went back to my home, where, blocking my path to the garage was a black mini-van. I couldn't find the driver and honestly, I couldn't care less considering everything.

I drank water from the bottle on the kitchen counter, put it back into the refrigerator where it should have been in the first place, walked up to my bed room and fell on my bed. I think I heard some mumbling and a noise wreck, but everything was a blur. I must blame the neighbours, house owned by the rudest boys, hosting a frat party every alternate weekday. I blacked out straightaway. I must have overslept, for the next morning, I was late to work. And when you're a school teacher, the headmaster never allows any excuses. After 30 minutes of well-versed discussion on why education is important to young minds, I was filled with regrets on joining this school. No sooner than later, I was reminded of Michael. How he could have gone missing out of nowhere and only to be found stranded all alone, oh the poor boy. Luckily, I had the following hour free, giving me enough time to contemplate with the sadness. I made a quick call to officer Burns, leaving a voice mail that I wanted to contribute as much as I could to help and I really wanted to do this for Darcy, and I ended the call. Maybe this is a wrong time to ponder over our past.

I used to like Darcy more than I would like to admit and that was until the charming, Matt Damon Roberts, came and swept her off of her feet. Yes, I went through a sad rejection which is probably why we drifted apart. But all of that is in the past and we are no more than good friends bringing out the best in each other.

On my way back home, I witnessed the frat party boys picking on the little kids playing on the park. As I was driving, I didn't stop but it gave me something to think about. What if the boys had done something terrible to Mike? What if, they were trying to pull out a prank, which turned out more harmful, caused his death and dumped him off-site, thinking they could get away with it?

I parked in my garage, called officer Burns, and left another voicemail stating my assumption. I was almost sure of this until the next day when I noticed the same mini-van I saw the previous day parked a few doors away. What was more intriguing was that, the van came right after Matt left in his car and the van left just before Matt came back home in the evening. I noticed this pattern the next few days and it obviously irked me into telling officer Burns. I left him a voicemail again. You would think that he might respond to the strangeness of all of this, but he didn't. Maybe I dialled the wrong number…. No, the number was same as what his card said. I called him once more and he didn't answer.

I looked out the window. Darcy's home looked dull without Mike playing in the front yard. I sighed and put my phone down and tried to distract myself from all the chaos. The next few days, I practiced a routine of work and then television, accompanied by a bottle of beer and cheap takeout Chinese food.

The following Sunday, I was awoken from my sleep by the loud thumping on my door. I opened it to find five officers, one of which claimed that he had a warrant to check my house related to Michael's case. At first, I was confused and then infuriated of false accusation. I saw Darcy a few feet away from my door, looking pale with her robe on, trembling with fear, holding onto her husband as her staff. The police raided my house. They found a box of Michael's belongings in my attic. It also had a map of the state, a rope, and a detailed plan of the execution. I was staggered as much as everyone else. "You are under arrest for the murder of Michael Roberts, Mr.

Richard. Anything you say or do will be used against you in the court," said officer Burns and handcuffed me. I was chilled to the core, dumbfounded. Darcy came up to me and said, "How could you?" After giving me a second to look at her pained self, she slapped me across my face and screamed, "HOW COULD YOU?!!" The officers took me away to the police station.

Everything that happened next escalated very quickly. During the questioning, I tried to convince the officers as much as I could that I was not the murderer. I mean, I loved the boy. I would never want to hurt him. I told them that I had only seen the toy or Mike's shirt when the boy had them and I also never used the attic because it was filled with the possessions of the previous owner and I still am a huge claustrophobic. They didn't believe me. They stated that I had two possible motives. The officer pulled out my old records and said that either I was still madly in love with Darcy, that I wanted to remove others from the picture to get closer to her or that my psychosis had rebounded which could have led me to committing the crime without realising. They wanted the truth and I firmly believed that it was neither. I called for my lawyer.

We went to the court the next week. Like they said, it was my own words against mine. The jury's verdict was that I must be sent to an asylum for my lawyer made them believe the latter was the possibility.

And that's how I landed here in this Medical Institution for the mentally ill. For over 6 months I have been here, with daily medication almost as if you lot want me to believe that I committed it. And hey, congratulations, it's working. Alan visits me sometimes, usually in the night. Right before leaving he whispers to me, "You are a murderer" or "You deserve this."

△▼

Richard was done reciting his entire story to the nurse for yet another time. He was lonely, stuck within the four walls for so long that every chance he got with any human, in this case, a nurse, he made sure to talk. In his defence, the nurse seemed new and he must know the story. With no response, Richard proceeded, "When do you think Dr. Smith will be back?" The nurse replied softly, "Do you remember me, Richard?"

Richard could not place him anywhere in his memory. The nurse removed his glasses and the clinical mask. He then took the bottle of water from the table, poured a little to his hand and bent down. He applied the water over to his hair and slicked it back, repositioning himself. And when he met with Richard's eyes again, he had that sly smile plastered over his face.

Richard was taken aback for a moment because the medications often swirled his brain and he began to believe this was one such time. He said, "Doctor..."

"John. Yes, we met at the hospital," said the now revealed doctor. "I have been watching you, Richard. For a very long time. Since the day lil' Michael died."

Richard nearly cried on his words, "But I didn't kill him. I couldn't have."

Hugging him as he wept like a child and rocking him, Dr. John said, "Shhh now. It's okay. I know you didn't kill the boy."

"You believe me?"

"Yes, I very much do. Now, I am going to tell you secret, okay? But you cannot tell anyone," John paused for a minute and said, "I did it. I am the murderer."

Richard was muddled with fear. "Wow, it feels great to finally let go off the weight!" exclaimed John. Richard had a million questions pondering his head but couldn't utter any. Dr. John continued, "This is the part where you ask 'why'. Fine! I'll tell you. You see, I have always fancied fragile little boys. And this was one of those times where everything goes wrong. But I couldn't suffer for it now, could I? With my name and profession on the line, I just couldn't risk it. I'm sorry, definitely not meaning it, for framing you. As for how I did it, I learned your routine, drugged you, planted the fake evidences and sent in an anonymous tip to the police." Richard still had nothing to say. His face clearly expressed that he would immediately shoot John in the head if he had a rifle. "Well, I loved spending time with you, Richard. But duty calls," said John and was about to leave.

Richard was stoked with rage. He got to his feet, cursing, as his only thought was to choke John to his death. Since he was chained, he couldn't move far. John's reflexes were quick and he easily pushed Richard to the wall, holding him firm. He brought a syringe to his neck and injected him to put him under sedation. Then he muttered in his ear, "You can try, but they'll never believe you" and with that, he dropped Richard on the floor. That was the last Richard ever saw of John, walking past and locking the door after him.

THE ALMIRAH GHOST

by Midhun Harilal

I was scared of the night and nightmares that followed. As soon as mom laid the plates on the table, I would realize that bedtime was closing in on me. And for that reason alone, I never rejoiced in a mouthful of good dinner. With every gulp of food and water I took, I consistently stared at the lights around the dinner table that slowly went dim. And this teased my blood to run cold.

Silence took its toll once the TV was switched off. From there the house gradually descended into darkness until it was pitch black and the family, after the last bit of their small talk had gone down, was on bed.

Cursed with asthma, I could barely sleep at night. This was so because a night's sleep to me, regardless of how people usually perceive it as a suspension of one's own consciousness after a tiring day, was defined by the horrendous nightmares I was thrown into. And the thing about nightmares is that, you run when you're being chased. When you reach the dead end, you turn back with fear, waiting to be eaten, no matter how absurd all of those might seem when you finally wake up. This deception of reality is what threatened me.

In most instances, I would wind up at the farthest depths of the sea. With murkiness, almost nothingness below and a fading, almost dying ray of light through the calm surface above, I was at where it was blue, bluest of all blues I've ever known, floating weightlessly right at the center of the gradient.

If not, my nightmares were of cold and scaly hands that snatched me from behind and dragged me all the way to someplace where my screams can never be heard by a fellow human. Nevertheless, in any case, I was suffocating in my sleep. It's almost as if my head wanted to conceive my own body that there was no escape from this condition, and that it had to give up. But I always eventually woke up, with a startle of course. Half the time, I broke down coughing painfully, waking my family up. Then there was this hustle of mom rushing to the kitchen to fetch me some water, my dad rubbing his hand at long stretches down my spine and my little baby sister wailing at the top of her lungs. Of nights I could faintly remember at that little house of ours, the most familiar ones are those. But there are those nights that I hadn't slept at all, the ones I remember even clearer.

With my eyes open, piercing through the darkness left behind by a fast-asleep moon, I saw things. I saw him.

He looked like an apparition – all white, remarkably pale like a cloud of steam at the verge of disappearing into thin air, just as though he hardly existed. I have nothing more to add to the description of his appearance, simply because I don't recall another notable feature. And as to what he did, he stood behind the almirah at one corner of the room, throwing his arm out and around as if he was trying to reach me, that too desperately with intentions unclear. Only a half of his body was out and seeable, while the other half stuck between the wooden panel and the wall closely behind it. Often, it seemed as if someone was holding him back from behind the almirah, him stuck like a fly in a cobweb. Some days elsewise, it looked as if he was mimicking his 'need for help', overdoing his struggle and taunting a helpless chap with eyes wide awake, staring at this very outlandish and unreal stranger from his bed.

I remember the first time I had seen him. That night, I, along with my family had laid down to sleep after a late-night premier of Rosemary's baby on the television. It's as if a movie night of that sort had to happen just to serve as or furthermore add to the eeriness that surrounded in the room of four the first of all times he appeared. The air cooler flushed and squealed in succession, from a worn-out fan belt apparently. The streetlights from a then silent street of Dubai that night had an odd tint to it. Its golden beam had alloyed with the silvery shade of the moon, which was then filtered out by the delicate linen curtains. My weary eyes followed the path of that stream of electrum to where it finally gleamed on one side of the almirah that was close to the wall at the opposite corner of my room. That is when I noticed a shoulder jut out from the other side of the almirah, the side close to the wall.

My half-shut eyelids fluttered open. My body froze. Then by degrees, a head poked out. Once the head was quite sure I had noticed it, it brought out its right arm and right leg out. And quite soon without any notion, he started tussling against nothing, beating his arm around and trying to get hold of me from where he stood between the almirah and the wall, as if someone was strangling him from behind. This made me shudder and lose control of my breath. As his struggle grew violent, my breath grew shorter. But then, the perplexing thing was, I couldn't move an inch. Nor take my eyes off the ghost behind the almirah. I heard the wall clock tick slower. This made me think that I'll be stuck suffering to suck in some air through my nostrils forever. I remember wanting to die, for someone or something to put me out of my misery. Soon after, my mom switched the room's light on to my muffled cries and he was gone.

This went on for a week or so until I learnt that he never truly was there to hurt anybody. In fact, he never took a teensy step out of that little space of about two feet of his. He never turned up in the morning either. I remember having approached the almirah one morning with a make-believe courage, all processed to face the phantom I thought would pounce on me, but for nothing. At days, I occasionally stood at that spot of his, aping his actions, staring down at the side of the bed I slept on, being the monster myself. That delivered an air of relief, laughing at the thought of a harmless monster in pain of some form or the other, so devoted to a teak wood almirah.

Then it happened. There was tumult and scurry in the house all day that Saturday until evening. The kitchen was being remodelled and things where so out of place. The night, nonetheless, seemed so stuck to routine except for the atmosphere of the bedroom with a few misplaced baggage and tools around the bed and the almirah. As it always had been, without any delay, he appeared once everybody else in the family was sound asleep. As per the protocol, he performed his act, giving his all to untangle himself from an illusory creeper that had bind around his body while I lay there motionless watching. That was when, capriciously, he fell to the ground, now breaking his norm of staying within the perimeter allotted to him. He then held onto his left foot so tight, crying in vacuum, which presumably looked like he was hurt. He groaned mutely, rolling on his stomach and back in unbearable agony before he disappeared. I, for reasons I don't recollect, chose to lay rooted to my bed all the while.

I remember having stayed up for hours muddled, stealing glances at the almirah every now and then. In the course of dawn's leisurely advent, I should've dozed off. I woke up a quarter or so past noon the next day to find myself alone at home. I hurriedly rang up mom on the telephone, only to know that the family had left early in the morning to purchase marble for the countertop and other essentials for the new kitchen without me, who was undoubtedly out for the count. But, you see, I couldn't care less. All that bothered me was what I had seen the previous night. I raced up to the almirah in my room, put my left hand around one of the curved edges of it and went on to impersonating what the ghost had done the night before, hoping I'd somehow comprehend what it meant. I remember being upset, even more frustrated about not being able to come to a conclusion as to what all of that implied. Why me? Why did I have to see a ghost caper around an almirah at night? My forehead grew hotter. My breath ran shorter. With both my hands, I vigorously shook the almirah, raising a ruckus.

Thud! The half-deafening sound of heavy wood on marble thundered all through the house, sending the floor vibrating. I was on the floor, wrapping my hands around my left foot in terrible pain, knowing I had fractured the bones. Gasping for breath, wheezing, I cried out loud hoping I would gather possible help. But they were of no avail. My surroundings grew dull and indistinct to my eyes. I felt death envelope its arms around me, promising relief. And believe me when I say that I know how it feels. It's partly agony, but for the most, it was comfort. And for once, I actually was fighting against the brevity of breath only not to breathe again.

Next thing I remember is waking up to a faint and compressed sound of relentless rain on window glass. I remember the smell of hospital clog my nostrils. The lids of sterilization boxes clanked feebly, followed by the sound of scissors cutting through elastic bandages. I was lying straight on a bed, and looking down I saw the cast on my left leg. Dad, mom and a few of the family's friends were also there. I hadn't responded much, but from their talk it turns out that a heavy wooden plank from the top of the almirah fell on my foot, wounding it badly. Staring at nothing in particular on the blank white wall of the room, I remember realizing that things were starting to clear up, that the fog was giving way.

I spent weeks at the hospital, day and night, and the ghost never once showed up. Stepping into home at the end of the third week, I knew I was expecting someone. The whole house smelled of longing too. But I knew I had to wait until night to see him. And I also knew that that night was going to be different.

After a light dinner of kubus and fried sausage, I made my bed so very fervently, aching for the lights to go out and everybody else in the house to crash out. The longing for about a month then had this unusual dry and rusty taste as if it had lasted for as long as I can remember. With every second that passed, my gaze tightened itself to the almirah. Soon, the family was asleep except for one, the room was dark and he appeared from behind the almirah.

He then walked out an open door, and stood there still for a while, retorting to the improbability that I and the night was looking forward to. On seeing him start to walk across the living room, I got up from my bed and silently followed. He walked into an open balcony oddly slow, and I lumbered along his path with enough of a gap. He halted at the fence to glare at the blunt air of the city for a while, climbed on top of it, only to evaporate without even turning back to look at me.

Hobbling towards the fence of the balcony, I too heedfully stepped on the baluster to climb on top of it, managing to find balance and stand upright with a casted leg. Looking down, I realized that a five-storey building was taller than I had imagined. Lifting my head up, I embraced the chill breeze that had gushed all the way from somewhere happier in this very world to meet my face that moment. I closed my eyes to another pair that wasn't watching me, a pair of hands that wasn't stopping me. I closed my eyes, once and for all, to the gleaming city of Dubai.

STORY EIGHT

LETHE

by Vishvak

CHAPTER 1: IDENTITY

Your memory has been wiped," I told him bluntly, interrupting the usual talk session I was having with him. Mr. Ken having had his mind occupied, clearly did not hear what I said, but aware that I had said something, paused for a moment.

"What?" asked Ken instinctively.

"Your memory has been wiped," I reiterated, followed by an air of silence and a very inconvenient echo of the fan screeching. I could feel the uneasiness in the room as I saw Ken having trouble breathing as if the air around him grew heavy.

Mr. Ken is a very practical man, although flawed, he has desirable qualities. He's a young man in his early 30s with the right conscience, earning a decent pay as a software engineer working tirelessly to improve himself. Despite having everything that would allow him to be perceived as a successful person by society, a tragedy did come his way. Ken never had a family but he only earned for himself and did not voluntarily contribute to charity, choosing to ignore the harsh realities of people beneath him. As I said, he is a man and not without his flaws.

I met Ken several weeks ago when he reached out to me for help. We have been having therapeutic talk sessions ever since. Ken, despite growing up in an unhostile environment, seemed to show signs of psychological trauma. He had issues with stress and anxiety as well, but he was fully sociable. When I asked him about his childhood, he had trouble remembering most of it. He also claimed that he had been experiencing flashes of memories that never happened to the best of his memory.

Ken has been alone for the most part of his life because he has trouble being in a relationship and expressing himself to others. He is also extremely Phono phobic; he is very sensitive to the sounds of his surroundings. It is for this reason that he is allowed a cabin to himself, isolating him from the others at work, which has put him at a disadvantage of socializing with his co-workers. He has never seen most of his co-workers, except for a handful, and feels almost as if he had been kept captive at his workplace.

The screeching of the fan and the incomprehensible discomfited face of Ken only added to the uneasiness. He turned my way as I said, "It's a lot to take in and it is alright to be in a state of denial."

A confused Ken murmured, "What?" again in disbelief of what he had just heard.

"Look, Ken. Breathe-in and breathe-out, calm yourself down. I am going to tell you something out of the blue that will throw you off again. Memory wipes or as we say, drug-induced amnesia, is a very common practice unbeknownst to the common public. I know, this might sound absurd, as unbelievable as it may seem, it's what happened to you."

"I'm sorry," interrupted Ken. "I made a 30-minute drive here so that I can talk to you about my problems and you are trying to play games with me? Is this one of your psychological mind tricks? If so, I am not amused, this is not working," he said with a burrowed frown on his face as stood up to leave.

"Mr. Ken, I can assure you I'm not playing mind games, this is not a psychological mind trick. It's the truth," I said.

Ken with a startled look on his face stood motionless. His face twisted as his mind went blank. "Why should I trust you on this?" he said growing curious.

I reached for the shelf on the left corner of my cupboard, where I had placed the file anticipating this exact moment.

"I want you to listen carefully. This is classified information known only to a handful of people. This information cannot leave this room," I said, firmly.

"Alright," whispered a muddled Ken hesitantly.

"Memory wipes were experimented at the time of the war. It was largely successful in containing information breaches. Since then, experiments on memory wipes began unfolding with the permission of the state to deter national threats. Unmotivated and circumstantial criminals were the very few of the public to have their memory wiped. Secretively uniformed officials of higher ranks, holding valuable information have not been spared," I said.

"However, your case Mr. Ken is a bit more complex. Your memory was wiped and replaced with a simulated memory, not of your own. In other words, Ken is your false identity given at the time of your memory wipe," I continued, curiously awaiting Ken's response.

A seemingly detached Ken, still startled with his eyes dizzying, grabbed the file I handed him impulsively. He opened the file in an unpremeditated fashion. His eyes grew wide as he read through the file.

"What is this?" he exclaimed.

"Your previous identity, Mr. Ken"

△▼

CHAPTER 2: TRUTH

Ken's psychological stress is an extension of the trauma he had experienced. There is a truth about him that he is yet to be aware of, which is what has been causing him a lot of problems, and it is intricately tangled. In any means, the truth could not be put forth in a way it is digestible for Ken.

"This is absurd, give me one good reason to believe you," said Ken, frustratingly.

"Ken, I would like you to meet Dr. Stephen," I said as I called in Dr. Stephen through the ringer to my right on my desk.

Stephen with his white lab coat swinging freely, entered the room immediately, seemingly nervous. I continued, "Dr. Stephen here, one of the very few people aware of the wipes, is also the one who knows about your case in detail."

"Mr. Ken, I am Dr. Stephen, a neuropsychologist." said the doctor introducing himself.

"You look a lot like my co-worker Anthony. You must be his relative, do you know him?" asked Ken, curiously.

"Who? No, I don't think so," said Dr. Stephen, briefly and continued. "Mr. Ken, as you may know by now when Nations waged wars, information at the wrong hands meant definitive defeat. The warring nations to protect information at all costs, conducted experiments on drug-induced amnesia. Over the years, the secretive practice perfected into selective memory suppression by destroying neurons to interrupt the memory trace and then stabilizing it to revert the effects of the disruption of specific molecular mechanisms, establishing synaptic connections or simply put, your memory. The process, however, has not been proven to be hundred percent efficient - loss of memory and flashbacks are common side effects of the process. Mainly, it failed its purpose in treating trauma patients as it did not undo the effects of the trauma. Your case Mr. Ken, is one of such cases."

"Your flashbacks are traces from your previous memory and your trauma is the result of a failed memory synapse after your memory wipe," I said as Ken's face turned gloomy yet eyes grew bright, with his heart pounding fast, anxious to glimpse at his past. Ken still casted a look of disdain.

"When new memory synapses are created, a new identity is given to the person. This allowed circumstantial criminals to be reinstated back into society with their new identity. However, with a fully grown adult, repercussions are not uncommon. The most irreversible memory synapse is the name of the person. With an adult, their new identity has the same name as their previous ones," continued Dr. Stephen.

"Who am I? You are just my psychiatrist, I reached out to you. How could you possibly know all this about me?" exclaimed Ken.

"You are not just my patient, Mr. Ken. You'll know the answers to that in a while. It's best for you to know more about yourself if you'll need the answers to those questions," I said enticingly, persuading Ken to ask the question.

"Who am I?" mumbled Ken distressingly again.

Everything I had set up worked perfectly, leading Ken to this exact moment. I glanced at Dr. Stephen standing at the end of the room for his approval. The disquieted doctor slowly nodded his head back and forth approvingly, with a dubious look on his face. An air of silence possessed the chamber, Ken awaiting the story of his ghost, gulped the heavy air.

I began, "Mr. Ken, you were formerly known as Alex." I paused anticipating an impulsive flicker in his eyes. Ken, however, made no gesture of such. I quickly turned to the doctor by my side in a brief manner and continued.

The truth about Ken unfolded before his eyes. Ever since the age of 6, he had a rough childhood mostly because of his abusive father, who paid no attention to his family. His mother was a beautiful lady, who unfortunately became psychotic after losing her firstborn in an accident. Stricken with sorrow, she led to live her life believing that she has lost her only child. His father tried his best to cure his ill-fated mother but eventually lost hope, and to cope up with the stress, engrossed himself in his work. Poor Alex, terrified by the hysterical cries of his mother, spent most of his nights muffling his ears with the only friend he had, his fluffy blanket. With no one to care for him, Alex grew emotionally depressed at an alarmingly young age. Days passed but the intense screams never stopped, but only grew.

One night, a 12-year-old emotionless Alex stood next to the lifeless body of his mother with a gun by his side. The horrified father's face contorted into a horrendous look of disgust, as his eyes grew wide with the sight of the ghastly murder. He looked into the lifeless eyes of his son, stammering with pain, and asked him what had happened.

"I did what you did to the doggy when it was in pain daddy," replied the 12-year-old Alex.

His life, grown into an intolerable ordeal, the father realized that he had no other choice but one and did the unthinkable. With no one by side, Alex was left alone, uncared for. I, accompanied by Dr. Stephen tried the memory wipe stimulant on the traumatized 12-year-old Alex.

Ken grew pale with his eyes turning cold, his lips formed a hard line, a gulp stuck in his throat as I told him the truth. A shiver ran down his spine as his flashbacks kicked in. With a perplexed look on his face, Ken was clearly aware of his truth. Even so, there is more to the truth that he will never know. A cold air of ghostly silence fell upon the room. Dr. Stephen was intensely observing him, yet Ken made no sign of response, he was slowly detaching from reality as his memory synapses convoluted.

"Ken," I exclaimed suddenly.

A phono phobic Ken impulsively turned still. It was time for him to make the ultimate choice.

"What will it be Ken? Would you rather live as Alex, knowing your past or have your memory wiped and go back to being Ken?" I asked unassumingly.

"Wipe my memory, I can't," stuttered Ken with a frozen face, as he sat there emotionlessly.

Two staff nurses walked in and escorted a possessed Ken, who left showing no restraints.

"This is the sixth time he has chosen to have his memory wiped," said Dr. Stephen. Moving the chair beside him, he adjusted his glasses and continued.

"Even after a complete memory wipe, he still shows signs of trauma, his stress levels elevated. It didn't work as we expected. We should have tried it on patient 3, or someone with a lower trauma level. You don't try a newer simulant with someone like him," said Dr. Stephen, glaringly.

"If it doesn't work with him, how would we able to get this approved?" I exclaimed.

"He does not have a name; he never had a name. That's the most consistent memory synapse. Not a lot of people are without names, almost everybody has a name," countered Stephen.

"I wanted to have the stimulant tested on someone with a higher trauma level," I said.

"I think we both know why you chose him. The only proper memory synapse he has is his fear of loud noises. Nothing will work on him," blurted Stephen.

"We'll run a different simulation, this time, with a different name. Maybe as a soldier suffering from PTSD and try this simulant again, with a much higher drug dose. We'll completely wipe his memory this time," I said, reassuringly.

"It doesn't matter what name you give him. You have to give up on him."

"I can't give up on my own son, Stephen."

IN SEARCH OF HIS FATHER

by Spandan Nath

Memory is like a mirror lost in time, you never know where you will end up and meet yourself without recognising.

He had never met his father. As a child, he still remembers his mother being called a whore for having given birth to a fatherless child. The man had walked away on her the moment he found out about her pregnancy. Yet she never held a grudge and always told her son, "Your father wasn't from here. He needed to go away. He had to take care of the world or else it would fall apart." As he grew up, he started believing that his father was probably a spy, a secret agent who needed to save the country from several attacks that the citizens would never know of because he thwarted them.

His mother never corrected him, but once she told him, "You are thinking too small. He is a lot more than that."

She had moved to another town with her son and even assumed new identities so that the stigma of her being an unmarried mother doesn't carry over. In his new school he was the son of a man who died during his wife's pregnancy. He hadn't seen his father's photograph before that. His mother always kept it locked in the cupboard safely. But to prove her son's legitimacy, she produced this photo just once...at the school. He tried to take it in as if it were a forbidden cuisine, that he might have the chance of having only once. That was his only memory of his father's physical form.

He tried to convince his mother several times to let him see his father one more time. Just once. He would never ask for it again, but she always got extremely worked up whenever her son would breach this topic. What was so wrong about it? Why was he never allowed to see his own father? And she would reply, "Because someday you will leave me and he would be responsible!" He never understood what she meant by that. He would convince her saying, "Mama, I will never leave you. Never. I promise." But she never believed him. She would sit hours staring at the wall after this conversation every time. Then she would cry relentlessly, and sometimes she would not remember why she started crying.

As he was growing up his mother was diagnosed with Alzheimer's. Gradually he saw her drift away. Every day a part of her would disappear. He knew that soon there would be a day when she would be gone completely. He would not leave her; she would leave him... and perhaps herself.

She had to be taken to the asylum for her own safety when he was about sixteen years old. On his eighteenth birthday, he went to meet her. It was very fortunate for him that she was having one of her better days. She recognised him, or a part of him. She hugged him and said, "I remember you. You are so dreamy now. I see you in my sleep sometimes. Am I awake?"

"Yes mama, you are."

"Good, then I need to tell you this, under the lamp there is a key. Take it out and burn that. He should not see it. Do you understand?" He understood nothing much but nodded. "Now go, go do that." As he began to leave, she murmured, "See I told you...you will leave me, and he would be responsible!" He couldn't hold his tears and left, trying to hide them.

He went home and sat thinking about what she had said, "Take it out and burn that." What was she talking about? Then it struck him... "Under the lamp, oh! How had I not understood this?" He rushed to what used to be his mother's bedroom and moved the bed-lamp which didn't have a bulb anymore. Yes, there was a key. He knew what it would open. He unlocked the safe in his mother's cupboard. Yes, yes ... There was the photo. He took it out and broke down. Someone had burnt his father's face. It smelt of cigar. Someone had extinguished a Cuban on his father's face! But why? He looked at the wall and sat for hours. Then the phone rang. He let it go to voicemail. When he stopped staring at the wall. He checked the voicemail. His life had changed.

He wasn't a big believer of rituals. His friends and the priest took care of the cremation. He was so blank that it hardly seemed he had lost his mother. When it came to scatter her ashes, he decided not to do so. He took it home and locked it in the safe where the photograph of his faceless father was kept. Then he went to a cafe and sat there reading. He sat there four hours gulping down an exact 34 cups of coffee. By the time he had finished the book, something was cooking in his mind. Something new, something sinister, but all for the good of mankind.

He kept returning to the cafe everyday... and each day he would finish a book there.

"I know who you are looking for!" He was startled by a middle-aged man, one day. He wasn't sure who this man was. Something familiar about him, but he couldn't place him.

"I am sorry, do I know you?" he asked.

"No, not yet. Listen, I don't have much time. I need to tell you something very important." He looked at this man carefully. What would a stranger tell him that was so important! "He will meet you. But you need to know it's him. You need to recognise him, you understand?"

"What? Who...? Who are you talking about?"

"I don't have much time. You will have only a moment with him. Unless you stop him. You need to ask him to stay. Ok?"

He couldn't understand a word this man was saying. He turned towards the counter and asked the waiter for another cup of coffee. Then he turned to talk to the stranger. But the man, where was he? He had left. What was he saying? What was that all about? He thought about it for a while.

"Here's your coffee. 26 so far." The waiter interrupted his thought.

"26 already? I haven't even reached half the book." He smiled and replied.

The waiter enquired, "Why didn't your father stay?"

The question hit him like a punch. "What? How do you know my father? How do you know he left?"

The confused waiter asked, "What do you mean? He was sitting by you and then when you ordered the coffee, he walked off. Wasn't that your father? He looked so much like you... So, I thought..."

For a second, he was relieved, "No, no. That was some...." and then the realisation hit him harder. "I know who you are looking for...You will have only a moment with him."

"Wasn't that your father?" What had he done? He hadn't recognised his own father. The man he has been searching forever. The waiter looked at him confused as he placed a few notes settling his dues for coffee of the day.

Then he took the book and rushed out. Running on the footpath he looked hard if the middle-aged man was anywhere nearby.

An old man came in the cafe that very instant and enquired from the waiter about the boy who sits and has coffee there. "Oh, he ran after his father, I think. Something wrong with that chap... I say."

The old man said in a frustrated voice, "Yeah, very wrong. Now that he has met his father." Then he took a cigar out of his pocket, lit it and stepped out. There was a sudden commotion outside. The waiters of the cafe rushed out to see that a bus had run over someone. A half-lit cigar rolled away from the crash site.

Eight years had passed by. He never saw his father again. But now he had started a new quest, a quest that would definitely take him to his father. Just a few more years, and all that reading at that cafe would bear fruit. He was about to crack it – time, that's all he needed.

Five years down the line, a very select few from the scientific community and a few government officials accompanied him in a bunker. It was time for the trials. He had agreed to share this technology with the government on one condition. He would be the first to travel. After much resistance, he was finally going to fulfil his dream. He was going to meet his father and also make sure that he would not have to work this hard for this, again. He looked at himself in the reflective door. Then pulling it he entered the space. He couldn't help but think, he was going to a journey within himself...his identity, his origin.

When he returned, he was about a decade older. "Someone is chasing me. Whom have you told about this technology?" He looked at the government officials accusingly. "No one. What happened to you? You look so..." He completed the officer's sentence. "Old? Yes, I am above forty now. I think. It gets difficult to keep track." The people in the room were shocked. They had never seen a man age a decade in a manner of minutes. One of his colleagues approached him and asked, "Please tell me you did not do anything." He smirked for a moment and said, "I think I knocked up someone. But that's not the problem. I told you someone was chasing me. Almost all throughout the journey." The colleague wanted to punch him in the face, "You knocked up somebody? You mean there might be a child out of her..." He quickly replied, "I don't think so. She wasn't too keen on the child. She was in love with the idea that I travel in ... You know." The entire room went in an uproar. "You idiot. How can you be so irresponsible?" But he said, "Calm down. We met at a wedding where I know my mother met my father for the first time. I was looking for my father. You know that was my only concern. I was trying to befriend her to find out if she knew my mother. Something led to something and I don't know. I don't remember everything." The colleague was concerned now, "You are suffering from side effects. How many times did you travel before returning?" He replied, "I don't remember. I told you I was running from someone. I couldn't lead him back here. I had to take a detour to warn someone. I had to make sure that all this wasn't for nothing. I will meet my father, now." After a minute of silence, he enquired curiously, "Why aren't you worried about the person chasing me?" The colleague calmly said, "Because no one else knows about it. Whoever it is, is from within this room. And he hasn't left yet." He realised that was true. He was suffering from side effects. The colleague continued, "I am more worried about the woman..." "She will abort. Don't worry," he said. "For her sake I hope she does. Giving birth of your child out of place. That's not good for her. Her memory. It's going to be fractured. The child will have to leave her and you will be responsible." The words suddenly made him go grim. He wanted to say something, his eyes went wide and then he fell on the floor.

He had slipped into a coma. Years of travel out of his true place, had an effect on his brain and body. Unfortunately, the team didn't have enough information about his travels. His journal used a code he had devised himself so no one could crack it without his presence. The team later created a covert ops unit around his technology. They would recruit fitting people for the job, who weren't as reckless as him.

Years passed by. When he woke up from his coma, he was quite grey. His colleague now headed the Mirror Unit as this covert operations group had come to be called. When he was well enough, they brought him to the Unit. He told his colleague something the moment they met. A day later, he was sanctioned a journey back into the Mirror. They gave him a warm farewell. The head of the Mirror Unit gave him two cigars - a code in the unit when someone was going for a suicide mission.

He travelled back to the woman to make sure she doesn't give birth. The technology wasn't exactly like the films. It could fix on a year perhaps, but not on the exact moment. Destinations were a bit uncertain. Owing to this flaw, he reached her when she had already given birth. He visited her and saw his son in her arms. "You came back," she said when she saw him. "But I am old now. In a way, you must know now that I hadn't lied to you," he replied. She didn't know what to say. She hugged him and wanted him to hold his son. He replied, "I cannot hold him. There are some things you need to know. I would not have done this if I knew. I did not know. But you must remember." She could not fathom his mysterious talk. Then he sat with her and explained. When he ended his explanation, both of them were in tears. Before he left, he told her, "You have to remember... He will have to leave you someday, and I will be responsible. Tell him that. He needs to know the sins of his father so that he knows of his own sins someday."

Next, he travelled back to the woman, years later. He disguised himself as one of the doctors at the asylum. He stayed there taking care of her for a few months. The night she would die, their son visited her. He came to bid her farewell. When she was talking to their son, he realised something and excused himself. He had to do something before his son discovered it. He lit the first cigar as soon as he left the hospital premises. This was the first part of killing himself.

He was done with the first part. He had to stay in this time, for one more mission. He went to the cafe of his youth and had coffee. Then he saw his son come in and sit at one of the tables. It was almost time now. Just a matter of days. He lurked around the cafe from then on. This part of his journey from the past was in the mist of his memory. He had to rely on his journal. And all the journal said was that he would meet himself... He would teach him to know his father. He laughed at his own naivety... Reading it. A few days later, as he waited for the meeting to happen, he waited on a bench at the bus stop nearby. He didn't realise when he slipped into sleep. As he lay sleeping, a middle-aged man walked past him. He entered the cafe and located his son. He slowly approached the son and said, "I know who you are looking for!"

THE GAME OF TRUST

by Soumya Srivastava

Shoot! Amie! You've got to run for your life! Quick! Run!"
I could hardly hear her. Eyes set on the white ribbon, my face was beet red. As the sweat dripped from my forehead, I sprinted at full pelt.

"Congratulations girl! You did it at last!" rejoiced Lizzie. She kept scrolling her phone on our way back home which was a ten-minute walk from school.

"I came fourth. Anne injured her ankle, so she was last," I said in a dead voice while pondering that only five of us had enrolled for the sprint in the Sports Club. Sprint was not a very popular choice in high school.

"Weeks ago, you were last and now you're not. That's an achievement. The least you can do is acknowledge me for the valuable advice I gave you," she smirked.

I shrugged my shoulder with a tilted head.

She watched me in horror. "Don't you remember it was me who noticed that you made efforts to breathe and then filled you in with all the medical information about your Lora?"

I nodded in approval and smiled, not in a mood to stretch the conversation.

I waved her goodbye and turned right towards my home. Lizzie and I had been friends since I moved to Atlantis. Having no memory of my last home or friends, Atlantis became my home since and Lizzie my sole friend.

I opened the door to our home, changed my shoes and called out for Mamma.

Whiskey, our dog greeted me with an exuberant lunge and when I entered into the hall, I endured him until he was contented.

Mamma called out from the kitchen, across the hall, instructing me to change my clothes and come for lunch.

I hurried to my room upstairs, showered, changed and returned to the dining hall.

Mamma was ready with the boiled vegetables, fried egg and bread for lunch. According to her eating green vegetables was good for my health.

I was a weak child since birth and hence my health was her first priority. Cycling, playing outdoor games with friends, and joining the sports club among others were all prohibited for me. The only time when I was allowed to go out was for school with Lizzie. She was the only one who used to come home while we played board games, studied for exams, completed projects, gossiped, tried make-up tutorials, dug the internet and every other nonsense thing that girls could possibly do in a room.

As Mamma passed me bread, she questioned about my day and I told her about our History lecture and Maths homework that we were assigned.

"Which book did you read today in your sports class, Amelia?"

"Huh?" I blinked a few times trying to avoid eye contact with her.

"I……" I staggered.

"Amelia, what happened?" Mamma had an influential impact on people around her. She had the ability to stare you in the eye and get the truth out of you.

I don't know if all the mothers could do this, but for Mamma, surely it was her ace.

To sit across her at that table and serve a lie in her face was more dangerous than walking in the lion's den.

I lifted my head up, fixed my eyes in her direction and answered, "Pride and Prejudice. I started reading the Pride and Prejudice today."

She grinned shaking her head, "So it's Jane Austen again."

She was right. It was my third in a row. It was supposed to be my third Jane's novel only if my newly discovered enthusiasm for sports hadn't taken over.

Finishing my lunch, I asked Mamma to pass the jug to me. She could hardly hold the jug full of water steadily. Her hands trembled uncontrollably. The jug was about to drop, but I reached for it in time.

"Looks like I need veggies too!"

I forced a smile, thinking how frail she was. A woman in her early thirties, who was not even able to hold a jug, was burdened with the responsibility of a weak child's upbringing. After her husband went missing under mysterious circumstances years ago, she became the man of the house.

I empathised with Mamma's gloomy state and tried my best never to disappoint her in any way, no matter what.

I got up from the dining table to leave and turned towards the stairs when she called from behind, "Don't forget to take your medicines Amelia!"

"Yes Mamma, I won't," I answered and ran to my room.

Medicines were an integral part of my life. I had to take them as per a strict schedule and Mamma made sure that I did. There were sticky notes all over the house, reminders on the phone, and calls in school office during classes - all to ensure that medicines were not missed, even for once.

Lorazepam it was. I called it 'Lora' or at least Lizzie did.

△▼

The next afternoon after waving Lizzie goodbye, as soon as I turned right, I spotted a tall and muscular built man standing at the gate, gazing at our home. His hands were in his pocket as his dark and short hair fluttered in the wind. I walked towards him apprehensively and tapped on his shoulder. When he turned to face me, I froze with dropped jaws and raised brows.

"Amelia!" his narrow eyes twinkled as he threw his arms around me and swirled me over.

I barged into the hall, overjoyed, "Mamma! Look who is back!"

"What is it Amelia? Slow down," She rebuked as she rushed out of the kitchen.

Stunned, she glanced at me, "Amelia who is…."

"See Dad has returned Mamma! My prayers have been answered. He's back," I interrupted.

A cold chill went down her spine. Dad had died for us years ago. His unexpected appearance left her speechless.

She plodded towards me and hugged me. I could hear her sob. As I hugged her back, she whispered loudly in my ears, "Yes dear, your prayers have been answered." She stroked my hair, "Go shower yourself, then we'll all have lunch together. Meanwhile I'll talk to your father."

I hurried upstairs and changed. It had been ten years since Dad died. At least we believed so.

Consequently, we moved to Atlantis to start afresh. Mamma worked as an editor in a local newspaper to make the ends meet. She worked day and night laboriously, taking up every part-time job available.

I dashed through the stairs, thinking how things would change; now that Dad was here.

"Dad, where had you been? Why didn't you ever try and reach us?" I enquired as soon as we sat for lunch.

"Amelia, stop bothering your father with questions. What matters the most is that he's here. With us. For you. Let's take a minute to thank God and eat without stressing yourself," She advised in her silky voice.

"Yes dear, eat your veggies, I mean lunch!" Dad grinned.

I smiled back and ate the lunch in content with my entire family, for the first time.

After lunch Mamma was busy in her reporting work while Dad and I played Frisbee outside in the lawn. Whiskey followed us wagging his tail. I threw the Frisbee towards Dad and he grabbed it mid-air. He returned it at a ferocious speed, such that I lost track of it and it fell on the ground.

He giggled while I picked it up and threw it for Whiskey, who chased it and leapt forward to catch it. He then brought it back to me.

Each time he would bring the Frisbee to me, though he was supposed to give it to Dad. I even tried directing him in Dad's direction, but all in vain. Whiskey was used to playing Frisbee with Lizzie and me. No new player allowed!

Every time he would snuffle me all over and then plant his muddy paws on my palm. I wondered when he would extend this friendly gesture towards Dad.

At night Dad oiled and combed my hair. He was sitting on the edge of my bed and I was sitting on the floor with legs crossed when Mamma entered the room.

"Amelia, you're not asleep yet?"

"No Mamma. See I got my hair oiled today."

"Hmm, I see that you are enjoying a lot with your father," she smiled and then continued, "You were with him for the entire day, why don't you sleep with me tonight?"

"NO!! I want to hear all of Dad's stories that I missed all these years."

"Amelia, why don't you tell your mother that I'll come to her after you're asleep?"

"Yeah, that's right. Dad will join you in a while after I doze off, which will be soon I promise," I pleaded.

She pursed her lips and rolled her eyes before shutting the door with a thud.

"So long back there was a girl named Kimoko in a village…….." Dad narrated a story as I tucked myself under the blanket.

"Dad!"

I woke up startled in the middle of the night. He was sleeping next to me, one hand supporting his head and the other on my blanket. I looked at the clock, it was half past two.

I realised how infuriated Mamma would be to find that Dad never turned up. I opened my door, careful not to wake up Dad, to check up on her. As I stepped outside, I heard someone murmur. I carefully tiptoed, moved past my room towards Mamma's room.

"I have no idea. I clearly remember burying him in the woods. The injury was grievous enough, there's no chance he would have survived."

A long pause.

"Yes, today in the noon…….. Never before, not that I know of."

"I'm sure she has skipped. The seal is not broken yet."

"How can I reverse it? Are there any long…."

"Okay, I'll call you again soon. Sorry for disturbing you so late. Good night."

She hung the phone and went to the washroom.

The earth beneath my feet began to crumble.

Why did Mamma bury Dad? Was she the reason why he was missing?

I grabbed the edge of the door with my hand. With every question that popped in my head, the heavy feeling in my stomach soared.

I turned around and trudged towards my room. My intestines twisted in agony and heart throbbed against my ribcage.

"Amelia, why are you strolling around at this time?"

I was surprised to see Dad standing at my room's door.

Dad do you know who buried you? Were you really buried? How did you escape?

My mind screamed silently.

"You should rest dear, come."

I followed him sadly.

Next morning as I walked down the stairs everyone was already awake. Dad was reading the newspaper and sipping his morning coffee. I heard Mamma washing dishes in the kitchen.

"Good morning Amelia," she called out, "Sit I'll bring you breakfast."

It was a constant wonder how she'd sense me without seeing. I sat quietly next to Dad and she sat opposite to us. Her ginger brown hair was neatly tied in a bun.

"Had a good sleep sweetheart?"

I nodded.

"I'm so glad to see you cheerful. When your green eyes sparkle with joy, I am on the seventh heaven!"

I stared her in the face trying to decipher her words. The joy in her words seemed so pure. She loved me in real. Then how can she?

"You've had your morning pills?"

My eyes widened and my mouth went dry. She knows I'm not taking them…

"Let's have breakfast first ladies!" Dad intervened and I was rescued.

I started gulping the cornflakes in my bowl.

As she started getting up to fetch more milk, I questioned, "Why don't you two go for a movie today?"

"Two? And what will you do alone?"

"Oh, I'll call Lizzie over. We have a project to complete."

Mamma lowered her brows, "You said Lizzie's cousins came over and so she wouldn't make this weekend. You forgot?"

"Oh! Yaa! It just slipped from my mind." I scratched my head realising how meticulous she was.

"Anyways, I have to go for grocery shopping today. How about a movie the next weekend?"

"But we can…."

"Oh! I put the milk to boil!" she hurried towards the kitchen.

Dad grinned behind the newspaper.

I was flabbergasted to find that I had just seen Mamma get edgy. Something that I had not seen in years. No matter how worse the situations were, she never lost her calm. However today was different. Or maybe it was always before my eyes, only I could never understand.

She loved me earnestly and I knew that. She raised me like a lioness. She never did anything to arouse fear or suspicion in me.

Then how can she be behind this horrendous crime? How can she bury the man she loved so deeply? I've seen her eyes turn moist every time we talked about Dad. She told me stories about how they met, he proposed, they married.

It seems there was more to what my eyes could see, and I had to get to the bottom of this.

△▼

In the noon I sat in my room at the desktop. Mamma went to fetch groceries and Dad was experimenting with his gardening skills in the lawn outside.

I typed 'Lorazepam' in the search box.

Whiskey was sleeping near the window. He shifted in his sleep and licked his muzzle with one slow sweep of his tongue.

Lizzie's absence bothered me. She was the one who helped me search last time that Lora caused respiratory problems and that's why I wasn't allowed to attend the sports club. Consequently, when I stopped the medicines, I could stand fourth in the sprint. She was a curious soul who would individually search every medical term that turned up, to make sure we didn't miss the tiniest of the details.

I clicked on the very first link that appeared on the screen.

Lorazepam cures anxiety, sleeping troubles, nausea, vomiting....
Longer use can cause weakness, decreased respiratory efforts, amnesia......

So, stopping Lora helped me with my breathing.

I scrolled down.

Withdrawal causes headache, anxiety, hallucinations, confusion, smell, and sound disturbances....

Confusion and sound disturbances? Is it possible that I misheard the telephonic conversation?

Amidst all these complex calculations, I heard Lizzie calling out my name.

As I dashed out of the door, Whiskey followed me wagging its tail. Lizzie peeped out of her car's window, "Hey Amie!" She was accompanied with her cousins.

I smiled and greeted them.

"You texted you wanted to talk, anything important?"

"No, actually I heard this…"

"Oh, if not then why not we discuss it tomorrow in the school? We're going for a movie and we are already running late. You want to join?"

I declined with an excuse and waved till they moved out of sight.

As I turned around to leave, Dad was standing behind me with a spade in his hand.

"Dad were you here all the time?"

"Yes surely, why?"

"Then why didn't Lizzie or any of her cousins greet you or ask about you?"

Lizzie knew about Dad, she'd seen my childhood pictures. She was the keeper of all my secrets. Then how couldn't she recognise him?

"Maybe because you never introduced me to her. Or maybe because she confused me for your new gardener?" he giggled.

When I looked at him closely, I was convinced that he would make a good gardener. Spade in one hand, other hand on the waist, a long towel put on one shoulder, wet clothes, and mud all over his face. Even I wouldn't have recognised him at first sight.

△▼

I sat at the dining table with newspaper in hands and eyes at the door. Waiting for Mamma. Dad and Whiskey were out for an evening walk. Soon the car parked itself in the driveway and Mamma entered with multiple bags. She gave me a smile and went for her room.

"Amelia! Oh dear! You scared me," she exclaimed as she came out of her washroom. Her hands trickled as she reached out for a towel.

I entered the room and closed the door behind me.

"Where did Dad go earlier?"

Her eyebrows furrowed and she twisted her ring. "Sweetie let bygones be bygones. Don't bother yourself."

"Mamma, I heard you talking over the phone about burying him."

"It is not what you are thinking."

"Then what it is? Who did you bury? And, my medicines? I also know that you know I am not taking them."

"Yes, yesterday I checked your room and found that you still haven't opened the new bottle. I strictly advised you to never miss your medicines."

"Medicines? Huh? Why do you always fret over my medicines? And I asked you about Dad! Why did you bury him?" I hollered.

My high-pitched voice made the glass kept on the table tremble.

"For you Amelia, for you!"

I stared at her, wide eyed, without blinking.

She exhaled and dropped on the floor with head buried in her hands. Weeping. Her dark large eyes swelled, and oval face was puffed up.

"Your father could never handle his liquor, Amelia. During the day he was a saint and at night, a scoundrel. It's always a woman who has to face the true colours of her man, when the world sleeps."

After a short pause, she added trembling, "That day was no different when he battered me. Only that you weren't asleep." Tears poured down her cheeks. "You my angel, came to rescue your Mamma."

I tried to look her in the eye, but she swiftly looked away. "You bashed him right over the back of his head with your baseball bat repeatedly, till he lay on the floor motionless. He bled like an open faucet."

I tilted my head and furrowed my brows.

Baseball bat? I played baseball? But I don't remember!

Wait, what! I killed Dad? He bled to death?

Then how is he back? I've seen him, talked to him even! How is that even possible?

There was so much conflict in what I knew, what I saw and what Mamma just said. Millions of questions erupted in my brain like an active volcano.

"Then how did Dad come back Mamma? And why didn't he say anything?"

"Because," she gasped for air, took a deep breath, "Because he's not here Amelia. You are hallucinating."

I could feel the hot lava flowing down my body. My breathing quickened as I kept swallowing.

I covered my mouth with clammy hands, while my brain scrambled to make sense of every detail that was thrown at me.

"After that accident you started having anxiety attacks. The doctor prescribed you medicines which helped you forget the events and subside your symptoms."

Never miss your medicines Amelia.
Long term use causes Amnesia.

"However, when you stopped them abruptly, your first withdrawal symptom was Hallucination."

"For all these years your most treasured dream was to meet your father. Consequently, you started hallucinating about him."

Everything clicked into place. Mamma didn't sleep with him; Whiskey didn't acknowledge him; Lizzie didn't greet him.

"My connections in the media and police helped us get away with the legalities. We moved here so that your past doesn't haunt you."

Dumbstruck I sat on the floor across her.

"Don't worry dear. The doctor said your condition is reversible. He has prescribed new medicines for you. I brought them today," she consoled me.

Realising how unfair I had been to suspect the very woman who protected me, I wailed. I held on to her tightly. My head against her bosom, I felt so safe.

She caressed my hair and kissed my forehead.

Deep down, my heart reminisced how safe I had felt even when Dad hugged me.

△▼

It's been over a month since Dad went for the walk. He never returned. Not that I wanted him to.

I quit the sports club and renewed my library membership. Not a single pill has been missed since then.

"Mamma, I'm going to sleep," I announced and closed the door. My energy was completely spent. Lizzie's birthday was always the most exhaustive day of the year.

I tripped over the bed and lay with my limbs stretched out.

"I've to change, eat my pills…," I mumbled to myself.

As I felt my consciousness ebbing away, I decided to give myself away to my exhaustion.

"Dad, let's play hide and seek," exclaimed the young girl.

"It's midnight sweetie. Your Mamma would be furious."

"I don't want to sleep or hear anymore fairy tales. Dad Ple-e-e-e-a-a-s-s-s-s-s-e-e-e-e-e," she squeaked revealing her broken front teeth.

"Okay fine! But you're allowed to hide only in the living room. Go, hide."

She jumped up and down like an alarm clock and ran towards the living area.

He put his hands through his dark and short hair and began counting till 10.

He checked everywhere – behind the curtains, behind the couch, under the table – but nowhere. Just then his eyes fell on the chest kept across the room in the corner.

As he tiptoed towards it, he saw a pair of emerald green eyes sparkle from the keyhole.

Just as he was about to open the lid, he sensed someone approaching, and turned around.

"You're awake?"

"Yes, I couldn't sleep." A silky voice was heard from a few meters away. "James what you saw in the attic today…"

"Look we'll talk about it, but in the morning. You have to answer…."

"I was saying that," the hands reached for the pants' pockets, "what you saw in the attic today is none of your concerns and I'm not answerable to anyone."

"What? Really? You still…." He began to snap when he paused suddenly, horror visible all over his face. His narrowed eyes widened.

The person raised their hands pointing the gun towards the man.

"How can you even?" He stretched his arms towards the person with palms forward and moved a step ahead, slowly.

The dragon engraved in silver on the holder of gun shone as the 4-year little girl watched in horror.

The trigger was pulled and…

"No!!"

I woke up screaming. I was sweating profusely. My head throbbed and spinned. I was in bed wearing my party dress. I wiped the sweat off my face with my hands when I noticed a tall figure standing near the window.

"Dad? You were…"

"Believe in yourself Amelia, in your instincts. Dad loves you a lot and so do you," his voice echoed.

Before I could deduce anything, I turned my head to the right when I saw a woman at my door.

Strong built. Long ginger brown hair. Her dark large eyes sparkled. Her hands were raised, pointing the gun towards me.

"Mamma?"

She swiftly curled her fingers around the trigger. The dragon on the holder shone.

"What are you doing?"

"I realised I forgot to kiss you goodnight honey."

TOO LATE

by Nena Patel

While I was in my room, someone called Riya and told she was sorry in hesitating voice. Riya replied, "What happened dear, why you are crying? Tell me"

"Riya, Dia died in front of me."

"What are you talking?"

"She was crushed under the wheels of a car. I am really sorry."

Her heart skipped a beat as the weight of those words dawned on her heavily. Stammering, she replied, "You are mistaken Kiara. Just a minute ago I came from her room and she is reading a book. She is safe and ALIVE!"

"No Riya her dead body is right in front of me. Cops aren't informed yet about the accident."

"Wait, let me check here again."

Riya rushed into my room to make sure Kiara was just joking but she didn't find me here. However, she found my novel which I was reading. She heard the sound of running water from the washroom. She frantically banged on the doors of the washroom, continuously calling me out, "Dia, DIA. You in there?" I didn't reply. Instinctively, she pushed opened the door and started crying loudly while taking my name continuously. Kiara, still on the call, asked her if everything was alright. She replied, "Dia, she is.... she is... her body!!"

"Yes, that's what am saying. She is dead and her crushed body is right in front of me."

"NO, NO, her body is drowning in the bath tub here, right in front of me."

"That's just impossible."

"She is drowning. Dia, get up!"

Suddenly she heard some footsteps approaching her. Without turning around, she kept asking who it was, without getting any response. Her eyes were transfixed on the sight of the dead body of her roommate.

When the sound of footsteps grew closer and louder, she slowly turned around and nearly collapsed in fright. Her sight went up to the ceiling and finding her voice finally, she screamed. But this time a little louder.

My body was hanging to the fan!

Riya was in shock; she couldn't understand what was really happening there. She turned towards the bath tub again and looked over my drowning body and then she turned towards the fan and could see my body hanging there, all the while on phone Kiara was continuously asking my roommate if she was okay.

But how could she be? I KILLED myself!

The footsteps she heard earlier were now quite recognizable of who the intruder was. Slowly she turned towards the door and guess who she found?

To add much chaos to Riya's mind, I was standing at the door, walking right in front of her. She was howling – in fear, in sadness, in confusion and her hair was all messed up. I asked her why she was crying and all of a sudden, she hugged me tightly. After calming down a little, she pointed towards the washroom, then towards the ceiling while telling me that I WAS DEAD! I laughed right at her face because how could I be dead if I was standing right there?

To prove me wrong, she held my hand tightly and pulled me towards the washroom and showed me the overflowing bath tub. I stopped laughing and said, "Sorry. From next time I won't leave the tap open." But the look she gave me was an expression of disbelief, as if I couldn't look past what she was really trying to show me. It was clearly not the overflowing bath tub.

When I still didn't react the way she had expected me to, she turned and looked towards the bath tub and could still see my dead body. Sweating profusely and being visibly impatient, she pulled me towards the ceiling. When I still couldn't see or understand anything she was trying to tell me, Riya tried to grab the vanishing sight of my dead body. Out of nowhere she heard a light eerie whisper in her ears, "She can't see me." It was as if my dead soul was telling Riya that I couldn't see my own dead body. She again checked both the spots but now the dead bodies had vanished. She was totally at a loss now. The strangeness of it all was quite scary in itself. Without speaking a word, she handed me her phone and on call was Kiara, crying. I asked her, "Hey Kia. This is Dia here, what happened? Why are you crying?" Just then, I heard a crashing sound. Kiara didn't answer but hung up the phone.

Sweat droplets rolled down my neck and there was a sudden jerk in my body. Something clicked my mind and I asked myself, "How was I talking to Kiara? She met with a car accident three years ago, crushed mercilessly between the wheels of a speeding car and was dead on the spot." I again tried the number from which the call came but no one picked up. The uncanny voicemail spoke back to me, "It's too late now."

I confirmed with Riya if she really was talking to someone on the phone and she replied, "I was speaking to Kiara and she was crying, telling me that you are dead."

I instantly flipped and screamed at her, "Riya, have you gone mad? What nonsense is this? It was Kiara on call, the one who died three years ago in a car accident! And how come I am dead if I am right here before you?"

I checked the call duration and it showed 30 minutes from then. Then my sight went on the call date and it was of the same day, same timing, but… of three years ago! My hands started shaking and the phone dropped down to the floor. I saw myself in the mirror right in front of me and I could see, not myself but the reflection of dead and crushed Kiara. From nowhere, carvings of tears formed on the mirror and they read, "IT WASN'T AN ACCIDENT BUT A MURDER." When I tried to touch the tears, they evaporated - just like my dead body to Riya.

I didn't mention about this bizarre apparition like event to Riya, lest she might lose her senses. Instead I consoled her that I am not dead, and she should just lock her room and take a nice nap. When she was all tucked in, I hurried to my room and locked it as well. I stood motionless in front of the mirror. Just then my phone beeped and I checked my cell, but there were no calls and no notifications. Assuming something was wrong with my device, I switched it off to check the batteries. While I was at it, I heard someone knocking, but it took me a moment to realise that the sound wasn't coming from my door, but from my dead phone!

My whole body shook with terror. The knock got louder and louder and finally when I switched on the phone, an anonymous video automatically started playing.

The video was of Kiara which must have been shot when she was alive. No, the video was of when she was about to take her last breath. Kiara was continuously knocking on the door of the car she was sitting in. Her face was covered with sweat and tears as she cried for help, in vain. The car was filled with some kind of smoke due to which she felt suffocated. Suddenly, someone choked loudly, but it wasn't Kiara, there was someone else in the car too.

No! This can't happen! Someone can't be this cruel and that too with Kiara. I was unable to see who the black cloaked person was, but his hands reached out for Kiara's neck and closed his fingers tightly around her radial artery. Now, he was covering her face with a garbage bag, holding two broken glass bottles in both his hands and now, sliding down the wine bottle's sharp cut end from top of her hands to her wrist. Kiara was continuously pleading for help but she was not much audible as her breath slowly faded away. The murderer clearly wanted a painful and slow death of Kia, not a fast one. He banged one bottle over Kia's plastic covered head and she started bleeding profusely. The sight was more than the word gruesome could be as the murderer had no mercy left. He cut the line below her diaphragm with a knife and put his hands under her open body and took out her stomach and some extra veins with it. He even cut her fingers, one-by-one. She was almost dead by then. The murderer then took out some blood from one vein and drank it like a monster.

My head started spinning watching the video and I tried to shut it off, but it wouldn't let me. I heard slamming of the door of the car, a speeding vehicle, Kiara's body being thrown under that, crushing of the body. It all happened in seconds. No one could tell it was murder. It clearly looked like a road accident.

As soon as the video stopped playing, I felt someone watching me from the window. When I turned, the mirror near my window caught my eye. Instead of my reflection, there was the plastic covered face dead body - just like that of Kiara in the video. This was so unnatural and I started screaming loudly.

Riya started knocking on my door, asking me to open. I threw away my phone and rushed to let her in – I could look at my phone no more.

While Riya tried to question me what happened, I stayed numb. She picked up my cell that was thrown on the floor and saw that it was broken, but the video was still playing. I warned her not to see it but she didn't listen. She even saw the reflection of the dead body in the mirror. To my surprise, she was calm in this uncanny scenario we were surrounded with.

She walked towards me and slowly whispered in my ear, "The murderer left one clue which you couldn't erase." I turned pale. As the message on the mirror started reading, "It was too late," a knife was pushed into Riya's intestines. Struggling, she spoke in broken words, "You are a monster. You don't deserve to live and you don't deserve a friend like Kiara nor me."

"I am sorry Riya, I couldn't save her. My want for blood neither saved her nor you."

As Riya felt my knife in her intestines, some intruder pushed a burning cigar in my neck and broke a wine glass on my brain. I felt a rope wrapped around my legs and a free fall down the building.

What happened to me, Riya and Kiara in that mirror remains a mystery till this day. It is now 'TOO LATE' for the world to understand.

But, what about your mirror? Does it hold the answer you desire now, or does it hold something else which you don't?

SOULONOSIS

by Sachin Shanbhag

The knock on the door made Sameer jump. He was enjoying his alone time this evening with a book and a drink by his side. He came to his bungalow in Lonavala often to escape the city life and guarded this part of him zealously. No one other than Seema, his wife of 15 years, knew he was here and maybe that was why the knock startled him.

It was nearing 8pm and even the birds had stopped chirping; the wind whistling occasionally through the trees outside was the only sound around. It was a nearly moonless night and being set a little away from the expressway, there weren't too many people around.

Sameer opened the door assuming it may be one of the villagers from nearby, who helped around his home usually. But other than a bat lurching around drunkenly from tree to tree, there was not a soul around. Shrugging, he walked out onto his driveway and looked around but still couldn't see anyone. A small shiver ran down his spine – Sameer was not particularly superstitious but what if it were burglars trying their luck. However, he had this home for over 10 years without any incident and he was wondering who could have knocked, and where they were now. Looking up, he could see the dark sky blotted by the sudden entrance of even darker clouds heralding the build-up of a summer thunderstorm.

He turned around and walked back thinking he should get more lights installed to dispel the gloom around here. It was then that he heard the soft shuffle of steps – from INSIDE the compound! Sameer's heart was thumping hard as if he had just run a 100-meter race. He peered towards the source of the sound. It grew louder and just when it felt like he could not take it anymore, a dark shadow emerged from around the right side of the house and came straight towards him. Fighting the urge to scream, Sameer stared at this apparition and as the feeble light fell on it, he saw a tall man with a dark shawl around him walking slowly with a hunched back. His swarthy face was adorned by a thick black and flowing beard with long matted dreadlocks to match. A cloth bundle on his shoulder and vermilion smeared on his forehead completed the look.

Sameer was still too stunned to speak and the man, if it was one, didn't help by standing silently in front of him with his dark eyes half closed. Regaining his composure, Sameer asked, "Who are you? Where did you appear from? You weren't here when I opened the door!" Looking at Sameer as if scrutinizing him carefully, the man replied in a slow but imperious drawl, "You should answer your door sooner if you want your guests to wait outside it. I walked over behind the house to see if there was another door there. As for who

I am, they call me Baba Dayashankar." Resenting the tone used by Baba, Sameer answered with some asperity, "You might be a Baba elsewhere, but you are definitely not my guest and not welcome here!"

Raising his palms in front of him, Baba smiled and said, "We got off on a bad start. Let me try again. I live in a small ashram downhill from here deeper in the forest with a couple of disciples meditating and honing my own specialty of hypnosis. Sometimes, I walk up the hill and go to the village to get supplies and earn some goodwill there if possible. I had never seen a light in this house and that is why I knocked. Now that I'm here, could I request you for some water to drink?" Sameer was a genial person and now that his initial fright had worn off, he was feeling a lot more generous. It would start to pour soon and the rain here was usually savage. In a much softer voice, he said, "Baba, I am Sameer. Please come in. You can have water and stay some time till this storm blows over."

Sameer led Baba towards the open door and into his house. After settling Baba in a chair, he returned to close the door and as he was doing so, he heard the sizzling rain approach in waves from the far distance. When he got back, he saw Baba looking over some books in his bookshelf with great curiosity. Sameer shrugged and went to get a bottle of water and a glass. He also filled a plate with some dry snacks and walked back to the living room. Baba nodded his thanks and sat back with a couple of books in his hand. One was titled Hypnosis by Liam Andersen and the other was Powerful Mind by Cathal O'Brian. Seeing Baba's quizzical glance move from the books to him, Sameer smiled. In his mind, he was surprised that the rustic looking Baba seemed to understand and read English. "These books are not mine. My wife is very interested in hypnosis. Personally, without meaning to offend you, I think hypnosis is humbug. Just some tricks played on minds too weak to realise they are being muddled," said Sameer.

"You don't believe in the science of hypnosis? Have you ever had a direct or indirect experience of being hypnotized? Or are you just being biased?" Baba asked.

"I have seen many "hypnotists" ply their illusions online and get millions of views to show for it. But I think they are exactly that; illusionists with their subjects in cahoots with them," answered Sameer.

Baba cocked his head as he heard Sameer out and said, "That's one big thunderstorm, let's hope it ends soon. But in the meantime, would you object to undergoing a session of guided hypnosis with me? So that I can prove my point to you?"

With a rueful shake of his head, Sameer said, "I will not get convinced. But just to humour you, let us do it. However, do tell me what exactly you are going to do."

"Scared already?" Baba smiled. "Hypnosis is a general term, but it is a vast and obscure science with many applications. For a true master, the sky is the limit. To laymen, hypnosis is nothing more than being put in a trance and letting your actions be controlled by the hypnotist. If that is what you think it entails, then you know nothing. What I am going to do today is different. I will start by helping you relax to the extent that your current surroundings may be lost to you. Guided by me, your soul which is now free to roam unfettered will be able to traverse some parts of the spirit realm; after that, who is to say who you may meet there? There may be moments when some soul you meet might temporarily make its presence felt. Also, if there is some strong hidden wish deep inside you to meet some long-lost person, it may just get realized."

Sameer was a little taken aback. He had not expected this. In a weak voice, he said, "Baba, what you are saying is unheard of and can definitely not happen. I repeat, I do not believe in this mumbo-jumbo; it seems to be a waste of time."

Baba's response was quick in coming, "Then why are you so afraid? Go through with it just as an experiment. Shall we start?" Feeling cornered Sameer just nodded and leaned back. Baba cleared the small centre-table and from the bundle he carried, withdrew a large bronze bowl, ladle, and a few incense sticks. He lit the incense and fixed them upright at one corner of the table. Asking Sameer to relax with eyes shut, he started running the ladle around the edge of the bronze bowl beginning slowly, but gradually increasing the pace muttering some incantations under his breath.

Even with his obvious discomfort with the idea, Sameer consciously relaxed as the incense filled the room suffusing the atmosphere with fragrance. His body went lax and settled deeper into the chair as Baba's low-pitched droning intensified while a thrumming sound arose from the brass bowl. Sameer was now completely motionless, only an occasional twitch of his arms indicating life. Baba now fixed his eyes on him and the pitch of his chanting rose feverishly as he called on all of his considerable power to exert control on Sameer's spirit - which was now free of the chains of his body and was hovering around restlessly. The next stage of the session was crucial where Baba would take control of Sameer's soul and release it into the spirit realm briefly before it returned and let itself get re-attached to his mortal body. Baba had done many such sessions before and was supremely confident of his ability to do it one more time. All those who had gone through this exercise with Baba always spoke about how it had rejuvenated them completely.

Reciting the incantation that temporarily released Sameer's soul into the other realm, Baba noted the shudder in Sameer's body with satisfaction. In the sudden silence, Baba sat keenly observing Sameer in the gloom. For a few minutes nothing happened and the storm raging outside suddenly made itself heard. A crack of lightning right then made Baba jump and look in that direction. The few lamps in the room went off with a crackle and then glowed back, much dimmer than before. In the dim light, Baba saw Sameer's body move; suddenly his eyes opened, and he slowly sat up. Baba had not yet started the incantations which would get Sameer's soul back and was puzzled with what had happened.

Hiding his surprise, Baba gently asked, "How are you feeling? How did you find your way back?." Sameer, still scrutinizing the room, spoke, "I am feeling very well. As to how I got here, you helped me do that, obviously!" With a jolt, Baba realized that while Sameer's voice was deep, cultured, and full of energy, the voice that spoke now was thinner, had used some vernacular and spoke with a slight lisp!

"Who are you?! You are not Sameer!" Baba asked, a slight tremor in his voice. Sameer gave a derisive laugh and said, "I am not Sameer. Look at me properly and you will see." Baba, looking at him carefully now, saw what he meant. Sameer was a stocky well-built man of about 40, with an open face, light brown eyes, and a confident manner about him. The man now sitting in the chair had black shifty eyes, a permanent smirk, and the unlined face of a 25-year old man. As Baba continued to stare, he noticed a continuous twitch in the right shoulder. "I am Chandan! And Sameer was kind enough to point the way," he said with a leer.

"Why did you come? You must have died and passed on to the netherworld. Then why did you do this unthinkable thing?" asked Baba. He was in uncharted waters and had to be very careful with his next steps. "Yes, Baba. I was killed by Thakur's thugs 40 years ago! Just because I came upon them looting the government granary in the valley. I begged and pleaded for mercy; told them I would not breathe a word of what I saw to anyone. Even swore upon my old parents and younger brother's lives. But they stabbed me then and there and left me to die. They went on to kill my parents and my brother too! What had we done to deserve this? Other than being poor, of course. They say God is watching but all of those killers are still alive and prospering while I am stuck in between this world and the next." Chandan was working himself up and angry tears seeped out of his eyes. Calming down a little, he continued, "Thanks for this second chance. I can pick up life from where I left off. I will claim my revenge and then go find..." He trailed off at that, blushing slightly.

Baba picked up on this and asked, "A girl in your life? A special one?" Chandan replied, "Her house is just 3 km from here. I can't wait to see her." For the second time that night, Baba raised his palms in a placatory pose, "Hold on, son. I completely agree that you have been gravely wronged. The perpetrators must be punished. I will take responsibility for that. However, what you want is not possible. There are some rules that this universe runs by; the dead cannot come back to life unless by rebirth. Doing this would be the most unholy thing ever. Think of your sweetheart; many years have now gone by since your death and she would be 40 years older.

Would you like to see her living with another man? What would she think if she sees you now, someone she loved and knows to be dead? She might be repulsed to see a dead man claiming her love! This is not something you want."

Seeing the irresolution on Chandan's face, Baba continued, "Also, think about Sameer. He is innocent and does not have anything to do with any of this. He has a family somewhere and has his whole life ahead with them. You had your chance and God decided that it was your time to go. Please consider this and let me take you back so that Sameer can come back to live his life." Baba's earnestness was not lost on Chandan and he finally sat back closing his eyes for some time. Baba watched him and his reactions closely knowing that he had been very persuasive in his argument. He had seen the flurry of emotions flitting across Chandan's face going from initial ecstasy and aggression to dejection and finally resignation. When Chandan opened his eyes, Baba knew he had won the argument and could expect no further resistance from him now.

To reassure himself, Baba gently asked, "Shall I take you back then?" Chandan sat up, as if rudely awakened and with some reluctance, nodded. Baba asked him to relax and sit back. Seeing Chandan sinking back slowly, Baba lit fresh incense, feverishly chanting the mantras to do what was needed. Again, the room filled with fumes and Chandan's eyelids got heavy and slowly his head lolled on to his chest as he became motionless. Baba continued the invocations using the ladle again, this time in the reverse. The thrumming sound reached its crescendo and the thunder outside accentuated the instant when Sameer stirred and opened his eyes. Baba looked at him closely and asked the same question, "How are you feeling?" He replied, "I'm feeling good. Just as if I am waking up after a long nap. How long was I out for anyway?"

At that, Baba realized it was nearing midnight. Still a little perturbed from all that had happened, Baba asked instead, "How was the experience? What happened to you there?" Pausing before he answered to collect his thoughts, Sameer replied, "I can't describe the place exactly as nothing was clear. Everything there has blurred edges as if someone used a strong eraser on them to smoothen the roughness. The few people I ran into were like wisps, white or black in colour, floating around. A couple of them talked to me but communicating there means telepathy, no actual words were spoken." Baba listened to all of this flabbergasted as this was a first in all the time he had been practicing that he was hearing what the other side was like. Most of the earlier ones either remembered nothing or had very vague recollections of large open spaces.

While Baba's conscience was battling with him about whether to tell Sameer the entire truth of what had happened, Sameer stood up and said, "I've been cooped in there for too long. I need fresh air, so I'll take a short walk. Thanks for the experience, Baba. This was worth it!" Baba jumped to his feet too and said, "Son, it is past midnight now and the storm is still raging. Why go out into this darkness now?" Smiling, Sameer started walking towards the door, "Don't you worry, Baba. A little rain is nothing. And I know this place like the back of my hand. I will not get lost." With that, he opened the door and walked out into the dark night and pelting rain.

Exhausted, Baba finally sunk back into the chair he had been sitting in, glad that the ordeal was finally over. As he rested, he went over the entire evening in his mind and got the feeling that he had missed something. He started muttering to himself, "Was I wrong?

What was different now? The way Sameer walked. He did not walk with a limp and a swagger when I met him first! Then why now? Sameer spoke to me in proper English now. Then why am I feeling there is something off? Was it the accent in which he spoke? He said he knew this place well; after all he has owned this house here for 10 years. But then, he is a city dweller who must have come here only occasionally for a few days. Then how can he?" While Baba was speaking out these innermost thoughts, he stood up with great difficulty and staggered towards the still open door. There he saw a pool of some reddish-brown liquid spread out on the threshold of the house and dribbling on to the driveway where it was getting diluted by the rain.

And that was when the horror of what he had done hit him!

Baba Dayashankar slid down to the floor as he started screaming into the stormy night!

RETALIATION

by Krishna Anap

I t's such a terrific storm!" Sameer yelled over the phone. "Hello? I'll be home soon. Stay indoors!"

Sameer turned around as he disconnected the call and frowned at the gloomy storm that had started to dominate the Mumbai skies. He was in his office while his wife Ruchika was waiting for his return. Outside his office, his employees complained about the storm as they sipped their last cup of coffee.

Sameer grunted and looked at the door with disgrace, as if the employees had bought him shame. He leaned against the glass and rested his eyes on the flooded road. He wasn't worried about his wife, his workers or the city which had surrender itself to the storm. Leisurely, he pulled out the only remaining cigarette from his pocket and lit it. The smoke calmed his mind and he closed his eyes as he puffed it out through his slightly cracked lips. The sky grew darker as minutes went by. The rainwater splashed on the window and killed the whispers that hung in his office.

His office door opened and a peon walked in.

"Sir, Saurabh sir has come to meet you," The peon said in his raucous voice.

Saurabh? At this hour?

"Send him in," Sameer said tightening his jaw as he glanced at the table clock. "And turn on the LEDs."

"Yes sir," the peon nodded and left.

Saurabh.

Sameer placed his cigarette in the ashtray and balled his fists tight to expose his pronounced veins. Just the mention of his name had ruined his mood; the way his intensions had ruined his life. He hated Saurabh, his poverty, and his never-ending desire; desire for Ruchika.

"Hello mate," Sameer forced a smile as he saw Saurabh's reflection on the window. He closed the blinds and gritted his teeth before facing him. His face made Sameer dig his nails deeper into his palms. "What brings you here? At such an absurd hour?"

"Hey Sameer. I thought you'd be here," Saurabh replied as he passed a hand through his long-wet hair. His overgrown beard suited his thoroughly chiselled face. "Um, I just wanted a favour, if possible?"

"Yeah sure!" Sameer exclaimed and motioned him to sit. He leaned back in his chair and smirked, "Do you want some donation or help for your firm?"

"Huh? No, I don't need any help." he replied in a tone of suppressed anger. "I said I need a favour, not help."

"Oh, my apologies. So, what do you want me to do?"

Saurabh spoke, but his words became inaudible as Sameer looked him in the eye. Something about Saurabh had changed which made him look ominous. His beard was wild, eyes gloomy with an unnoticeable smile on his lips that made his presence look disturbing. Unexpectedly, Sameer's face turned into frown.

"Is something wrong?" Saurabh questioned.

"Uh? No, no." Sameer looked away. "What were you saying?"

"Can I stay at your place tonight?" Saurabh requested in a flat voice, his eyes on Sameer who got up and removed his coat, occasionally fanning himself with his hand. "Funny how a simple storm made you realise how it feels to be warm."

"Stay at my place? Why?" Sameer crossed his brows in ignorance, disliking the way his poor friend had addressed him in a sarcastic way.

"The storm has blocked the roads and I can't make my way to my apartment. Moreover, I've got a flat tire." He pulled out his car keys and tossed them across the table at Sameer and shrugged. "I'm not lying."

"You can… stay," Sameer stammered, shocked with the dark tone of his speech. Though he wanted to deny his favour, his lips opened into an affirmative yes. "Let me pack up."

Sameer picked up some files and stuffed them into the shelf. He couldn't help but look over his shoulder with a suspicious look. He got a good view of Saurabh, who was staring at the window, smiling with a malicious grin. Hesitation dissolved into Sameer's mind and his face started to flush with the deepest anxiety.

"Are you done mate?" Saurabh walked up to the door and stopped. "The storm is scaring me."

△▼

"Saurabh? What a surprise!" Ruchika exclaimed and clasped her arms around him. "It's so good to see you!"

"I know, right?" Sameer snapped and walked past by her. He just couldn't bear the sight of his wife touching Saurabh, her ex-boyfriend.

"Come in," Ruchika looked away and adjusted her saree while Sameer threw himself on the couch and untied his shoes.

Saurabh sat beside Sameer, admiring the mansion and its towering walls. High quality furnishing, big chandeliers and expensive paintings made it look luxurious and unrealistic.

"It's a beautiful place," Saurabh complimented as he rolled his eyes from one corner to the other.

"Yeah, I built it. Most of the things you'll see are imported," Sameer smirked at his friend whose eyes seemed to drool at the sight of luxuries which were out of his league.

"Why don't you get fresh Saurabh?" Ruchika said as she sensed the unborn conflict. "I'll get the dinner ready."

"Yeah sure." He shrugged, knowing there was a tinge of grudge and anger in his voice, which remained unnoticed by them.

Mary, a young house worker guided him through the corridors towards the guest room. No surprise that the room was insanely huge with facilities he had never imagined. He realised how small his apartment was where clothes would lay all around, dirty and crumpled. His apartment had no aroma like his friend's house had. It had stained walls, smelly sheets, and nibbled carpets. Sameer's luxury, his success, and the fact that Ruchika was his wife had started to vex him. Irritated and tired, he clutched the tiny study table and looked at himself in the heavily bordered mirror, where his reflection seemed to brainwash him.

That man snatched everything from you. Your love, your reputation, your dreams. He constructed himself by destructing you. Yet you watch him grow every single day? Shame on you, coward!

He grunted and slid his hands over the table, knocking down a wooden statue that clanked against the reflective tiles. His knuckles had gone pale and his palm was beaded with sweat. Frustrated and exhausted, he threw himself on the bed holding his head and running his fingers through his thick hair. He knew he wasn't calm for he could feel the chaos that had started to haunt his insides.

"How dare you touch his body again?" Sameer growled as Ruchika entered the room with a basket of clothes. She walked into the closet without answering.

"Answer me."

"What do you want to hear?" she hissed as she slid the closet doors.

"I don't want you to get closer. He's here for a day."

"Your words are cold and cheap."

They argued for what felt like an eternity. Every word was harsh, every accusation was disgusting. It intensified, both of them unaware of the feelings and secrets the other person held.

When Ruchika stormed out of the room, she bumped into Saurabh and gasped while he adored her face with a guilty pleasure, petrifying her with a stupendous feeling that washed her body with a rousing wave of love. She froze and so did time. Unable to get her eyes off him, she loved the way his warm breath felt on her skin. He smelled fresh, just like a petrichor. He leaned closer, their lips inches apart.

"I'm sorry," she finally pulled away, regretting the closeness. Her mind shuddered with anxiety, her guts trying to clutch the butterflies that had awoke. She stepped away and looked at him one last time before walking downstairs, acting as if nothing had happened. Overwhelmed by the guilt that had started to fill her heart, she finally broke down, thinking about how beautiful her life would have been if she had never let him go. She quietly worked in the kitchen, feeble and helpless while Mary eyed at her, suspicious and curious about the new guest.

The dinner was no fun except for the worn-out casual interrogation. Purab and Kriti, their children, were amused by the presence of a new person on the dining table. Scared of the rumbles, they silently ate their food. No one looked up, no one talked. Everyone was holding on to an irresistible anger; the righteous one.

After dinner, the children gulped down their glasses of milk, complaining about how disgusting it tasted. Aware of how uncomfortable the dinner was for them, Sameer snuggled and picked them up, asking them if they wanted to hear any bedtime story as he walked out of the room.

"He is a great dad, it seems," Saurabh said as he watched him disappear behind the curtains.

"Totally," she chuckled and walked out. "He's just a great dad. That's all I love about him."

The words brought a bitter taste in his mouth. He had nothing left to say except to accept the fact that she had a great husband and beautiful kids. When she walked out, the workers barged in and started to pick up the used dishes and bowls while he sat there gripping a glass, angry and full of envy. He couldn't feel his satisfactory nerves. Sameer's pride was madding each of his senses while his mind blurred out all the happy thoughts. No matter how hard he tried to consume his hatred, it would pop up again. He didn't flinch until the glass broke in his hands, making the workers wheeze. He apologized.

Apologies.

No one apologized for their mistakes that day. And a mistake without any apology brews a sour consequence.

That night, Saurabh had the gaze of wilderness and plans as cold as ice. The night was slow, but not the storm. Everyone slept, unknown by the terrors that were about to unfold. A sleep so deep and undisturbed that no one heard the scream that echoed inside the mansion, reverberating the walls. The paintings looked humanoid but awfully still. It was scary because someone died, someone killed.

△▼

"And no one heard anything?"

"No one."

Mary couldn't stop crying and screaming. She would sniff, cry, then throw her hands in the air and scream as she saw her white apron turned red with blood. She couldn't forget the things she had just witnessed; the way she fell into the pool of blood that swamped the kitchen floor. Sameer's corpse was terrifying, his spine stabbed a numerous time, making his bones visible. His head was skinned unevenly, and a long knife was impaled laterally in his eyeball, with a force so intense that it broke open his skull.

Purab and Kriti bawled when they saw Mary screaming. They didn't understand why their house worker was crying or why there were police in their house. Though upset about her bloody apron, they were locked up in their room until their aunt came and drove away with them.

Ruchika was disturbed, stunned to the core, unable to move her lips which once chanted his name. Mary would put her arms around her and murmur prayers. But Ruchika didn't cry. She did nothing except to stare at the opposite wall as if it was an infinite stretch of hypnotizing imagination. Her eyes were numb and dry; expressionless as if they had lost their existence.

"Cry! Cry!" Mary would plead to her mistress.

"The murderer has to be a man, sir. It's not possible for a woman to stab someone so brutally."

Ruchika shifted uncomfortably at the mention of a 'man'. Thoughts had started to stir in her head, and she hoped they were wrong. Instantaneously, she clutched her yellow nightdress.

Upstairs, Saurabh woke up with a nerve cracking headache and numb limbs. His eyes were blood red, sore and heavy. Every muscle of his body throbbed with pain, urging him to lay down for some more time. But something didn't feel right. He wasn't in his bed. Instead, he found himself in a dark, musty room, lying on a worn-out couch which was surrounded by dusty furniture and piles of useless papers. Confused, he walked out the room and down the stairs, limping occasionally.

"What the hell? Ruchika?" He gulped as he walked down the stairs, shocked to see officers everywhere.

"Saurabh!" Ruchika gasped and so did Mary. The police officers quickly unbuckled their leather gun-holders and pulled out their pistols, aiming at Saurabh.

"Hands up. Hands up!" The officers commanded as they jogged forward, armed and alert.

"What?" Bewildered with what was happening, he glanced down at his body where everyone was staring. A gothic fear was induced in his body as he watched his loosely fitting clothes all covered in blood. No matter how hard he tried, he couldn't look away from the dark red stains.

"What did you do?"

"You killed him?"

He couldn't hear anything. His body stiffened as he remembered how cold the blood felt on his clothes that night. What he remembered was blurry, but true. The icy sensation of blood crawled over his skin.

△▼

"I don't remember anything!"

It was almost a week and a half since Sameer died. Saurabh was accused and arrested for murdering Sameer with a kitchen knife which had his fingerprints. Medical tests showed chemical imbalance in his body and he was diagnosed with BPD, borderline personality disorder, a disorder found in criminals.

"But I told you all, I don't remember anything!"

Scared. That's how everyone reacted. Ruchika found it hard to keep herself away from the social questions that arose after Saurabh had testified in the court. The love triangle wasn't bounded anymore and had managed to become a headline for all news agencies. It was more of a gossip than a news; a gossip about a cold murder, which had stupefied everyone's soul.

Everyone attended the funeral except Mary. She never hated him because he would always treat her with affection and what she felt, was love. She was young, raw and attractive with a curious heart. Along with time, he started to caress her palms and feel her warmth when they would be alone. It was their secret, a story about obsession.

The events that followed his death, sacred her more than his memory. She would see a silhouette move across the house at nightfall. A familiar touch would travel across her skin the moment she would be alone. Every night, someone would spill water all over the kitchen floor. Heavy footsteps would follow her as she moved around the house. They would get louder as if someone were approaching her. Then all of a sudden, they would stop and retreat. Things would change their position randomly and chandeliers would sway wildly without any wind provoking them. She would feel his presence and it scared her. She couldn't help, but reason it out, hoping that they were her hallucinations.

After the funeral, Ruchika headed home and swiftly walked upstairs. Mary couldn't help but leave the kitchen and follow her mistress who had locked herself in her room. Unknowingly, she carried a knife along with her instead of leaving it on the kitchen counter. She pressed her ear against the door, trying to grab any type of sound. When she couldn't hear anything, she got on her knees and peeped inside through the keyhole.

Her mistress sighed as she opened a hidden locker in her wardrobe from which she removed a blue nightdress. It was velvety and had deep red patches.

The blood had finally dried.

Ruchika undressed herself and wore the nightdress again, satisfied to have his blood touch her fair skin. She kissed her husband's ashes which she had brought home and felt his burnt flesh and bones on her lips, which reminded her of the detrimental night; the night when she had lost control over herself and so had her sanity. His resentful talks had irked her. She was provoked and insane. Never had his eyes adored her soul like Saurabh's did. His skin never brushed against hers affectionately. She regretted killing him. It wasn't hard for her to adulterate everyone's food so that no one would hear him scream. The hardest part was to skin his head, while he was still alive. She wished he would have moved a little less as she pulled out layers of his skin. Then she stabbed him again, not once or twice, but multiple time, and finally his head. She never wanted to frame Saurabh, but her panic-stricken heart did. She spent a sleepless night as she offered her husband an eternal rest.

"I feel dead, Sameer." She whimpered and placed her fingers in his ashes. "I shouldn't have killed you."

Dismayed and outraged like a broken lover, Mary's blood boiled with an uncontrollable anger. She shrieked, banged her fists on the heavy door and kicked it until her limbs hurt. When she stopped, the door opened, and she saw Ruchika standing in front of her. A murderer.

"Mary?" she mumbled as her eyes espied the dirty knife she held in her hand.

Mary shivered. She remembered she had been holding a knife as she watched her mistress gulp. The knife got heavier the moment she gripped it tight. Its blade was large and odd, with a shine of fatal repercussion. Her vision blurred as she heard a faint whisper which washed her with a familiar blue feeling. It was the voice of Sameer.

You know what you've to do? Retaliation.

"Retaliation?" Mary whispered as her lips formed an iniquitous curve. She finally knew what she had to do. Evil, rebellious, and profane, her soul had turned heinous.

Revenge. Reprisal. Retaliation. Mary's thoughts weren't lucid; maybe that's why she never questioned the things that scared her. She had all the signs and yet an unclear mind.

Was Sameer really dead?

THE ILLUSION OF LIFE

by Ranjitha Ravindran

Jaanvi, be careful in the woods. Don't hurt yourself my child, listen to me..."

Her dad's voice was still on her ears, as if he was right beside her, walking along the stream. The last time, when she and her dad came to the jungle on a hike, her dad made her walk all through the woods and beside the river, telling her stories of how the monkeys would survive the monsoon there. She was 14, but he made her understand all that a grown-up adult could. The hike and his stories will never get old for her. It was a bright and sunny day in mid-September, the early drizzle of the monsoon made the mud beneath her shoes swampy and hard to walk on. When both of them halted for a while, her dad made her ripened mushroom soup with some raw pepper and chilly available right there in the deep jungle. It was insipid, but she didn't want to disappoint her dad.

She exclaimed, "What an experience daddy! A forest mushroom soup out of nowhere!"

"Yes, Yes! That's the adventure you get in life. Aren't you my ever-loving darling girl? Yes, you're!"

He rejoiced as he held her in his arms and swung her around. He made sure everything's happy and good when they were together. She never felt her mother's absence at any cost with her father around. He made her feel strong, beautiful, powerful and happy, of course. "He was the best daddy ever," she thought. Yeah, he was. He is no more.

Jaanvi extended her arms in front of her, to feel the bliss of her dad's presence. Unfortunately, she couldn't. He wasn't there. She just wanted to have a hike by herself, one personal hike in the same woods where she had gone with her father for the last time. If only that incident hadn't happened, she would've still been with her dad, she mumbled to herself as tears blurred her vision. She made up her mind and entered the deep jungle.

Not many wild animals would be there to harm, her father had informed her already. Some civet cats or jackals might be there, but it's a mid-humid day and animals would more likely be resting and won't be approaching the borders, or that's what she thought. She has got her pepper spray too, cautiously. The sound of bubbling brook, buzzing insects, chirping birds, rustling leaves, all of those gave a thrill on her spine as she was the only human down there. Jaanvi paused and looked around amidst the withered dry-yellow leaves. She was alarmed by some unknown caution, but she couldn't find out what it was. Maybe a bear? Oh no! Not at all. What else is scaring her?

"Maybe I should've stayed home!

Why did I even bother coming here?

Should a teen come all the way deep inside the jungle, alone, just to relive the memories of her father's last moments?

Is it a joke or a torn memory?

So many questions, but she couldn't convince herself. Since she was already halfway, she thought of continuing her mission, no matter what happens. She moved further inside the forest.

The clock struck 2 o'clock in the noon, and her stomach grumbled reminding her of food. She tried taking the sandwich from her backpack, and then later remembered her father's trick of finding the way back home, if ever they got lost. She dropped tiny pieces of bread slices as she walked along. As Jaanvi spent another 30 minutes walking and panting deep inside the jungle with her hiking stick and heavy backpack containing three liters of water bottles, she found a deserted hut like the bigger ones appearing in Halloween Henry stories. She wondered who on earth would live in this hut with no basic amenities inside the jungle? Last time, when she visited the place with her dad, the hut wasn't there so how could someone create such a deserted hut within a couple of months? She decided to enter in, to find out what it was all about.

The hut was totally empty with no signs of human existence. Cobwebs and withered leaves were all over the place and few hatchlings from the bird nests were tweaking food forcefully from the mother bird. Jaanvi had a rough look all around the hut and sighed. What was she even expecting? Disappointed, she walked out and continued further in, not forgetting to drop the bread pieces one after the other.

On crossing the stream with wet boots, the swampy floor made her walk more tiring. At the end of the stream, she couldn't move her foot out of the mud. She groaned as the pain in her twisted ankle shoot up and wished that she could get help from someone around. She panicked since she couldn't move at all. It felt like someone was holding her foot firm under the water. Wait, what if someone or something's under the water, holding her for real? She was terrified at the thought. She began trembling and could barely stand.

"No Jaanvi, don't collapse and fall into the water. You would make it worse," she warned herself. She made up her mind to look at what's beneath her foot. She put her arms under the water and tried to free her foot from whatever was holding her. To her shock, there was nothing but mud. Her foot was as free as the flowing water.

"But why am I not able to take my feet off? Am I paralyzed? Did a bug bite me?" She was horrified.

Unable to move nearly for more than 20 minutes, she just stood still at the edge of the stream, feeling dejected. Her hunger and tiredness seemed to challenge her. She felt sleepy, bizarre and angry all together. Inside the forest, it gets darkened early and very soon she would be all alone in the deep jungle standing stranded. What was she going to do now? She wiggled her foot once again harder as a last try, but nothing happened. The clouds started thundering, the sky went dark and rain drops turned into downpour from drizzle. She was standing there shivering with wet clothes, with no clue what to do. Within 10 solid minutes, the rain stopped and the pitter-patter sound from the trees and bushes were the ones accompanying her.

Something alarmed her that she had some other company too. An adult male coyote was standing right in front of her. Panic-stricken, she didn't move a muscle. Even if her foot was released now, she was not supposed to make any sudden moves, since it would be an invite for the snarling coyote to attack her. She avoided eye contact with the mammal and remained as quiet as she could. The animal sniffed around her and made some peculiar noises. He was anxious and thrilled, but seemed to be harmless. He just came beside her and sat snuggling himself.

Jaanvi was taken aback. Why would she get stuck in the mud pit inside a deep jungle with a coyote accompanying her? And why was he very silent and unprovocative? The strangeness of it all made her pray fervently to go back home again, safely. As time went by, the coyote moved a bit closer to her and looked at her face. She was quivering but managed to see what he was really trying to do. He just sniffed her forehand and moved slowly into the dense shrub as if nothing had happened. The next moment, Jaanvi felt her leg being released. She was awe-struck. Was it something the coyote did to her or was it just the mud that got loosened up due to the rain on the stream? She was in chaos, but there was no time thinking about all these, she had to get back home before dusk and before something worse could happen. She looked back into the bushes to thank the coyote and made her way back home.

The stream was tougher than before due to the rain. She was also more careful now because she didn't want to spend another hour stranded in the water. Successfully, she reached the other bank of the stream and started running. But to surprise her, none of the sandwich droppings could be seen anywhere. Some animal or bird could have eaten them, or it was destroyed in the rain. Whatever it was, she wondered how she would get back home. Following her guts, she set about moving in a particular direction. When she spotted the familiar tall pine trees, she started running in full force.

She was starting to get hungry and dehydrated. She had an unnamed and unexplainable feeling that she wasn't alone in the jungle. She didn't know whether to be happy about it or feel scared. Even though she didn't feel any human existence, something seemed to be around her. People say, you can sense if something wrong is going to happen to you. She took a deep breath to calm herself down and looked around to check if anyone or anything was really with her. A cold breeze brushed her shoulders and made her hair wavier, as if someone just touched her skin; the dry leaves on the mud were rattling and breaking off the silence of the woods. Croaking frogs and the water droppings on the plants weren't poetic anymore. They seemed to be haunting her, as if some obnoxious persona was watching her every move around the jungle.

As she began walking slowly, she heard some indistinctive noises all of a sudden. It was like a lawn mower, like a beard trimmer, like coffee mugs clinking, like someone whistling and all kinds of strange noises. She widened her eyes to get a clear view around her and sharpened her earbuds to find where the noises were coming from. She cloaked her fear by walking hastily and pushed the nearby shrubs away to make her path clear. She felt the noises closer and closer as she walked. Now, some murmuring noises were added as well, some peculiar male voice was humming an ancient kind of Arabic. She thought perhaps some trekkers or campers might be there around. Jaanvi started running towards them.

"Please… Somebody help! Help me please… Over here…."

Jaanvi was screaming on top of her voice as she ran towards them with full force. However, she soon realized that she kept running towards the noise, but she couldn't reach them at all. She had been running for more than ten minutes, but nothing got her closer to anything. It was just the jungle and her. Jaanvi stopped. She looked around. And asked out loudly, "Who are you? Why are you scaring me? What do you want?"

The noises stopped. All of them. On a click. Jaanvi was terrified. She gathered courage to ask again, "I have nothing. Please let me go. I want to go home."

No response. Just silence.

"Maybe, it's just the woods and me and nothing else. Hunger and fear bring out unwanted illusionary series of events," she thought.

"Who am I talking to, what am I waiting for? A prince to rescue me, like in stories? How am I going to save myself from this mysterious place filled with void and fear? Am I taking some pills for these kinds of bizarre thought series happening in front of my eyes?" Jaanvi began walking back in the same direction, as she kept talking to herself.

She found a vacant space in the middle of the jungle, where the hut was supposed to be, which now vanished. Utterly scared now, she shrieked on the top of her voice confused of the chaos happening around her. She couldn't forget the sight of the hut, and how empty it was and how she still felt the smell of the permeated odour of the old wood inside it. She fell on her knees and started crying out. She was shaking and looked around her out of nothing but fear. She found the jungle haunted for the very first time.

This jungle had always been her favorite ever since she started hiking with her dad. She thought that she knew every corner of it, but the truth is only her father did and without him, she couldn't even find her way back home.

She was aghast when she found the same old stream just in front of her, as calm as it ever could be. She stood dumbfounded. It was the same spot where she was stranded for a long time and then got released by a coyote. She has been walking for so long and she was still in the same area? How could that be possible? "Am I losing the right direction? How can the stream be here when I just came from the opposite path? What am I even doing?" she was pathetically disturbed.

First the hut disappears (or was it even there in the first place?) and now this. There was no time to waste, she had to get out of there as soon as possible, never to return again. But how? She had no compass or a cellphone to call for help. She had been too confident on making the journey alone. All that she had with her was a backpack with water bottles and a cap and a flower to place on the wood where her father fell on and passed away. Thinking of the rock, her cry grew louder, she hugged her backpack and cried more aggressively, washing all of her stress away. She sobbed and thought of putting the flower on the stream, hoping that the river would flow it away to her dad.

While she was taking the flower out of her bag, something watching her caught her eye. Just 20 meters away, the coyote was standing, as if waiting for her. Was he trying to send her off or was he waiting for her to become his dinner? She had no idea. But this time she wasn't afraid of him. She moved closer to the mammal and kept the flower in front of him, at a safer distance. He didn't make any move. He was just gazing at her eyes as if she's an illusion.

"My dear Coyote! You're the only companion I have got here in this jungle! What do I do? Please help me, can you?"

No response. The mammal was just silently looking at her face.

Jaanvi started weeping again.

"Coyote, I don't know what's happening. I am lost and I want to go home. I want to feel my dad hugging me and I want to weep loudly in his arms!"

Jaanvi's cry got louder. The coyote was looking at her politely and slowly approached her. She had covered her face with her palms hence she couldn't see the coyote approach her. The animal tiptoed towards her making no noise, opened his snout wider showing his incisors teeth. His eyes were fixed on Jaanvi's face and he was slowly getting closer to her. As the distance shrunk between the two, there was a voice!

"Jaanvi. It's getting late my dear. Come on, let's go!"

She heard her dad's voice in the distance. Jaanvi lurched back to see where the voice came from. It was foggy in front of her, and it blurred her vision of something moving towards her. When she turned back to look at the coyote, he wasn't there; neither was the flower. The only companion she had, and the one whom she trusted was the coyote, and now he had disappeared. Where did he go? Did he also hear her dad's voice? Suddenly, from behind, someone tried to hold her forearm with a grip. Jaanvi panicked and tried to free herself, but couldn't. She wanted to scream asking someone or something to let her go. But she couldn't open her mouth. She was suffocating for breath. She was sweating and her heartbeats went higher. She felt traumatized.

"Hey Jaanvi, my child! Why are you so frightened? It's me. The fog is getting dense, come on we'll head out home before we lose our way. Come my girl!"

It was her dad! She couldn't believe her eyes. What was he even doing there? Or was she dead along with him? Is he existing for real?

He is wearing the same jacket that he wore the other day, his skin is still fresh and his new perfume feels the same. But where did the coyote disappear all of a sudden with the flower? Was it her dad reborn or did he come as a mammal to rescue her? Jaanvi went speechless with numerous questions lingering in her mind, but she couldn't ask any of them. She was silenced to thoughts. She couldn't help resisting but she was all there smiling at her dad.

She just followed.

FOLLOW WHAT YOU SEE

by Guduru Sai Bhuvan

On the midnight he was following the blood stains on the streets, he found his victim who was hiding from him. Victim was in a vulnerable state as she had lost a lot blood. He laughed looking at her and said, "Look at you. You look so pathetic and you are so weak that you can't even defend yourself." Still bleeding profusely, she started fainting and begged him to save her. He chuckled out loud and gave a deranged smile and said, "You pathetic human being, you think I will save you after what all I have done. Well, well you are a great example of what is coming next. You have done your work now so you can rest in peace. Dying is way peaceful than living and it is way faster than sleep." He then left her to die there, leaving a note behind. The petrifying note read, "It felt so good to kill the FIRST lady of this town. SECOND one can be beside you. Beware."

When people woke up the following morning, the lady's corpse greeted them and that's how they knew, they were doomed. Immediately the police were called to the crime spot, who in turn took the body to the forensic bureau to get more information. The dead woman's face and body were filled with scares and blood, almost making it impossible to recognize her.

When the Sheriff of the town saw the note which was left by the murderer, she opened and read it. First lady? Did he mean the number or Chloe Mathews, the First Lady of the town? But she was out for several days so that could be ruled out.

However, the forensic reports identified the dead body to be of Chloe. The horror-struck Sheriff informed the mayor about his wife's death and murder. After the cremation ceremony, she also informed him about the uncanny note and the forensic reports. The reports suggested that Chloe was hypnotised and was forced to come inside the town.

James Mathews was a rich business man who was also the mayor of New Orleans. He completed his studies from Harvard University and also did a special course in linguistic studies. He also had a great knowledge about physiology and hypnotism. You can't place James to be a friendly person as he mostly kept to himself. Among the handful of friends he had, there was Anthony Charles who was a successful business man and he and James used to practise hypnotism together in Charles' old property. There was Miss

Hannah Chase, closest to the James family and a specialist in hypnotism, Sofia Stan, the Sheriff of New Orleans and her husband.

Since Anthony was out of town, James was upset that he couldn't be with his best buddy during this unfortunate time.

When James saw the note, he was curious about who the next person could be. Meanwhile, the Sheriff was on the streets with her troops to protect the town from this psychotic killer.

Several days passed by and still there was no clue of this mysterious murderer as he didn't kill anyone except Chloe Mathews. Eventually people also started to forget about this mysterious killer and went on with their lives.

One fine day, a mysterious person walked into the Sheriff's office and said, "I saw what happened with the wife of the mayor that night." The Sheriff was very intrigued and immediately called the Mayor and Board of Council to hear what this person had to say. When everyone arrived and settled down, he cleared his throat as if assuming the role of someone important and introduced himself. "Hello everyone. My name is Arthur Dylan and I work for Elijah Stan."

Without stopping to receive the necessary greetings, he continued, "While I was walking back home after work, I saw blood stains on the road. At first, I thought that there might have been a typical road fight but those blood stains were everywhere. I walked two streets and on both, the blood stains were scattered. I got suspicious and followed the blood trail till the end. That's when I saw a man in a hoodie trying to kill a girl. I really wanted to stop him, but my instincts wouldn't let me go further as he looked dangerous. That man had strange tattoos on his hand, as if they were some symbols. From what I could see, the symbol was of wings, as if made of steel. He used a dagger to kill that lady and that dagger was a limited edition one, sold only at Elijah sir's shop. He gave the dagger to her and asked her to scar her face and also chop her limbs off. And she did. While murdering her he said, 'Well, well you are a great example of what is coming next. You have done your work now so you can rest in peace. Dying is way peaceful than living and it is way faster than sleep.' He was grinning all the while Chloe was harming herself."

As soon as the man completed his monologue, he took out a small note, gave it to the Sheriff and stabbed himself. While everyone got up in shock and backed off, the man slowly started cutting his neck with a sinister smile plastered on his face. He had the same limited-edition dagger.

The shocked gathering stood there transfixed for a while and only spoke when it got too much to bear. The mayor was the first one to break this silence. "The man was hypnotised. He never blinked his eyes once while speaking." After a long pause, during which everyone took in the information, he added, "This man, Arthur was also not feeling anything. He showed no emotions while he spoke. He was just used as a messenger to let us all know of what is coming next. The murderer wants us to find him. That's why he gave us so many clues."

James then asked Sofia to read the note which was given to her by Arthur. The note read, "Oh my bad! Did I kill the first person who gave you the clue to reach me after all your continuous failure attempts? Well, well the second one is also gone. Who's going to be next? Clue: Someone close to you."

Everyone was stunned after reading the note. But some action had to be taken, that too very soon.

Sheriff sent the body to forensic lab to find some more evidence. James was again scrutinizing the notes when he said, "There's something else in here; I think it's some kind of code language." They wanted to consult Elijah about this case but were a bit hesitant; after all he was Sofia's husband.

Elijah Stan was one of the biggest industrialists in USA and a very reputed man all around the world. He was also a Harvard graduate and a batch mate cum good friend of James and Charles. Elijah loved birds a lot, especially eagles. That was why Charles gave him the suggestion to keep his industry name 'Wings' and also put wings as its symbol. He also had a shop where he sold swords, daggers and guns. Sofia was his second wife. His first wife left him after two years of marriage.

While James and Sofia were discussing how to approach this matter to him, an officer walked in and gave them a bad news. Elijah Stan was found dead on the streets! As the words finally sunk in, Sofia fell down, numb first, then cried bitterly about her beloved loss.

Clue: Someone close to you.

Elijah's body was sent to the forensic lab and everyone awaited the results. Sofia took out the note which she found near Elijah's body and showed it to James. This time it read, "Knock-knock. Who's there? Sheriff's husband. Sheriff's husband who? Oh yeah right, I killed him! So tell me sheriff how does it feel to be someone's second choice and not the first? While you are at that, I must say that it really feels so good to kill some of the finest names of this town."

The forensic reports suggested that Elijah was forced to cut off his arm and make scars all over his body. Those scars represented a symbol - wings. They realised that the murderer was following a routine pattern. While killing Chloe, he left few scars on her face. Arthur while killing himself had showed everyone his wrist which had a tattoo and now while killing Elijah, he left some scars on his body. The scars and tattoos showed a symbol made of wings.

This was all getting very confusing. Elijah was the one who loved wings and birds. Who else in this town would love wings and is a psychopath, manipulating people and then killing them brutally?

A couple days later, Anthony Charles returned back to town and went straight to Sofia and James. He joined the cremation ceremony of Elijah Stan and mourned the death of his best friend. With a great wave of anger that swept across him, he vowed to help Sofia and James find the killer, who had hurt his closest ones.

Days went by but they weren't getting any clues nor were they reaching anywhere near. All they knew was that the killer is a psycho who kills people for fun and that the murderer loved birds and wings.

One day, Sofia and James were discussing about the murders in Sheriff's office, scratching their brains to get some clue. Little did they know that an unfortunate event awaited ahead.

After discussing this for a while, James got up from his seat to get a glass of water. He turned back to ask Sofia if she needed one as well, only to find her chair empty. Well, she must have gone to the loo, he thought and turned back. Like a flash of lightening, he realised something was amiss and ran back to her chair. Sure enough. There was a note, one left by the now serial murderer. Hastily he grabbed it to read when suddenly, the window glass in the room shattered.

Sofia had jumped and was now laying dead on the floor, blood splattered around her. Screams were heard, from a near distance an ambulance was honking their way in, a woman who was the closest to stand were Sofia dropped dead was vomiting and fainting continuously, police officers were rushing here and there frantically, trying to control the sudden chaos. The town had just lost their bravest Sheriff of all time.

Her body was sent to the forensic lab to find the cause of death. Reports suggested that she was hypnotised and was forcefully given drugs to make people believe that it was an accident. She also had the sign of wings on her hands, tattooed just a few minutes before her death.

Her cremation ceremony was one of a kind were people from all sects attended. There were the rich and powerful, the middle-class citizens and poor residents. She was given the highest stage of honours. Her close people spoke some beautiful lines about her helpful nature and lively personality.

Imagine the plight of James who was now left all alone. In a span of just a few days, he had lost his wife and two of his closest friends. Charles wasn't keeping too well and mostly kept to his home these days.

Very soon, a new Sheriff was appointed in the town named Katherine Ford. She was the ex-lover of James and ex-wife of Elijah. James welcomed her and informed her about the current situation of this town and warned her about the psych murderer who was still running wild. She was totally invested in it and promised to put an end to this. James brought all the notes and shared with her all the clues he had.

That's when he realized that he had missed one note, the last one he found in Sofia's office before she jumped to death. He had been in grief and shock that he totally forgot about that. Now was the time. He quickly opened it and read, with each word his eyes going wide. "It's sad to see the pillars of this town fall apart. Your best friend is dead Mayor, what are you going to do now? I killed the entire close ones around you. I guess it's your First time. Well I can be anywhere; I can be in any NAME. Follow what you see."

As James sat murmuring to himself, trying to decipher the meaning of it all, Katherine noticed some repetitive words in all those notes. She asked James to look into the clues once again carefully. He read them all again and discovered that the words 'first' and 'second' were in all the clues. They brainstormed hard on what the connection would be between these words, left deliberately as a clue for them.

Like a brainwave, James grabbed a pen and paper and scribbled the names of all the victims. He then wrote the clue as per the notes: Chloe – first and second; Arthur – first and second; Elijah – second and first; Sofia – first.

After thinking a lot, James found out that the murderer had been giving them clues from the very start and his name was hidden in his victim's names:

CHLOE - First and Second - CH

ARTHUR - First and Second - AR

ELIJAH - Second and first - LE

SOFIA - First - S

Merge all these letters and it would read CHARLES.

No, that couldn't be. James refused to believe that it was his best friend doing all these crimes, that too with people close to him.

Thousands of questions swarmed his head. Still in denial, he tried to connect the dots and dig deeper, hoping to find his friend innocent.

Charles was the one who suggested Elijah to name his industry 'Wings'. He also had a tattoo of wings made on his hand. Charles was fond of limited-edition daggers and mysterious old things and would collect them earnestly. He was close to both James and Elijah, so he knew what their weak points are. And how could they forget that Charles was also fond of hypnotism.

The dots indeed connected and it was sure that Anthony Charles was the psychotic murderer of the town.

After slumping down on a nearby sofa, completely stunned, James suddenly got up and rushed to the old property where he and Charles used to practice their hypnotism skills.

As soon as James walked inside, he heard a voice saying, "I have been waiting for you to come here for so long. Finally, the wait is over." He tried to find Charles everywhere but the noises came from every corner of the house.

Finally, he found him at the terrace, murdering a woman named Hannah Chase of their town. He couldn't behold the sight of Hannah being compelled to cut off her limbs. Charles was grinning at that sight and ordered Hannah to pass a note to James. She obeyed and gave a note to James and suddenly chopped her head right in front of him.

James screamed loudly at the sight as he could take in no more. He wanted to kill Charles for everyone he made to suffer.

Boom. Suddenly, there was a loud explosion, somewhere near the town. With the sudden explosion, Charles demeanour changed as well. He wasn't the murderer he was just a while ago. "Hey James. What's happening? Why are we here? Everything alright?" In response, James started kicking him, mourning for his loss and trying to avenge the deaths.

Boom. Another loud explosion and Charles' demeanour changed again, to the hypnotist murderer he was a while ago when he killed Hannah.

It was indeed a strange scene that was unnatural. Charles pushed James forcefully and then shrieked in a hoarse voice, "HE IS COMING; A PSYCH SOICOPATH IS ON ITS WAY TO COMPLETE WHAT WAS LEFT."

As soon as the words left his mouth, he jumped off the roof before James could stop him, and died.

Boom. Another loud explosion hits and Charles flips to his own self. "Help! Save me, please!" he screamed as he touched the base and died.

Perplexed of what just happened, James opened the note and read, "It's the end of a new beginning."

DEAD OR ALIVE

by Nayanika Chatterjee

I wake up to the cruel rays of sun pouring in through the only ventilator in the dingy cell. My spine no longer feels as rigid as it did in my earlier days of imprisonment. I get up and make my way towards the earthen water pot, the only piece of evidence of some inhabitation, besides a blanket that lies crumpled on the floor. I drink the tasteless water by cupping my palms because there is no glass. That is all I get for breakfast. Water and sunshine. I move to the only part of the cell that receives some light in all day and sit there to bask. Head bowed down; my eyes closed - as if in meditation. The pictures move in a reel, like a movie. The same that I watch, every day. For the last twenty months.

△▼

26 November 2012

I married him. Chetan Garg. Handsome, rich and powerful. To be marrying one of the most successful and established business tycoons was a matter of whooping pride for all I knew. Not that I wasn't ecstatic, who wouldn't be - with a castle to rule, a ferry of cars to line up as soon as I step foot outside, and all luxuries at the click of my fingers... little did I know that my castle was a mere fragment of my fairy-tale imaginations.

Things seemed to be in a dream sequence when I moved into his house. With just the two of us in that gigantic house and all the time in the world, love and ecstasy achieved newer heights every day. Every moment that brought me closer to him took me farther and farther from those that I had known. I reached a point where my family and friends had moved far below my priority list and my husband stood at the receiving end of all my time and mind-space. A few months, hence, things seemed to be finally falling into place and we weren't out of breath all the time. As work pressure gravitated him more and more towards his office (or so I thought), he seemed colder every night. I thought I understood. While Chetan was away for days at length on business trips, I wandered around the house - exploring room by room, getting acquainted with all the nooks and corners. I often tried to spark a conversation with the staff, but they rarely met my eye and never engaged in casual chats. Their replies were always one-worded. No matter how hard I tried, I couldn't close the gap with them. In fact, Chetan disliked my empathy for them. He would always say, "You should know your place. They are your servants, don't try to befriend them."

Chetan was a man of fine taste, and I had a lot of upgrading to do to match him. Most of my possessions were expensive things he brought for me from his business trips. He was generous, but he hated sharing. And, was extremely possessive. His wardrobe, his bar cabinet, and his study were the restricted areas in the house. Chetan cleaned them himself. No one was allowed inside, not even me. Once when he was away, curiosity got the better of me and I set out to explore his study. I tiptoed to the room at the far end of the hall, escaping the prying eyes of the staff as best as I could. The white door with its golden knob resembled the other doors of the house, and yet gave out a sense of forbiddance. As if something dared me to come in, I took a deep breath and turned the knob. Locked. Obviously, how stupid of me! I panicked. It would not be good for a staff member to see me trying to break into my husband's study.

I decided to brainstorm. I had done this before, and I knew I could do it again, now. I had a knack of unjamming locks with hairpins and then jamming it back - no one could know that the lock was tampered with. I quickly surveyed my surrounding, took out a hairpin from my bun, and entered the room within ten seconds.

Once I closed the door behind me, I let the shock wash over me. The room had cream coloured walls and the sunlight bathed more than half the floor area, which was covered with an ancient and beautiful handmade rug. Everything about the room was warm, soft, and radiated happiness - nothing like the rest of the house, which was all about sharp lines, edges, and masculinity. I stared in awe at the paper birds that hung near the window. The birds danced with the breeze. There were children books, stacked neatly in shelves. I ran my fingers over the little library and pulled out a book at random. The book had a partially broken spine but was otherwise in perfect shape. I turned the cover and on the right top corner of the first page, I read - Chetan, 2000. He was ten years old, then. I smiled and put it back. There was a blue plastic table, right by the window, with a red plastic chair. The set did not fit Chetan's taste of pure mahogany wood furniture. There were only three things on that table: a toy car, a greeting card, and a brown-coloured box. I opened the greeting card first. It read "Happy Birthday, Mummy!" and a cartoon on the left page - a woman, a man, two kids, and a dog. I kept back the card and opened the brown box. Inside, there were pictures of Chetan. Baby Chetan holding a telephone receiver to his ear, his first school day, a birthday party, college graduation.

"You shouldn't be here," the voice was so cold, it cut through the space and hit me with such an impact that I dropped all the photographs on the floor. I turned around as my hair stood on end. It was Madan, one of the staff members. I was relieved that it wasn't Chetan, but Madan's icy stare made me extremely uncomfortable. For a staff to look at me in the eye and speak so sternly was a first. There was a pregnant silence in the room and Madan's frigid look axed any chances of explanation. I quickly bent down to pick up the photographs. He followed every inch of my movement. With my back to him, I tried to arrange the photographs in the exact order as I had found them so that Chetan would not get suspicious. That is, if Madan doesn't open his mouth. Baby photo, school, birthday, graduation… I paused on the next photograph. There were two kids on a see-saw, one was Chetan but the other?

"Hurry Up!" the voice cut through again like a sharp blade. I immediately stacked the rest of the photographs, put them in the box, and left the room without meeting Madan's eyes even once. I walked as fast as I could and hid myself behind a pillar near the room. I wanted to see what Madan does. Will he go in? If he does, then I can turn him in too. But what happened next was baffling. Madan came out of the room with his usual calm stance, took out a bronze key from his breast pocket, and locked the door knob. He took out a handkerchief from his trouser pocket, wiped the knob, and went back to the kitchen. I don't know how long I stood there, trying to make sense of what happened.

My curiosity died down in due time and I almost forgot about the whole incident. Madan never complained and between us, we pretended it never happened. Chetan was back, but different. The fire at the start of our marriage had given way to this strange emptiness and I didn't know what to do with it. Over time, the differences between us grew how mountains grow from flat lands. Slowly at first, and then all at once. We seemed to be fighting over everything. We had conflicts of interest - major, minor, and even as trivial as what to have for breakfast. Our kingdom of peace was battered with loud arguments and abuses very often. So many things broke during that time - mobile phones, table lamps, cutlery, our mahogany coffee table, trust, love – you name it.

Chetan had always been a short-tempered man, but I wasn't ready for his bouts of violence. We, once, had an argument about shoes. Chetan said that my sandals were not matching my saree and wanted me to change into the stilettos he recently bought. I tried to explain to him that my feet hurt in them and I didn't want to wear them. Just that, and I never saw the slap coming. His right arm extended in a wide arc, gained momentum as it slashed through the air, and fell flat against my cheek. It was so sudden that I don't think I realized what happened for the first few seconds. The burn in my cheek gave way to a jolting sense of awareness. I would have revolted, but the way he looked at me said more than he could put in words. It was better to be silent. But far more often, silence is understood as submission. I was no exception. The episodes became more and more frequent, and I stayed mum to dilute the impact. The staff went about their duties as if they did not see or hear anything. I had never felt lonelier or scared. What happened to our love? Was it just an illusion? Nothing felt real anymore.

One night, Chetan came home drunk. It was unlike him to stagger up the stairs and leave his clothes in a messy pile by the bed. I was lying on my side, my back to him. I was aware of his movements, but kept my eyes closed and tried to breathe easily, but Chetan did not care. He grabbed my elbow and pulled me to a more convenient position. He shoved his mouth into mine and the strong stink of whiskey numbed my senses, until he roughly spread my legs. I was so scared by that time that I thought it wasn't possible to be worse. I said, "No." He paused, looked at me squarely in the eye, and said, "What?" I replied, "No, please." My eyes had already filled with the inevitable doom of marital rape. Then, came the obvious part - the rape. After that, came the unobvious part -he beat me all night till his hands became soar. I screamed and begged, cried and yelled but nobody heard. That night, I thought this was the end of the world, but this was only the beginning of the end. I couldn't move a limb in the morning when he kicked me hard to make him his morning coffee. Frustrated, he got up himself, kicked me thrice again before leaving the room. Just at the threshold, he turned back and said, "I'm not done with you yet."

I don't remember much of the next few days or months. I was in a prolonged state of trauma. I tried contacting my family and friends, but the Call for Help went in vain because all telephone lines had been cut off. All servants and house help were indefinitely suspended. All doors and windows were bolted from outside. I was trapped. The days and nights merged into one another - I would be beaten, whipped, kicked around the house and Chetan said if I screamed, he would break my teeth. I tried breaking free - but he said he would kill my family if I did. He was powerful, he could if he wanted. Who was this animal? I married a different person. I did not know this monster and worse, I did not know how to escape.

Every time I closed my eyes out of sheer fatigue or pain, I wished I never had to open them again. Sometimes I even wished I would wake up from a horrible nightmare to find my husband snoring softly beside me. But most mornings were the same, I laid like a broken doll or a crumpled piece of paper somewhere in the house. That morning too, I was lying on the kitchen floor, a dozen cockroaches crawling near my face. I wanted to scream but did not open my mouth, scared that Chetan was home. I laid motionless on the cold marble floor, with blood oozing out of the gashes on my body. The sunlight from the ventilator sparkled in the blood. When I was sure I was alone, I dragged myself up - staining as many surfaces as I stumbled on, for support. I caught my reflection on a broken mirror as I was making my way to the bathroom. A face that was bruised beyond recognition, stared back at me through her hollow blood-shot eyes. Torn clothes clung to her at minimal places and bloody deep wounds that covered her body screamed for help. That image was my turning point. The courage that had been extinguished by the first whip against my back, rekindled. My line of tolerance had been crossed long back but it was time to fight the war. It was time for freedom. Time to raise my voice. I had to be my own hero.

Several months of sharing the house with the devil had made me perfectly acquainted to his timings and habits. I knew that the front door padlock would be unlocked at exactly nine thirty at night. That gave me ten hours of preparation time. I stood under the shower and let the water trickle down my pain. I put on fresh clothes, combed my hair for the first time in months, and applied my favourite lipstick. By eight-thirty, I was ready. Ready for the final showdown.

When the knob turned at exactly nine-thirty, the lights were off, and it was dark. Chetan stepped into it, amused. He always left the lights on and I was not mobile enough to regulate the light switches. As soon as he turned to flick the lights on, I struck him on the head with the heaviest vase in the house. He turned around, the shock in his eyes giving way to the cold animal anger that no longer intimidated me. He raised his hands to strike me, but I was ready and before his fist made contact with my chest, I had plunged the butcher knife into his gut. Blood pooled down around our legs. But the monster wasn't dead yet. He pulled out the knife from his abdomen in one agonizing, but swift, motion and struck me on the face. I had no time to react to the pain. I grabbed the curtains on the door and pulled them over him in one rapid pull. He was confused for a few seconds and that was all the time I had in hand. I had no time to think or strategize. I picked up the heavy curtain rod and hit on the round protrusion under the fabric that I presumed to be the head. I hit and hit and hit till my hands felt sore. I screamed every time the rod hit a part of him, as if making up for all those times that I had shut up. When the rod fell out of my hands, I stared at the river of blood spilling out of the soaked curtain. I lifted it up without a flinch, looked at those hollow, bloodshot eyes and the lifeless limbs which seemed to make me feel alive! I murdered him and I was not sorry.

I had conquered the evil, and I was pleased with myself. After several months, I felt alive.

I walked out of the doors, not looking back even once. I had earned my freedom.

I was charged against third degree murder. I did not deny it but put forth both sides of the coin. The court seemed to be in two minds about my decision, so they sentenced me to five years of imprisonment. I had already completed half my term in the jail, when one day a lady officer came to inform me that I would be released early on grounds of good behaviour. I was ecstatic.

A week later, I stepped out of the iron gates - closing yet another chapter of my life.

I began picking up the pieces of my life I had left behind and gradually started a new journey. Everyone at home were supportive and no one spoke of the past. It was so liberating. I ate well, slept well, and even walked the dog.

It was a Thursday and after a long walk, I sat on a bench in the park to catch my breath. Life moved around me happily, there were people running, the laughter of children, the melodious song of birds. Despite the peace around me, my guts didn't feel alright. I had an uneasy feeling of someone watching me. I tried to ignore it at first, but my discomfort grew. I turned my head and scanned my surrounding. Everything seemed perfectly normal. And then, I stilled. On a bench diagonal to mine, sat a man in black suit. He had the same pair of eyes, the exact crook of nose, and the unmistakable shape of jawbones. How could it be? I killed him myself. I did not understand.

Suddenly, I could not feel the ground under my feet. Our eye contact remained, and my numbness gradually faded into a lazy consciousness. His animal-like stare sent my mind back to the sunny afternoon when I had stealthily barged into Chetan's study.

THE ANIMAL WITHIN

by Veddansh Kapoor

Young Chase and his father Dan crouched in the woods, still and silent. The birds chirped as the duo hunched behind a rock, the smell of fungi, dirt and some muck at their boots keeping them aware of the presence of the jungle and its raw earthliness.

His father had taught him to pull the trigger several times when he practiced his aim and controlled the recoil on cans of previously eaten beans or bottles of cheap beer from the village market. This was different, a real deer, a living thing. Chase froze, a finger on the trigger but fear in his heart for the irrevocable judgment he was going to pass to an innocent life. Dan saw his boy contemplate his actions, but as his father did to him, Dan put his hand on Chase's shoulder and gave him a reassuring nod as they firmly believed that the world was a food chain, eat or get eaten. With a tear in his eye, Chase pulled the trigger.

A boy had entered the woods and got down in the dirt, but a man arose. His innocence had finally gone. The pain, the remorse had their wings clipped. He felt powerful and with a gun in his hand, unstoppable. He had passed his final test and entered manhood. He now carried himself with pride and understood the value of the family name and the honour that comes with it.

The young lad and his father returned to their farmhouse where Kelly, the master chef and Chase's mother had prepared pancakes for the family. Chase ran and hugged her with all his might, "I did it mom, I finally did it!" he exclaimed. "I know you did honey, I believed in you. You're strong and brave. I love you," Kelly said hugging her son tightly. "Let's sit and say Grace," commanded the captain of the house and they all sat down to eat.

Mid-way through the food, the door to their house banged open with a loud explosion and Chase's vision went completely white. From the fading distortion and his quick reactions, he noticed several men with guns rushing in. He saw his father being dragged out while his mother tried to pull back the kidnappers hurling abuses and swinging for the fences at the heads of the kidnappers, only to get knocked out by a vicious strike from one of the guards' guns.

Chase got up and started hurling kitchen appliances at the intruders but to no effect. He rushed out to see his father being dragged and thrown into a cage like a wild animal. Weird enough, a look on his face said that he knew this day was coming but was in shock that it came so soon. They locked eyes for a second, the pain, fear, and confusion in Chase's eyes were evident as a black bag covered Dan's face. That was the last he would see of his father, for a while.

That day was burned in his memory. Standing in the heat, he would reminisce the dirt where many footsteps almost like an army had mashed the well-kept ground. A tear rolled down his eye, he knew he was the man of the house now and he would do anything to make the bastards pay for the pain they caused to his mother and father.

The cars and the men drove away from the house leaving behind a hysterical woman with her confused son. Chase walked up to his mother and hugged her. He was frightened. In a flash his life was thrown into a dangerous abyss from which an escape would be tough. A happy but disciplined life in the woods was all he knew. His father always taught him how to love and respect others while still having the ability to defend yourself in a crisis. Everything that happened, proved otherwise, he felt weak and ashamed of himself for not being able to defend his father. He picked his mother off the ground and took her home. He closed the door and sat beside her at the table.

"We will get him back mom, I promise you." said Chase as he consoled his mother.

"They took him, how did they even find us? We kept it all a secret, a new life, a fresh start is all we wanted," said Kelly as her sadness turned to anger and determination.

She continued, "There's something you need to know about us Chase. Your dad wasn't always a simple farmer, in his youth, he had joined the army and was one of the most handsome, sophisticated and strong men I had ever met. He was a Captain."

"Dad was in the army? Why haven't you told me about any of this? What has this got to do with what happened today?" Chase started firing a machine gun of questions at his mother.

"What did you do before? A spy for a government?" he probed further, slightly agitated about being kept ignorant of this family history purposely.

"I was your father's childhood friend, we stayed on the same street and often looked outside our windows to catch a glimpse of each other. I loved his coy smile, it won me over. After he returned from the war in Afghanistan in 2003, that smiled had disappeared, his charisma, his happiness was replaced by alcohol, cigarettes, and a lot of anger and regret for his fallen comrades engulfed him. His father was a gambler and had bet his house on a drunken night in the local casino. To get the money, Dan needed to do some job, but since he was always with the army, his set of skills were not required by regular jobs such as a bartender or a counter server and being bad at math, didn't really help. After being contacted by Vaas Monte, a local gangster, he picked up the gun and put his skills to use," said Kelly. "That's all you need to know, let's get down to preparations."

"What preparation?" questioned Chase.

"We need to get your father back. It's up to us now, we are our only defense and your father's only hope. I know someone, we need to go meet him."

Kelly pulled out a phone from a secret cabinet in the kitchen and dialled a number. The person on the other line said something, Kelly agreed and hung up the phone.

The duo started their journey outward.

"So where are we going? Who is this guy?" inquired the young man.

"His name is Victor Sullivan. Back in his old job, your father was hired by Victor to rescue his child, Drake from the clutches of a rival gang. After a lot of bloodshed, Drake was rescued. We need to talk to him, I'm sure he'll help us."

The road to the village was absolutely magnificent. Lush green trees all around formed an arch up above to protect the earthlings from the heat as their dried leaves scattered the road like a welcome and the beautiful crunch of the leaves as they walked past was almost therapeutic. The road lifted up sorrows and instilled you with love and mindfulness. As they walked in total silence, sometimes breaking into a tear as they dealt with their emotions, they drank in the finest nature all around them. Not a word was spoken but they felt each other's warmth. The feeling of being alone together filled them, the primal link of mother to son in this moment of intense commotion of emotion could be felt. The birds sang songs for them healing the wounds of the passer-by giving harmony in death. The wind blew in their faces like Mother Nature wiping the tears of her child and blowing a kiss of comfort.

When they reached their destination, they gathered themselves and gave each other a reassuring nod.

"Don't say anything, let me do the talking in there. Got it?"

"Yes ma'am," replied Chase as Kelly knocked on the door.

A slot on the door slid open, two eyes peeked through.

"Who are you? And why are you here?" asked the person possessing those eyes.

"I'm Kelly and he's Chase. We're here to talk to Mr. Sullivan."

The panel slid shut, after a few murmurs, the locks unbolted and the door swung open.

A big man with military-grade gear stepped out into the light. An M16 rifle in his hand, a MK-29 sidearm holstered by his thigh and a bulletproof vest. Muscles shining under the sun, broad shoulders and thick biceps. He looked like the cheap version of Captain America.

He approached Kelly, spread her arms and patted her down and then Chase.

"We are in a safe house. Don't try anything stupid, we have guards everywhere. I'll have my eye on you."

"We understand. Let's go, Chase."

They walked in.

Sullivan sat in his chair smoking his cigar just like he used to.

"Seems like not much has changed. Neither has your shirt, I can smell you from here."

Sullivan got up from his seat and cracked a smile as he approached Kelly.

"You're a big talker aren't you? Come here."

Sullivan hugged Kelly tight.

"I've missed you. How are you doing? And how's this little troublemaker doing?" queried Sullivan

"I'm concerned about my dad. We need to plan his escape and execute it to perfection."

"Big words from the little one, I like it."

"It's been a tough morning. Some armed thugs came in and grabbed Dan. I think it may be Vaas," replied Kelly

"That piece of shit, really I hate that kid. He's messed with my people before, killing a few good soldiers and now, we can honour their memory properly. By exacting some revenge."

"Let's get down to planning then," replied Kelly with the happiness of achieving firepower to save her husband.

"That's the spirit kiddo, let's do this thing."

"I knew I could count on you Sully, thank you."

Kelly and Chase left.

△▼

A blow landed on Dan's face as he woke from his sedation. He realized that his arms were tied and so were his legs. He weakly sat up straight and tried to look at his attacker. A large light flashed straight into his eyes blinding him; he tried to cover his eyes but failed. When he looked away, on his side, he saw dark grey walls, water could be heard dripping in the background. The silhouette of a man walked up in front of him.

"Remember me?" said the silhouette.

"Vaas. Cut the crap, tell me why I'm here. We had an agreement."

"We are here because you have a pen drive with a certain video in it. I want it."

"I told you, I don't have it."

"Then you're going to tell me who has it. You're going to call Sully. He'll know where to find it."

"What? No. Leave him out of this; he's got nothing to do with any of this."

"A little birdie told me that he's the one who has it. You're here so that when he comes to rescue you, he gets captured. Then let's see where we find the pen drive. And you get beaten up because you're a prick."

He was gagged and a bag was put over his head. He felt a needle prick his arm and, in a few seconds, everything went dark.

△▼

A few days passed by while Sully and his men did a reconnaissance of the place Dan was being held. They noted the area, the routine of the soldiers, the entry points, the exit points, and where to stash emergency weapons. After gathering all the required information, Kelly and Chase were invited back to the safe house to discuss the plan.

After a long and tedious discussion, the group made up their minds about the POA (Plan of Attack). They left the same night to the prison of Dan.

It was a windy night, a storm seemed to be in the making. The group of soldiers, Sully, Kelly, and Chase reached the outskirts. Being dead silent, they sat on the grass. As two patrol guards walked by, the group slowly advanced while the soldiers knocked the guards unconscious and dragged them behind a few barrels of homemade wine.

"You and Chase go and find Dan, I'll deal with Vaas," commanded Sullivan.

"Alright Sully, let's do this."

Sully sent his guards with the mother son duo, while he went on his mission to find Vaas. Sully and his team had acquired the blueprints of a building. He noticed a room which was quite far from the others and had a look. He approached the backside of the building. As he turned the corner, he saw two guards and instantly hid behind the wall hoping he wouldn't get spotted. After a few long breaths, he peeked from the corner and noticed that the guards had their backs turned as they puffed on a cigarette. Silently, tiptoeing towards the staircase, Sully went in. The ground underneath him had puddles and was soft due to the rainfall earlier that day. He slowly climbed up the stairs, a rather shady entrance with dirty and semi-broken stairs and just one lightbulb to cover the entire stairway. This was designed to hide the light from being spotted from a distance.

As Sully walked up, he saw a door and approached it. He swung it open. There lay Dan, connected to some needle in his arm presumably a sedative, and he looked hurt. Sully rushed to detach Dan's wires and remove the needle when he got hit on the back of his head. When he turned around, he saw Vaas, smiling, and grinning through his teeth.

"Vaas, why are you doing this? Dan has retired from his work," questioned Sully.

"The pen drive, old man." replied Vaas, "I want it and I want it now." He said pointing the gun to Dan's head.

"You either give me the pen drive and go away with this vegetable or I end his life right here," he continued angrily this time as he pushed the barrel of his gun against Dan's forehead.

"Alright, alright. I'll give you what you want. Get the gun away from his head please."

While falling down to the ground, Sully noticed an injection on the floor underneath the bed.

"Please, I've agreed to help you. Let's be civil about this," begged Sully as he crept his hands towards the injection.

Vaas kneeled to look at the old man in his eye, and pointing the gun at him he said, "Alright old man, so where is it?"

"It's in a safe a few miles from here. I can get it to you."

"Alright, let's go."

"I'm an old man now, please give me a minute. You hit me quite hard."

"Fine."

"So, why did you come for this pen drive now?"

"I've been a spoilt brat all my life. Money, power, and women overpowered me. All I did was directed towards that. But recently my father died, and after him, all I want to do is start afresh, move on from this world. But to do that, I'll need to destroy this last piece of evidence. Enough chat, let's go now."

Vaas approached Sully. Suddenly, Vaas felt his legs being swept from under him. He fell down and a striking pain rose in his shoulder.

Sully did this to take away his gun. Now Sully had the power. Vaas cowered in front of him.

"Sully, I told you what all of this was for, I just want a fresh start. I'm unarmed, please don't shoot."

"You're a coward and a piece of shit. You don't deserve to walk among us," saying this, Sully pulled the trigger.

In a flash, the bullet pierced through Vaas's head and he dropped dead.

The guards downstairs heard the shot and started rushing up the stairs. Hearing these footsteps approaching rapidly, Sully hid behind the door. The first guard barged in and noticed Vaas on the ground and rushed towards him, the second was close behind. They failed to notice Sully behind the door which led to both of them getting shot. Sully approached Dan; he had awoken from his slumber.

"Welcome back to the land of the living Dan."

"Sully, I need to ask you something."

"Already? Let's meet with your family first."

"No, this is important. Do you still run drug distribution networks and some human trafficking networks?"

"Who told you this shit? This dead guy here? He's a liar. Don't trust him."

"Then where did you get all this money from? I'm sure your cab business hasn't taken off that well to afford all this fancy equipment."

"Let's talk about this later, you need some rest."

"Before Vaas tortured me, he showed me pictures of you making those deal. We agreed you would drop all of this a long time ago. You said you'd never kill again, yet I saw you assassinate three people just now."

"But I did that to save you."

"No, I saw the look in your eyes. You didn't need to fire the shot, you wanted to. You've come back to being the animal you always were."

"Stop. Stop talking. I've come here to help you," replied Sully as he started getting angry.

"No, you came here to take your revenge on Vaas, my rescue is just a by-product."

Smashing his foot down in anger he yelled at Dan, "So what if I'm back in my old ways? I get all the money I want and more. I have power and fear. The world didn't care about us growing up, I'm not going to start caring now."

"You sell people because you never could have a daughter. You irresponsible, drunken piece of shit of a father. You're so emotionally distant, you don't realize what you've done to so many innocent lives. Your greed for money has driven you insane."

"Shut the fuck up, you know nothing about my daughter or my wife," exploded Sully in a fit of rage and pulled the trigger.

The sound of the trigger snapped Sully out of his rage. He realized what he had done. A tear rolled down his cheek as he looked at the lifeless body of Dan.

Kelly and Chase heard the gunshots and started sprinting towards the building. Seeing them arrive, one of Sully's bodyguards went up.

"They're almost here, sir. Do we need to fix anything?"

"No, it is fine, I'll handle it. Go down and stand guard," ordered Sully.

With a polite nod, the guard returned downstairs and saw the duo sprinting, one ahead of the other.

Chase reached the stairs and instantly flew up with such haste, the guard was scared that the stairway would break.

The door burst open with Chase entering and seeing the lifeless body of his father, the blood seemed to drain from his face. He swung his gun behind him and sat beside his father. Kelly ran in soon after, she walked slowly.

"Dan? Dan?" she said as her emotions flooded her eyes and the dams holding the tears back, broke. Weeping she fell to the ground beside him.

"Finally, I had everything I wanted, my husband back, my farmhouse, my son. Now everything is gone," she said sobbing by his side. The tears didn't stop.

Chase was in tears as well. He held his father's hand and kissed it.

A thought appeared in Chase's mind, a strange one, one he hated but knew it could be true.

"You killed him," Chase said softly.

Rage boiled in his eyes. He fixed his eyes on Sully like a hawk.

"You killed him." This time a little more audibly.

Kelly turned around and looked at Sully, "He's no killer, he left that life years ago."

"The gun is still in his hand, and he's the only one here," said Chase as he got ready to charge.

"You piece of shit I'm going to kill you," was the battle cry as he rushed towards his adversary.

Sully sidestepped the young bull while grabbing his neck and kicking his leg to make him fall over. Sully had him in a rear-naked chokehold.

"Listen to me objectively, I shot your father. I won't lie. Things got heated and I lost control. I'm sorry."

Chase tried his best to get free but Sully's hand was wrapped around him like a Python.

"You killed Dan? How could you?" said Kelly as she rose from her husband.

The guard had heard the commotion upstairs and rounded the corner as Kelly stood up. Her intentions were clear so, like a good bodyguard, he came close to the door and caught her hand and restrained her.

"Thank you, Suarez. Please wait downstairs," said Sully.

Light sparkled in Suarez's eyes, he thought to himself, "Sir knows my name." With the grin of achievement, he headed down the stairs.

"So, as I was saying," continued Sully, "Your father is dead, and nothing is going to bring him back now. You're young, you'll be the best ever. With regular money provided to your mother, she should be able to live life comfortably. All you need to do is accept, and all your worries will vanish. Your future will be looked after through the work we do. As long as you're the strongest in the room, no one will dare lift a voice against you. Your mother will never shed a tear again, all her whims and fancies will be looked out for. You have the choice, right now, to lift up, higher than the mere sheep of the planet, be the shepherd, not the sheep. You would never like to die the death of a helpless man tied up in some dirty room in a far-off farmhouse. He didn't leave enough to support your future. Rise up, and take what is rightfully yours."

"Don't. Please don't listen to him Chase, he's the White Devil. He once took your father away from me and now it is you," replied Kelly as streams of tears flowed down her cheeks. She was in hysterics.

"Your father lived his glory days and now it's your time. You've been taught well. Join me, let me help you hone your skills. Money will never be a setback. Your father left the game, abandoned his post and now he is dead."

Overwhelmed by emotion, Kelly fell to the ground, she didn't know what was happening to her. All these emotions were too much for her to handle.

As she stared into the ground helpless and broken, she heard Sully's voice, "Follow me if you want this gift of life." as he walked to the door.

A second of silence followed and then, she could hear the second pair of footsteps walking behind...

THE DISGUISED PAST OF SARA

by Karvi Gupta

1. INTRODUCING THE LEADS

Johnathan, Sara is out of danger. But there's a problem with her," said the doctor. "She has lost her memory and it would be better not to force her to recall anything otherwise it would lead to a panic attack."

"Why is all this happening, this accident, now this memory loss? I am moving out of here, we are not safe here," Johnathan kept muttering to himself as the doctor tapped his back and asked him to go inside.

Sara was sleeping relaxed, with no worries, no sorrows, nothing. Little does she know that this could be the worst phase of her life.

Johnathan entered slowly into the room and she got up. She got scared and asked who he was. Johnathan replied, "I am Johnathan, your husband Sara. Well, the doctor says I can't force you to recall anything. So, we are moving out of here, to Sydney. You should get ready; Esteban is waiting outside."

Sara was confused but decided to accompany him, she had no choice left. She wanted to ask Johnathan so many questions, but he already left the room.

Outside the hospital, next to a big range rover, a handsome man dressed in black suit was waiting for her. He opened the door for her where Johnathan was already waiting inside. He told her about the young man, Esteban. He's French and one of the best. "Best driver?" She asked. "Well yes!" he replied.

And they drove far from the hospital to the airport.

2. OFF THE ROAD

As Esteban drove them to the airport, three of them took the same flight to Sydney. All the time Sara kept staring at the clouds, not even once turning anywhere while Johnathan kept looking at her.

When they reached their destination - Sydney, Sara was still very silent. She wanted to ask where they were going and why. Johnathan asked her to move into the car while Esteban took them to Stacy's house.

When they reached there, the trio was welcomed warmly. "A big and beautiful house, at the seashore. The same as you wanted dear,"

Stacy welcomed Sara into her new house. Sara, still confused, finally asked Johnathan, "Johnathan, where we are?" Johnathan, smiling at her, replied, "Stacy is my sister and wife of late Mr. Phillip, the owner of the entire Phillip industries here in Australia. I have been her manager for a while. It's her house. Doctor suggested I take you to a place where you find peace and I thought her place would be the best. Isn't it?"

Sara hesitantly replied, "Of course. I love the place. I am sorry Stacy you have to be in trouble because of me. I just don't remember anything. I am helpless!"

"Don't worry dear, that's what we do in a family, right! And you need to rest now. Come on let's go upstairs to your room," Stacy consoled her.

"I want a favour. For some time, could we get separate rooms for me and Johnathan? Please." Sara uttered in a low voice. All of them agreed with no arguments.

Sara entered her room and started crying. "It's all so beautiful here, but I can't remember them, just nothing!" She started crying louder. Hearing her cries, Johnathan knocked on her door softly.

Sara opened the door, finding Johnathan in his pyjamas with a little kid in his arms. But he never mentioned kids, or wait, did he? She wondered.

3. THE CONVERSATION

"Sara! Why are you so upset? Look little Mike is here, Stacy's son. He was sleeping when we arrived." Johnathan knew that she would not ask anything, so he started by himself.

"Do you know, Sara, we used to live in Melbourne but after Phillip's demise you urged me to not leave Stacy to live here alone. So, we moved here for some time. One day, you went to visit the orphanage that you always visit on your birthday. And on your return, you faced a terrible car accident. And then, you lost your memory," Johnathan kept saying.

"Mike was just one year old when Phillip died due to cardiac arrest. I did not want him to live as an orphan because we lost our mother when I was 16. She died due to breast cancer after which dad started drinking. He began to think that mom could have been saved. Which is somewhat true, because he was so busy in his work that he never cared for mom. Then you came, a doctor who treated my mother and told dad to not to worry. You knew from the start that he won't survive long but you still helped him to recover not only physically but emotionally as well. He asked you to marry me and that's how we got married. Just after our marriage, he died due to liver failure."

He paused and continued, "Ever since then, I have only loved you. You're my love, my life and everything. Doctor told me not to talk about anything, but I couldn't resist myself."

Sara came closer and hugged him. She knew it wasn't easy but seemed so true. Yet she asked Johnathan to go to his room to sleep and he went away with Mike.

Sara considered sleeping a better option. She took the blanket, switched off the lights and fell asleep.

4. THE NIGHTMARE

Sara has been tied to a chair, her mouth covered, and she feels terrible, trying fiercely to get up and run away but nothing seems favourable. She tried to scream but couldn't even talk a bit. Then comes a tall man with an even taller shadow. She gets frightened as he touches her chin. Dear Sara, you know it doesn't matter whatever you think of me. I know that I have won. With blurry vision she tries to look at his face, but nothing happens. And then she heard a loud sound of an explosion.

Scared and sweating heavily she woke up with a start and realised that it was a nightmare. But that's not the first time this has happened. She realised that this nightmare means something to her, and she should ask Johnathan about that. That time she realised that she forgot to take medicines, maybe it's because of that.

In the morning, Stacy and Johnathan were all set to take Sara on a road trip. He asked her to get ready. She also wanted to spend some time with them, to know them better, her family and obviously her loving husband. They drove to her favourite spot where Johnathan had proposed to her for marriage and went to her favourite restaurant.

"Mike is hungry and I think we need to buy some toys for him," Stacy said and asked everyone to get in the car. But Sara was mesmerized by the sunset and didn't reply immediately. When Stacy repeated her statement, Sara jerked with a start and said, "Sorry, I just got lost for a minute."

They drove to the toy shop and went in. There were so many toys for every kid. "Mike loves cars, I think we should go to the cars section John!" Stacy said. But Sara was more interested in the dolls section. And there, she heard, "Mumma?" a girl's voice, calling out to her softly and hopefully. Sara turned back. A small girl with blue eyes. She was so beautiful that Sara kept gazing at her for a while. "I am not your Mumma, dear. Who are you? Sara asked her." The little girl hesitated and moved back saying, "You look just like my Mumma."

5. THE RELIEF

"Hey Sara, let's get back honey!" Stacy said. Sara finally asked Johnathan, "Do we have a child?" "No Sara, Phillip's demise made my shoulders heavy," Johnathan replied with a gentle tone.

"But why do I have these stretch marks?" she asked. Johnathan remained silent. "Sara, ask him once when we reach home. I will make sure he answers well," Stacy broke in trying to pamper her.

When they drove back home, while Johnathan was parking the car, Stacy urged him to talk to Sara. "Tell her what makes sense, not to force but to help her," she said. John nodded and went to Sara's room.

Johnathan entered Sara's room: "Sara. You asked me about our child, I have to tell you something. We lost her even before she was born. You had a miscarriage and then this all happened." Johnathan was almost in tears.

"But Johnathan I feel like I was a mother. A girl keeps calling me Mumma in my head. I can't sleep, I have a nightmare every night and suddenly something explodes. I don't remember anything. I don't remember anything," she started crying.

"Sara, I can't force things upon you. You'll realise slowly what's true and what's not. Now we should sleep," John replied.

"Wait, John! I want to ask you for something. I want to go out. Alone! I want some time for myself," Sara asked for the most difficult thing.

"OK go tomorrow! Go wherever you want. Esteban will drive you to your destination. But don't go too far," Johnathan told her and left the room.

6. ENROUTE

"I don't know this place nor the people, but I have to go, so that I could know myself better," muttering to herself, she fell asleep.

Next morning, Sara woke up smiling and got dressed. Everyone except Johnathan seemed happy too. "John cares for you more than anything," Stacy said, serving her breakfast.

"Thank you, Johnathan," Sara said. He smiled and told Esteban to take care of Sara. She got into the car and waved to them.

On their way to the city, she asked Esteban about his family. "Miss, I am a servant. Mr Johnathan is like my God brother." "Esteban is so faithful," Sara thought. "But Miss Sara, I want to advise you that whatever happens, don't believe anything until your senses are sure, even if it seems perfect," Esteban made a mysterious statement. "Well where should I drop you Miss Sara?" he asked Sara as they reached almost 10 kms away. "I don't know many places, but you can drop me at the toy shop we visited yesterday," she replied.

They were just about to enter the parking lot of the toy shop when she saw a reflection on the front door glass. It was a man in his early thirties, a dad maybe, and a caring husband, not so handsome but smart, I guess. This reflection got stuck in her head. She could feel many things happening inside her mind. As if she knows him. As if his imperfect world is related to her perfect world. But who's he? Who's he? Who's he...She kept thinking and reached the shop.

7. MEMORY LANE

"Esteban, stop the car now! I think I have got a fellow acquaintance." As soon as Esteban stopped the car, Sara rushed inside the shop. But that man was not there. She went to the second floor, almost behind every rack. But no clue. "Was he really there? The man? Or is it just some hallucination due to those medicines?" Just when she was wondering this all, she heard a voice. "May I help you Miss?" A girl, perhaps of similar age as that of Sara. Young and beautiful! "Yeah sure! I want to buy some toys for my nephew but there are no cars," Sara replied. "Oh! I see but the cars section is on the first floor and you're on the second," the girl answered.

"Hey, can I ask you for something?" Sara hesitated because she remembered what Esteban told. That never trust someone until your inner self says so. But this girl looked trustworthy.

"You can ask me anything," the girl, smiling, replied.

"You saw that man, who was waiting on the side of the counter. Well can you tell me who he is? I feel like I know him," Sara finally spoke.

"He was my friend; he was waiting with his daughter for her school bus," she replied. "But how do you think you know him? He's from Melbourne," she asked.

"Well I worked there. After marriage I had to move to Sydney," Sara made up a false statement to avoid further questions. "By the way, I am Sara," she introduced herself.

"Oh! Hey I am Lily. I work here as a customer service provider," the girl told her.

"Ok! Nice to meet you Lily. Now I have to buy some cars." Sara took those toys and went back. And Lily came back to her house where that man was waiting for her.

8. WHO AM I?

On her way back, Sara seemed tense, thinking about the man and his daughter. Perhaps she could be that pretty girl, she met that day. "What if she knows me? What if I really look like her Mumma," she thought.

When she reached home, Johnathan asked her about her day. She told him that it was great. "I made a friend and I would meet her on Monday. She's really someone who can understand me, and I could spend some time when you're not home." Johnathan nodded in a yes and Sara entered her room.

Meanwhile at Lily's house, the man was lying on the sofa, his daughter playing beside him. Lily came and called the girl. "Sky! Look what I have got for you."

Sky is a girl with beautiful blue eyes. She's just 4 years old and already lost her mother. "Aunty! I missed you," Sky rushed to her and hugged her. "Hey Andrew! Some lady was asking for you. Do you know someone who has worked with you in Melbourne?"

"Not really, he has never worked in Melbourne," Druke, Lily's husband came out of his room. "Yes Lily, I never worked there. Annie used to work in a hospital in Melbourne, so we shifted. But Melbourne had been unlucky for me," Andrew told Lily. "But who was that lady? How does she know me?" he asked. "Well! I will ask her tomorrow if she comes again. Now let's have dinner. It's too late," she said.

Lily was about to switch off the lights when she saw Druke staring at Sky. "What happened?" she asked. "You know honey, I think Sky needs a mother. Andrew should admit Annie's death and marry someone else," he replied. "Druke! But he believes that she's still alive. Who knows that explosion never happened, or she was not inside the hospital at all. He never found her dead body. And anyway, as soon as Andrew finds a good job, he will become engaged in his work. Maybe then, we could talk about his marriage. Now let's sleep," Lily said and switched off the lights.

9. ENCOUNTER

Johnathan did not seem very happy with Sara. "Why does she need to go out every day?" he entered Stacy's room and asked her. "John, you knew it even before. I told you back then, you can't always keep chasing her," Stacy asked Johnathan to keep calm and let her go.

Sara was not insecure anymore. She decided to tell Lily everything. She thought to take her help in knowing about this nightmare.

Sunday evening, Druke and Andrew reached home, the latter being totally drunk. "The whole party he was just missing Annie," Druke told Lilly. He never talked about her much, not even had a photo of her so that Sky does not ask. But this day he showed them a photograph of their marriage. Lily was curious to see Annie because she had never met her.

And at that moment - when she saw Annie - she got speechless. She was beautiful, simple yet pretty. The photograph was of Sara. Is Annie alive? Is she hiding something? Has she left Andrew for a rich guy? Is that why she was asking about him? She kept asking questions to herself but only one person could answer them. It was Sara herself.

10. NOT A HAPPY ENDING

Lily arranged a meeting to reunite Sara and Andrew. She called Sara, which in turn gave her confidence to tell her everything. "Andrew can you please drop me? I have to meet a close friend and I will take Sky along with me," Lily asked Andrew. "Why not Lily. Sky will be so happy to hear this," Andrew answered. Sara was walking downstairs when Johnathan came. "Let me drop you today," he said. Sara was just silent in the car when Johnathan said, "Sara trust me. You can tell me anything that comes to your mind." Sara smiled and they arrived at the cafeteria. Sara and Johnathan got down from the car.

There was Lily, the pretty girl, and that man! Sara was shocked to see them. She asked Lily, "What's happening?"

"I don't know Sara, why are you doing this, but you are Annie, he's your husband and she's your daughter," Lily said. "Don't you remember what you used to call her? Why Sara?"

Sara had tears and she hugged Sky. She still didn't know who was truthful, but she knew a kid would never lie to her mother. Crying and sobbing, she replied, "I remember you Sky and you're my reason to live. I don't know enough about my past, but I can trust you."

"Johnathan, I don't know the truth, but I know I could not be your Sara and I don't want to be. I'll rather live as Annie."

Sara started moving forward to hug Andrew when Johnathan replied, "Sara, you were always free, but when you know the truth, you will come back. I will not chase you, but you'll come back."

He got into the car and drove away. Sara hugged Andrew but that nightmare still haunts her.

What is the truth?

LOST

by Hari Pudipeddi

Rushali never intended to kill her.

She first thought of doing something about the matter after she saw them together in a restaurant, hugging each other, like a *couple*. With tears welling in the 'Baby Girl's' eyes, he was comforting her.

She turned away from them, quit her plan of lunch and shopping with a friend, and took an auto back home. Tears welled in *her* eyes then; she held them from spilling out.

By the time she was home, they rolled down.

She wasn't spying on him, of course; just chanced on him – with her.

Thoughts swirled in her head.

He went to office. Or she thought so. But he was meeting another woman.

BITCH.
Cheating on her.

Infuriated, she let out her anger on the house.
He would never cheat me, she thought. That bitch might've cast a spell on him.

"I'm going to find out from him. Tonight," she told herself.

△▼

That night he came home late. Tired and exhausted. Yet, somehow, he seemed to be 'in the mood'. He asked her to join him in the shower and she didn't deny.
Had to act like she knew nothing.

Then later, as she was searching for words to question him, he tried to take her into his arms in bed but she was reluctant.
He knows that I know, she thought, so he's trying to make it up with his – fake – love.

Still, she gave herself in. One look into his face – his eyes - at that moment, melted her heart. "I love you, baby," he told her, coming at her to kiss, and she couldn't pull away. So, they kissed, for a long moment.

She doesn't care now. That look in his eyes – hypnotized - assured her of his love.
How could I doubt him and his love?

With that, she let him roll on top of her. Then she forgot all about the bitch. After a long time, they made love. And she felt good.

She was awake till the morning hours, cursing herself for the suspicion. But, still, there was an affair. She was sure of that.

He's incapable of such a betrayal, she thought.

Blame the bitch.

"I'll have it out with her," she decided.

Then she slept.

△▼

They met for the first time when she had accidentally dashed into the men's washroom, back in college, eight years ago.

After college and a year of live-in, they got married.

As Rushali herself was an orphan, they agreed on adopting one, but he wanted to wait for a financial stability.

Three years passed. It was a happy marriage.

Except, of course, until three months back.

First came the late home-comings. He would be late for an hour, then it was two; and slowly it creeped to 9 or 10 at night. Hardly an hour's drive from office after the shift, he used to be home by 6:30 in the evening before.

"The Metro Rail project, baby," he'd told her, "Extreme pressure and workload."

She believed. Though, there was a doubt in her mind.

He never came home tired; never looked like he spent time amidst the metal and concrete; he always seemed calm and cool.

Next were the messages.

He hardly used his mobile previously, but it changed. His phone constantly CLINK-ED or BRRRR-ED now. There were only a dozen in a day at first, and gradually they increased.

He used to smile into the phone, reading them.

"Group of school friends on WhatsApp," he told her once.

There were calls too. He spoke on phone for never more than two or three minutes before; he'd liked talking in person, with anyone, but now he was on-call for more than 10 or 15 minutes. Then, the durations went up to even one hour.

"Calls from office, baby," said the man who never brought work home. "Desperate times, desperate measures."

But always he was smiling or seemed jolly while on those calls. Only on few occasions he'd been serious.

He did love his work, she thought.

The final blow came some three weeks back.

One Sunday, while he was away to a barber shop, there was a message on his phone. He forgot his phone, she thought and peeked in.

Just like a good suspicious wife.

And she found a treasure trove that sprinkled fuel on her suspicions. There was only one chat in WhatsApp - contact named 'Baby Girl' – which itself increased her body temperature. As she scrolled up the chat, there were a bunch of – hell, a herd of – 'love you' messages, for which he replied, 'love you, little one'. She gritted her teeth at them.

And also, there were the KISS and HEART emoticons.

She could – should – have stopped there but did not. In the call log, there were calls mostly to and from the 'Baby Girl'.

Next in photo gallery, she found more than fifty pictures of a young girl, with a boyish haircut, fair-skinned, and a smile that made

Rushali's heart go cold. Mostly there were selfies. In a few he was with her.

And, my god, one or two pictures showed him planting a kiss on her cheek!

With that she threw the phone, which landed behind the sofa, and ran to her room, where she cried for more than an hour. That last pictures brought tears in her eyes. And also made her heart sink.

Later, when he asked about her red eyes, she told him, "Dust. I smudged them."

Once she decided, it wasn't hard to find the Baby Girl, she tried to spy on him. She followed him, wishing that he'll meet the 'Baby Girl', for four straight days. She waited for him around his office, watching his bike.

On the fifth day, he came out at 1 in the afternoon. She went after him in an auto. He met with the 'Baby Girl', and at around 3:30 they split.

Rushali went after her.

She lived in a remote area. The colony was deserted and silent, with houses set apart. At around 4:30 in the afternoon, the Baby Girl went into her house.

Rushali waited, lingering in the streets, observing the neighbourhood, for some 20 minutes, then walked and knocked on the door.

The door opened and the Baby Girl stood there, in tiny shorts, and a t-shirt. She smiled at Rushali, with an expression of surprise, and exclaimed, "You?"

"Wasn't expecting me?"

"No," she stepped aside and Rushali walked in. "He was going to tell you and introduce me. I didn't know you knew about me." She added, "I just came home. Sit down. I'll get you something."

Rushali just stood.

Giving a bottle of water, she asked, "How come you're here?"

Rushali put the bottle on table and said, "To talk about the spell you cast on him?"

The smile quivered a bit on the Baby Girl's face. She said, "What spell? On whom?"

"My husband, dear. You're his secret lover now, right? How'd you trap him?"

Smile vanished now. Shock on her face, "Lover? Trap him? I don't understand."

Rushali cut in, "You do, bitch. I see it on your face."

"No…no…you misunderstood."

"Yeah I did. I thought he was cheating on me for another woman, but one look at his face - into his eyes - and I knew he had been cheated into cheating me. He loves me still. If not for you, he'd never think of another woman."

"Oh shit," she said, slapping her hand on forehead.

"Yeah. Shit, dear. I found you now and your game is done."

"He was going to tell you. It is not what you're think…"

"Yeah, it is not, may be. It's beyond my imagination. He might've already slept with you. Or filed for a divorce with me. I was going to be served the papers, eh?"

At that, the Baby Girl turned angry. "Aww… shut that trash mouth. You are not what he thinks of you; talks of you."

"Shut up, you bitch."

"Stop calling me a bitch. Shut your filthy and dirty talk and get out, you suspicious dog."

"How dare you call me a dog?"

With that Rushali pounced, her hands wrapped around the Baby Girl's throat, choking her. Her face turned red.

She started taking steps backwards into the kitchen, while Rushali continued to strangle her. Finally, she managed to catch hold of a knife and slashed at Rushali, cutting her arm.

Rushali let out a scream, let go of her, who was coughing and gagging now.

"You whore," Rushali said and pounced at her again.

They both were instantly on the floor, in the narrow kitchen, struggling. The knife flew and fell to the floor. Rushali slapped her across the face.

Then, suddenly, the Baby Girl gained. With a grunt, she pushed Rushali aside and was on her, pinning her arms to the floor.

Rushali wriggled her left arm free, found the knife, and swung it, making a deep cut on the Baby Girl's face. With that she fell away to the side, blood pouring out, screaming.

Rushali was taken over by a sense of pleasure and rage in that instant. She attacked the Baby Girl, flooring her, and hitting her head on the floor repeatedly, creating a pool of blood.

The Baby Girl's hands fell to the side limp; her eyes wide open.

A smile spread on Rushali's face. She now held the knife with both hands, raised it, and brought it down into the Baby Girl's breast.

△▼

She sat in the Starbucks café, sipping her coffee, and staring out of the window. It was 6:30 in the evening.

After she was sure that the Baby Girl was dead, she washed herself in the bathroom, changed into one of Baby Girl's decent clothes. She gave one long stare to the body. Then, as an afterthought, she pulled the knife out of the breast and left the house.

Now, the blood-stained knife was in the handbag next to her. She didn't know why she brought it back along with her.

Just to help cover what I have done.

I never intended to kill her, she told herself. It happened in the heat of the moment.

But, in her heart; in the back of her mind, she knew that she *did* want to kill her.

The Baby Girl was the dust in my marriage. And I smudged her. I murder-

Her phone rang, interrupting her thoughts.

She answered the call. It was him. He asked her where she was. She told him she was out with a friend. He said he was home, waiting for her. He sounded excited.

"I'm on the way," she told him, getting up, and carefully shoving the knife into her handbag.

"I'll tell you a secret. One I've kept for very long," he said.

They were sitting facing each other on the bed. He'd been struggling to get those words out, but did it finally now, at 1 in the mid-night.

"What is it?" she asked, tensed.

"But you'll forgive me, won't you?"

"Yes. My word."

"Right." He drew a deep breath and started.

"This is about a girl lost long ago. I knew her from my childhood. I was six when I first saw her and fell for her instantly. She was the first girl I loved after my mother. She was younger than me but I admired her beauty. The smile, those curved lips, her hands, and also her words. Everything she said and did was magical for me."

"This girl grew up as a rebel. She hated cartoons and fairy tales; read superhero comics. A kind of tomboy she was, loved action and horror movies. That was at the age of eight or nine. Her toys were never miniature cookery sets, but guns and trucks and cars. I introduced her to rock music, and she fell in love with it."

"I remember her learning to ride a bicycle without the balancing wheels, hurting herself. Even her hair was short, boyish. I loved it."

"But when she was ten, her mother died. Her father remarried. And the stepmother hated this girl and her ways. Beat her and shouted at her. The girl hated her back."

"She couldn't take it anymore and ran away on her bicycle. They searched for her for days and weeks and years. Only the bicycle was found. She was lost. And forgotten."

"I used to think of her during those early days. Then I too lost the memory of her and moved on. I met you in college and you know my life from then on."

He stopped there. He was struggling. She placed a hand on his and patted.

"I forgot about her until my father reminded me of her a year ago. Lying on his deathbed, he wished that I found her. I gave him my word, though I didn't know how I'd do that. Over the years I also sometimes believed that she might've died."

"Who was she?" she asked, unable to resist anymore.

"My little sister," he croaked.

"What?" she said.

"Yes.

Then he continued, "But because of a photograph of a travelling program crew on their Facebook page, I found her three months back. I knew the instant I looked at the photo. I compared a childhood photograph with that one. And my hunch was true. I finally found her. I got to know that she worked as a camerawoman for that program and was staying in the city. I went and met her. There was an odd silence at first between us. She believed me after a lot of convincing."

"She was very reclusive. Living alone, away from people. 'Liked it that way,' she said. I started meeting her often. Talking to her, texting her, I brought her back a little into the world. We caught up on each other's lives. When I told her of dad's last wish, she broke down. My heart wept to see her like that."

"So, I stayed with her as she came out of her shell – recluse - in the past three months. After a lot of disagreeing, she finally agreed today to live with us. I've been waiting for this moment. To tell you all this and get the burden off my chest."

Now, tears were rolling down his cheeks.

"And I did."

Rushali said nothing. Her mind went berserk. Her heart should've burst out. Her body was hot and cold. But then he got up and went for some water. When he was back, she was lying inside the blanket, crying.

Early morning next day, he was informed by the cops about his sister's death – murder.

At that same time, Rushali was in the bathroom, holding the knife in her hand.

"I'm the bitch," she told the Baby Girl's dried blood.

THE HOUSE THAT NO ONE VISITS ANYMORE

by Aastha Gupta

It was a normal morning like any other day – the father was busy scanning the newspaper, the mother listening to her favorite *Bhajans*, the house-help cooking breakfast and the two teenage daughters, like every day, were struggling to get out of their beds to go to school. Both the parents were working professionals – the father was an investment banker and the mother, a school teacher. The mother was the first one to leave for work, followed by the kids and finally, the father left the house around 10:00 am. The house-help was now home alone.

It was an extremely sunny afternoon. The clock struck two and the kids got down from their school-bus. Usually by this time, the lunch was ready and served on the table for them. While eating the lunch, they would watch their favorite Nickelodeon show and doze off to sleep. However, this afternoon was different than the usual. The kids opened the door of the house and what they saw next was astonishing. They saw someone hanging from the ceiling fan of the drawing room. Moments later they realized that it was the house help. Both of them were dumbstruck. There was a body hanging right in front of them and they were clueless on what to do next. They stood there, zoned out, feeling a loud shudder inside their hearts.

It took them some time to come to terms with the reality. They rushed to their neighbours (also very good family-friends) since the parents were away at work. They told the whole incident to the aunt there who immediately accompanied the kids back to their house. She then phoned the parents and informed them about the situation. By the time the parents came, the news had travelled to the other neighbouring houses. Large swarms of people gathered around the house to witness what was going to be a life-altering incident for the family.

Within a few hours, the police arrived at the crime scene and began their investigation. The house-help had hung herself from the ceiling fan with the help of an old dupatta that belonged to the mother. The dupatta was neatly knotted showing that a lot of practice must have gone behind it before executing what could be a probable case of suicide. The slippers were nicely tucked under the sofa chair just next to the ceiling fan. There were no signs of any commotion or disorder. The body was brought down and the police made sure that there were no signs of life. The body was spotless, the eyes still wide-open, as though asking for help. The entire house was scanned for any leads that might help the police in solving the case.

The house-help's parents were informed about the tragedy and they arrived at the house by late evening. Losing their only daughter had shattered them completely, although at this moment, they looked extremely docile and held-back. They weren't quite sure of how to react in such an excruciating situation.

The house-help belonged to a family from a small village called Phulpur in U.P. The major family income came from the money earned by their daughter and the three sons who were sent off to big cities to work. The police started questioning everyone around - the parents, the immediate neighbours, the relatives, close friends of the family etc. Everyone, including the police, thought that it was a classic case of suicide.

Next morning when everyone woke up, nothing felt the same. The room was filled with angst, fear, anxiety and despair, all at once. Everyone gathered for breakfast like the usual days, only today, one person amongst them was missing. Each of them exchanged occasional glances and eerie silences superseded the daily banter. When the kids returned home from school that afternoon, they felt a vacuum, the younger one felt more so since she was particularly close to the house-help. The family noticed an instantaneous change in the behaviour of their neighbours. Everyone started ignoring them and began gossiping behind their backs. Some even speculated that the father might have killed the house-help since he used to leave the house last. The kids couldn't stay alone at home and none of their friends came to play with them anymore. That fan was now dreaded to an extent that the father had to get it replaced with a new one. The younger daughter kept running away from that area of the house, the corner haunted her every night. The mere thought of a dead body hanging in front of her sent chills down her spine.

A few days before the incident, the family had hired some daily-wage workers to white-wash their house. They used to come to work only when the mother returned from her school. Their last day of work was a day before the incident happened. While everyone was investigating the case in their own heads, the mother revealed to the family that a few days back, she had seen the house-help talking discreetly to one of those workers. According to her, they were fighting with each other but as soon as they saw the mother looking at them, they ended the fight and got back to their respective duties. This revelation of the mother put a doubt in everyone's mind. Until now, everyone thought that the house-help had committed suicide but this new angle paved way for many more theories and the younger daughter, in particular, looked utterly distraught.

A day passed by and the family decided to report this incident to the police which meant more turmoil for the family in the coming days and increased trips of the police at their home for further investigation. The police interrogated the mother several times, not wanting to leave behind any trace of important information that might lead to a solid proof. After recording every minute detail, they decided to review the case again, this time, with much more vigilance.

The police started collecting all the particulars about the daily wage workers. When they spoke to the security guards of the area, they got to know that the same set of workers had worked in few of the houses, a few months back. There were three men who came every day and as per the security guard, two of them were old ones, the third one was new. While taking notes, the police realized that the physical attributes of the new worker matched the characteristics of the worker described by the mother. He was the tallest amongst the three, sported a small beard and had a mole on his right hand, close to the wrist. Further the police were informed that the workers had started working at this house roughly a month before the incident, they used to come around 3 pm daily and left after two hours. Before coming to their house, they also worked in two other neighbouring houses. The police went and spoke to the people living in those houses and asked them about any distant kind of behaviour that they might have noticed in the new worker, in particular. Everyone confirmed that they mostly saw him smoking a 'beedi' outside the house, sometimes even inside, while working. Unfortunately, there was no record of their names and addresses, although one of the security guard had a phone number which he had noted down in his register but he was not sure to whom that number belonged.

Everything looked normal on the surface, however the atmosphere in the house was quite tensed and only the family knew the criticality of the situation. When the other kids got to know about this horrific incident at the school, the poor kids were both mocked at. They hardly had one or two friends who were still talking to them. It was a real tough time for these teenage girls at the school as well as at home. The parents tried to spend as much time as possible with the kids, during the mornings as well as in the evenings. Their lives were now engulfed by an unsettling mystery and they had nothing much to look forward to until things around them got better.

Even after repeated attempts by the police, the phone number was continuously engaged when finally, one afternoon, somebody answered it. The voice on the other side was a little husky. "Who is this?" the person enquired. The police replied, "We were informed that you were one of the persons who came for the paint work in Sector-42. We want more information about the tall guy with a mole on the right hand. Is that you?" "That's the other guy sir, not me," he answered and hung up. Later the phone number became unavailable. The police traced the call to a house in a nearby village. They rushed their team to the house and smashed the door when no one answered. When the team entered, they saw a body hanging from the ceiling fan in front of them in a similar way like that of the house maid with a neatly knotted cloth around the neck. They checked the breathing pattern and found that the person was already dead. While bringing the body down, the police noticed a mole on its right hand. The landlord of the house shared the details of the deceased and confirmed that the person came to the city just two months back. While checking his identification copy which he had submitted to the landlord, the police realized that this person belonged to the same village as the house maid. The police were now sure that both the house help and the worker shared some history and the fight (as seen by the mother) led to their suicides. The case was closed.

A few more days passed. Things finally started looking better for the family. Kids were now more relaxed and people from neighbouring houses were beginning to behave normally with the family again. They also hired a new house-help (part-time) after doing proper background checks.

After a few months, the police got a phone call from the father. He informed them about an incident that had taken place at the house that morning. While everyone was away at work/school, someone had barged into their house. When the kids came home, they tried to open the main gate's hook but it was broken and the two parts of metal fell into their hands. They went inside - everything in the drawing-room looked orderly. When they entered the first room, they saw the wardrobe was open and there were piles of clothes scattered on the floor. The second room was also in the same condition. The drawers and closets were all open and things like cash, gold, papers etc. were on the floor. The strangest part of this whole incident was that absolutely nothing was missing from the house, not even a single penny. The family was still recovering from the previous tragedy and this incident was like another jolt for them.

The police arrived and questioned the security guards about any person they might have seen entering the house. They were clueless. The police and the family wrote the incident off thinking that some small-time, amateur robbers planned the robbery but didn't end up stealing anything, probably due to fear of getting caught.

Next morning, the new house-help was cleaning the messed-up rooms. While cleaning the second room, she found a 'beedi' butt beneath the pile of clothes. She casually lifted it in and threw it in the dustbin.

What could have been a game-changing proof in this case now lay inside a pile of the house-waste.

CALL OF THE GULMOHAR

by Spandan Nath

Darkness, it has a special place in certain people's lives. They stay awake at nights and find themselves dragging during the day. In silences, their thoughts wander into the depths of their minds, taking a plunge into deadly sinful desires and among people they are loved for their bright view of life. The masks are very carefully crafted over time with observations and experience, so that no one can get through to their real faces. But animals - they don't do masks, they deal with instincts and souls. They see the reality no matter how well hidden. And they love a person anyway, without judgement.

Arun was an insomniac. He stood at the balcony every night while it was time for the world to sleep, he looked at the sky, the moon, and sometimes the pavement below. He would imagine what would happen if he jumped from the balcony. There were Gulmohar trees planted beside the pavement. He would imagine if when he jumped, he would first have an impact with the branches of these trees. Would he break a branch and then fall on the pavement along with that? Would the pavement be painted red with his blood and the showering of the perished Gulmohar flowers? Would his mangled body covered with sensuous flowers be discovered by his best friends on the road – the dogs? Would they howl and cry and wake up the neighbourhood? Would it rain? Would it wash off all his memory like a petrichor?

When his mother died, he would often contemplate if he would meet her by a simple slashing of his own wrists. One fine night unable to sleep, Arun left his bed and sat in the balcony with a 12-year-old bottle of whiskey. He kept drinking till he felt his subconscious take over. Then he went to the bathroom, took his straight razor and sliced open his wrists. Then he calmly came back to bed and felt himself drain out, soaking his mattress with his heart. The last memory he had of that night was a feeling that someone was licking his wrists. It felt like one of his friends from the road. He thought some divine dog must have come to receive him.

When he woke up the next morning, he wasn't sure what happened! There was no stain of red on the bed, no scars on his wrists. Had he fallen asleep and merely dreamt of this experience? He went to the bathroom to check and found that the straight razor was indeed stained with blood. Everyone he told this about, people he trusted, told him this was a dream for sure. The razor must have been stained from one of his shaves when he accidentally cut his cheeks or something. But they all agreed that he needed help. After much convincing on their part, he decided to get psychological help.

At one of the therapy sessions when he decided to tell his therapist about this strange experience, she listened to it very carefully. She didn't interrupt or break his flow of thought. Finally, when he was done, she asked him, "What do you make of it?" Arun couldn't help but laugh, "Am I not supposed to ask that instead?" She smiled and replied, "You might! But you should have some thought about this incident." Arun let out a sigh of relief and continued, "Thank you for not calling it a mere dream. I am tired of explaining how real it was. Yes, I have thoughts regarding it but I don't know if it makes sense." Dr. Sonia replied, "It might or might not have been a dream. That doesn't mean it isn't an incident in your life. For instance, that was the triggering moment that led to you taking a step towards therapy. And about making sense, who says everything in life should make sense?" Arun was glad he had ended up with this therapist. She understood him. Their later conversation revealed that it might have been his subconscious telling him about something that might save him from his suicidal tendencies. No one really wants to die, but such moments make it clear what they want to live for. A dog? That's what he felt would save him? It could be... his love for dogs was known to all. Why would then this be surprising!? There are so many people with clinical depression who are better because of service dogs. Why would this be weird at all?

Not long after he went in search of a puppy to adopt. He looked for this friend at several veterinary clinics but was disappointed. When he was ready to give up, he found another such clinic and decided that this was the last place he will look at. As luck would have it, the doctor who owned the clinic had a female Doberman who had recently given birth to a litter. She was looking for dog lovers who were willing to adopt. He went in to meet the litter and select from one of them. Out of all the puppies, one of them was extra interested in Arun. He came and licked Arun's wrist. All of a sudden, Arun collapsed. His eyes wide open, as if he had seen a ghost. He felt it! That lick on his wrist from the night he had slit them open... it felt exactly the same. The vet rushed to help him get up. He got back his composure and said that it was probably low blood sugar as he hadn't eaten since morning. He said he was interested in that particular puppy. The vet said he should look for another of them because he is the runt of the lot. Smaller and weaker. These dogs have the least chance of surviving, but Arun was adamant. The vet finally said, "I guess Anubis found his match. What can I say, when it's right it's right." Arun's eyes sparkled, "Anubis, what an absolutely delightful name! How old is he?" "Well they were all born on 13th of May this year. That makes him 45 days old." Arun's shocked expression returned. That was the night he tried to kill himself and felt he was sort of healed by a dog's lick. Anubis! Of course, that's his name, it was the name of the Egyptian god of Death and also the patron of people who felt helpless and lost.

They say every person in our lives has a purpose to fulfil, and once that purpose has been fulfilled, they leave. Anubis was no exception to this rule. At least that's what it seemed like.

Noob, as Anubis was called at home passed away three months after getting adopted. But those three months brought a lot of changes in Arun's life. People who saw Noob in Arun's arms would say he was more like Noob's mother than father, despite his gender. And Noob returned the unconditional love in more ways than one could imagine. Despite his small stature, he was extremely protective of Arun. One night, the call of the Gulmohar was stronger than usual. Arun made sure everyone was asleep and then silently he slipped out to the balcony. He stood there, but he didn't look at the sky today, nor the moon... only the Gulmohar-bloomed-branch filtered pavement. He stared at it imagining what he would look like, what his father would feel when he found out and what would Noob do. Finally, getting the resolve strong enough Arun was ready to take the plunge when he heard a growling. Arun looked back. Noob stood there disapprovingly growling. Then he ran up to Arun and pulled his pyjamas. Arun tried to get off Anubis' hold of his pyjamas but couldn't. He decided to pick Noob up and set him somewhere inside the house before doing the inevitable to himself.

He was indeed unloved. His death would not affect anyone, not even his girlfriend Ria. Especially not her. She was tired of him. She didn't want him to cry when his mother died and called him weak for being suicidal. Whenever he would go to his therapist she would say, "Fuck your depression! Be a man, you pansy! Real men don't get depressed. They don't need help." Today she had cheated on him, or had she? By her logic she had not. She had warned him she was going to sleep with a friend of hers if he didn't pull his act together. And in her books, he hadn't, since he was still going for therapy. So, it was time to show him that these were not idle threats. She had sent him photos of them kissing in bed, so that he knew that this wasn't a lie. The photos were enough for him to know that love is a myth. So, he decided to die in the arms of the sensuous flowers staining the pavement.

As Arun bent down to pick up the little ferocious boy, he didn't expect any resistance or weight. But it almost seemed like some huge dog had put his feet down and it was very difficult to pick him up. Arun was surprised at how loudly Noob started growling. His sole purpose was to protect Arun, and at this point it was from Arun himself. Noob barked at him, almost scolding. Even in that morose mood, Arun smiled at this. When he tried to pick him up again, Noob started licking his wrists. He broke down and sat on the floor. The moment that happened, Noob's behaviour changed completely. He came and sat in front of his dad like a good boy. "Why won't you let me leave? I am not wanted, don't you get it? Nobody cares!" The boy answered this with one simple gesture. He climbed up Arun and started licking his tears off. He was wanted, and he was loved. He just needed to look closer.

A few days later, after Arun stopped all communication with Ria, she called him. She was crying her heart out. She begged him to forgive her. She said she had made a big mistake and now she knew it was karma. The way she had treated him, had only come to bite her back, as this friend she slept with had spread their photos among his friends stating her to be a lecherous woman. Arun felt bad about it. He felt every bit of pain from that night, but he decided to forgive her. She said she was afraid he might have done something to himself. He told her, "I would have but for Noob. He somehow understood what I was up to and stopped me. He held on to my pyjamas and wouldn't let go." Hearing this, Ria said she owes Noob a lot of gratitude and she would like to meet him. Arun decided to invite her home. He would also introduce her to his father and get his blessings for the match.

When she came home, his father gladly gave their match his blessings, but not Noob. No. Noob was an extremely friendly dog. He would get along with everyone. But when he saw Ria, the ferociousness of the other night returned. He barked at her and was extremely aggressive towards her. It almost seemed that he knew she was to blame for his dad thinking no one loved him. He even tried to bite her, as if trying to protect him from her. They had to finally lock him up in another room till Ria stayed. Arun's heart broke as he heard Noob's cries and howls. His mourning wail and scratching on the locked door was the only sounds his ears could focus upon despite Ria being there and chatting. After Ria left, Arun hurried and unlocked the door. Noob turned his face and wouldn't look at his dad. Arun had to pick him up and kiss him repeatedly and say sorry. And Noob couldn't hold his anger for too long.

Not too long after, he passed away. Noob's death was another shock to Arun. He was barely over his mother's passing, and now Noob had to leave too! Two days after his passing, Arun had gone to sleep crying. He was sleeping in a twisted manner and this would have aggravated his existing spondylitis. Arun dreamt that Noob was sleeping on his chest, as he used to. And when he heard his dad groan in sleep of pain, Noob took action. He got off his chest and started pulling Arun's t-shirt, so that he sleeps properly or wakes up. This dream pulling of his t-shirt woke Arun up for real. And as soon as he woke up, he started looking for Noob. It didn't feel like a dream at all. He felt his son's presence. He knew he was there. But he couldn't see him.

His therapist tried to convince him that this was a dream because he was missing Noob so much. Dr. Sonia explained in scientific terms how human brain uses images associated with personal protection to actually take care of the body and mind, but Arun knew what he had felt. They didn't know the bond Arun and Noob shared. Ria was back to being herself and started telling him that he was weak for being so affected by a dog's death.

Two months later, Arun decided to do something that would reunite him with Noob one way or the other. He answered the call of the Gulmohar. He stood at the edge of the balcony hoping that Noob would stop him. He looked at the pavement and wondered if finally, it had to be his red salvation. His eyes started tearing up. Why was he crying? Did he start loving his life? As he decided to take one step off the brim, he heard a familiar growl. He turned back but saw nothing. He tried to go ahead and jump but something was holding his pyjamas. Arun smiled. He turned to see where Noob was but only saw something invisible pull his pyjamas. Arun sat down and held his hand out, as he would call Noob. Slowly he felt something furry on his palm. He could make sense that it was a snout, but it was bigger than Noob used to have when he died. "I want to see you!" Arun said in a broken voice. Gradually he started seeing two glowing yellow eyes. Then his form appeared. Anubis looked bigger than when Arun last saw him, more handsome and far more ferocious if need be. Then Anubis stuck out his tongue showing affection. Arun smiled and hugged him.

After this Arun always felt Anubis' presence around him. If someone looked closely, when Arun sat idly, one of Arun's arms always caressed the air as if petting a dog. Ria was worried. She spoke to Arun's therapist to find out if this was a sign of psychosis. Dr. Sonia refused to talk about this with Ria without Arun being present, but she feared the same. Ria then decided that she had to find out herself. She stopped him one day from petting the air and asked, "What are you doing that for?" "Oh! Nothing, it's just a habit," he replied. Ria's worries were coming true, "Habit of what?" "Of when I used to pet Noob," was the reply. "Stop it now Arun, your bloody dog is dead." There was something extremely calm about Arun, "I know." Ria was further agitated with his calmness, "Arun, listen to me! We live together now and if such things continue how am I to feel safe?" "What things?" Arun disregarded her concern. "You petting your dead shitty insolent dog, you bloody schizophrenic!" Ria blurted out, "And your bloody therapist doesn't want to speak to me! She thinks it's unethical! Sometimes I really wonder why in the world I came back to you!" Not changing his demeanour at the slightest, Arun replied "You want to leave? Maybe you should. But be careful, it's dark outside. God knows what kind of ferocious creatures roam around the streets at this hour!" Arun's excessive calmness ran a chill down Ria's spine. She reacted the only way she knew...with abuses. "God knows what your mother bred you with, you mental shit! She died messing with your head and then that wild urchin died hammering the last nail. You belong in an asylum you asshole!" Then she turned and left. Arun patted in the air, as if patting Anubis' head and said "Go! Have your dinner."

It was pouring outside and the lightning added a sinister tone to it. The cab services were declining her request. But she was too scared to go back in that house now. She opened her umbrella and started walking in hopes of finding some transport on the way. As she walked, she had an eerie feeling that someone was following her. She kept looking back to see but there was no one. She had walked about a kilometre, but no form of transport was seen anywhere. She had reached Gulmohar Grove, the garden like place where she had first met Arun. She cursed that moment right now. She tried her cab app once more. A cab accepted the fare but it would take another 20 minutes. She decided to wait for the cab. Under the grove, the trees made the rain seem less fierce. Then she saw a figure coming up to her. Oh god! Had Arun followed her? Then she noticed it probably was some headlight. Two yellow glowing lights were approaching. The cab must have been nearer than expected. Yes, she could hear the roar of the car's engine. But then she realised, it was a roar indeed, but not of a car! Before she realised what it was, she felt something force her down on the street. Slowly she noticed that the raindrops weren't falling on her but sliding off something invisible above her. She could only see the glowing yellow eyes. There was a crackle of lightning and suddenly she could see him. All she could do was scream, "Oh God! You are real!"

When the cab arrived at the spot, the driver saw something fallen on the road. He came out to inspect what it was and threw up at its sight. A woman's body was laying on the street. Her neck had been torn off. Her limbs dismembered. Disembowelled, her intestine was scattered like the limbs of a lifeless octopus. The storm dropped Gulmohar flowers on her. They soaked in her flowing blood through the gutter... washing away a man's footprint.

CALF HUNTER

by Midhun Harilal

As absurd as this might sound, I have never been able to scan through the district news column of the DailyThanthi the same way ever since I received Aravindan's first postcard, three years ago. It said, "A healthy and sturdy calf" – pencilled on the thin vermilion cardboard of the size of my palm, in a spidery fashion. Thenceforward, I found two other postcards of the same, invariable layout in my mailbox, winter after winter, both apprising me of some poor calf's well-being.

On collecting the third one last mid-October, I gathered that week's supply of newspapers and had them spread out on my writing table. To my mildest of astonishments, I spotted that a couple of days prior to the dates I was delivered each postcard, the local news cried of a dairy farmer's grievance over his missing calf. Sadly, it took me about three long years since I met Aravindan for the first and supposedly the last time at an airport to ascertain that he hadn't been completely fooling around about this 'kooky' leisure sport of his.

I happened to cross paths with the aforementioned Mr. Aravindan at terminal two of Trivandrum International Airport, in the summer of '15. After having checked at the immigration counter, I quickly accessed entry to the Bird lounge, which was rather oddly empty then. Without a moment to waste, I chose a table at the farthest corner of the room where I will believably be least bothered by someone. Owning plenty of time of about two hours ingenuously gifted by a delayed flight for myself, I thought I would sit down to jot down the crux of the short story I had been working on. Around fifteen minutes had passed, and I was staring through the Pilkington textured glass partition at particularly nothing, wholly submerged in a sea of vague thoughts, when a voice approached me.

"Out in space, aren't you sir?" said a solid masculine voice.

"Huh?" I snapped out to see this.

A man who appeared to be in his early thirties, undeniably hunky and casually dressed, resting easy on a chair at the nearest table to my left with his head halfway turned to my direction. Once I inferred that the man had been waiting a little longer than required for me to address his question, I replied, "Oh hey, didn't see you there."

"Would you like some tea?" he inquired. "I'm getting a cup for myself."

I gave him a heavy nod in response, a fairly grateful one. I really felt that I could use a cup of tea to get my brain up and running.

He walked up to the Café Coffee Day at one end of the diner and walked back with two cups of what looked like Ethiopian coffee on a tray. I recalled having agreed to a tea, but I didn't go on to complain stating my distaste for coffee. With a moderate smile across his cheeks, he slowly set the tray down and joined me on my table. I picked a porcelain cup brimming with foam that seemed to steam a cloud of wakefulness. Before I could present my gratitude in words to atone for all the gestures I've been awkwardly throwing at the man across my table, he cut in, "How much of a listener are you?"

I shifted my gaze from the coffee to his face.

He continued, "You know, a writer not only ought to be a voracious reader, but also a good listener."

Firstly, I was surprised at the fact that his toss of the dice at what I did for a living was quite right. Then again, a laptop displaying an open barren white word document should have disclosed it.

"Sounds like you have something up there that I would desperately want to listen to," I replied.

"I'll let you be the judge of that," he said, after which he flung at me what I remember to have looked like a sardonic grin.

"I was born in Kanyakumari; orphaned at a very young age," he said in a rather soothing tone, hearing which I broke in, "I live in Kanyakumari too."

Paying no heed, he continued, "At the age of eight, a wealthy couple from up north Pudukottai adopted me. The couple owned a cattle ranch, acres of land, at the edge of which our Chettinad home stood tall and wide - with a marbled Thinnai in the front, a Mugappu stretching along the inner walls of the house and a spacious pillared courtyard within. This design in architecture traditionally served as the reason to why the houses of prosperous

Tamil businessmen lasted generations. In short, the couple that adopted me was wealthy enough that wayfarers and acquaintances in need passing by never once missed an occasion to courteously greet them aiyaah and amma, expecting alms in return. Hence my needs, cravings, and hunger were never once spared. And with the wealth I inherited, I traveled across oceans to make my fortune. I should say - a 'lot more than decent' one."

He took a moment to draw some air, what otherwise seemed to me like a window of opportunity to take a sip of my now icy coffee.

"If you were to ask me what I did for a living –," he started abruptly, then stopped apparently giving me the space to relocate my attention from the drink to my only companion in the lounge. Once he got what he wanted, he resumed, "If you were to ask me what I did for a living, I'd say that I'm a well-to-do Data Security Analyst, now living in Morristown, New Jersey."

I, by force of habit, raised my eyebrows - giving him the 'good for you' look. Soon after, I hoped he hadn't noticed.

"But if you were to ask me what I did – just like that, the first thing that would rush to my mind is, funnily, I steal calves," he said.

I gave him a baffled face, to which he returned a commiserating look. I mean, what else could he have been looking forward to on saying something like that.

"Yes. You heard that right," he said, rather proud. "You see, growing up watching a herd of cattle being raised at your very barnyard, I've always had a deep resentment to this one sight – the sight of calves feeding off their mothers."

You should have seen with what assuage he said that.

"I haven't been able to grasp on what grounds yet, I might never will. But I carried that bitterness at the tip of my tongue all throughout. Shortly after I could stand on my own feet, the landholdings and other properties were handed down to me. Unhesitatingly, I sold the majority of it, most importantly – the cattle ranch. Following that, I purchased a tract of land in the outskirts, to the more countryside part of the peninsula, built a home and a ranch there; and got my hands on a Maruti Omni."

I was clearly more than just intrigued now and he certainly saw that in my eyes.

"I rode down to Kanyakumari once every year, mostly sporadic, and abducted a calf back to my sweet new home. And I still do that, hence my visit this time," he said, leaning far back on his chair.

His aura smelled of strange confidence. Now becoming extra-prudent as to what slipped out of my mouth, with much concern, I said, "What do you do to them?"

Gathering some sort of deliberate blatancy from the cold air in the room, he said, "Nothing."

"And you never once got caught?"

"Come on, why would anybody even suspect someone like me for the crime of cattle theft?"

We sat there for a while; not having moved an inch, with both of us probably wondering what ran through the other's mind. Before the silence could grow any denser, he said, "The story is not finished yet. What I'm saying is that I'm not very certain of its future either. I'll write to you; in case you'd want to…"

"I undoubtedly would want to know," I admitted promptly.

With a warm smile, he handed over to me a card and a pen that he unhurriedly ferreted out of his little carry bag. I wrote my address on it.

"Where are you off to?" he asked, sounding as nonchalant as ever.

"Chennai. To meet a cousin of mine," I croaked as I passed the card back to him. "What would your name be?"

"Aravindan. I'll write to you." Saying that he strolled away. I sat there for so long, trying to comprehend all of what had just happened until the announcement bellowed of my name.

Since then, I had been on a lookout for a calf hunter on the news. I always wondered, and I still do, pertaining to why he briefed his outlandish and outlawed pursuit to me. I anticipated a letter for months, and then doubted his story for a cooked up one; until I received his first postcard.

If you should think that I call back on the conversation with Mr. Aravindan quite frequently; that I'm worried about what happens to a calf somewhere closed in the periphery of Kanyakumari, you're wrong. If you were to elsewise think that I have a reason to be reminiscing this today, you're right, but I would tell you there's more than just a reason to my now reddened curiosity.

I received a postcard two days ago, and for this year's count, the papers did mourn a little calf's disappearance. But my moment of epiphany happened this morning, right at my verandah, when I bent down to pick up the freshest of newspapers, I ever laid my hands on. Under the "SEARCH FOR MISSING" column were the photograph and other details of a boy, from Kanyakumari. I can't seem to discern why what flashed through my mind, did flash through my mind then – but I scurried off to the almirah in my room and pushed down the bundle of yesteryear's newspapers. With cold, dry, and forgotten news scattered all over the floor, I collected all the newspapers of a number of days prior to and following the dates the postcards hit my mailbox. Like I already cited, the news of a calf vanishing into thin air was reported about three mornings before the postcard, and like

I had expected, the news of a child from Kanyakumari being kidnapped was reported about two mornings after.

With a burst of indignation in my heart, I stormed to my telephone to dial the police. As the ring back tone buzzed into my ear, I thought of what I would tell the officials: That I had met the kidnapper at an airport, years back? That he writes me lovely postcards? I found my actions ludicrous in the view of the fact that all I now had were questions; questions that no one, but Aravindan bagged answers to. I slammed the handset shut.

I walked back to my Oakwood writing table where the postcard from two days ago lay. The pinkish shade of it seemed to have adopted a darker hue to my eyes now. My body for once trembled, sending shivers down my spine, as my lips mutely read what it said.

"Another calf - A weakling this time."

THE INTERTWINED CHAPLETS OF WILTING BLOOMS

by Akshara Bruno & Ranjana Reghunath

The fitful rain dashed against the window sill and Etsuko kept wondering if the clouds were just a veil to hide the treacheries committed beyond the skies. The elusive images of the misty night inside the pitch-dark cubicle came gushing to her as she watched the heavy clouds touch the earth.

It was confirmed, Etsuko was suffering from schizophrenia. The darkest train of thoughts and images have always ruled her mind for as long as she could remember. But the one image that haunted her the most, making it hard to be distinguished from reality, was of that one girl, in a wasted salmon yukata, waiting for her in the sunless darkness. Her face, unclear. The deafening silence masked her screams with the dripping water and the aroma of chrysanthemums lingered in the air. Sitting at the facade she reminisced soaking in the sun, or rather it was an attempt to pull together a happy memory that she wished to remember. Out of the blue she heard the roar of a thunder. In a blink, a jet-black sphere spread over the sky blinding her from the surroundings. Etsuko woke up with a pounding headache. She realized her condition was getting worse.

Her diary was filled with words crying for help. She penned every single detail, as precise as she could to help her gain clarity. Her words often left diminished for her tears swept the ink away. She possessed a letter hidden underneath the heaps of papers.

The letter was from a friend.

To my adorable Etsuko,

You are as vibrant as the hydrangeas. You are the bluish hydrangea with the sweetest scent that swells in the air. Your eyes have got the purity of the white, like no others.

Your face, a blushing pink, loved by all.

But why do I see the poisonous leaves growing all over your heart and soul?

Lovingly,

Your soul companion.

No name. Only an address. An admirer, perhaps. Five months to be exact, since she received the letter. Of course, she had the most absurd reasons for why she had obtained it in the first place. For the heavy bound of confusion in her own head, this letter was her only comfort. The paper was almost crumbled, a result of how much she relied on it. Because although she couldn't, someone out there, for her, was able to see through her. Should she try?

A letter she wrote.

Dear friend,

I received your letter a while ago. Pardon me for not replying sooner. I know not who you may be. Yet I believe you have the gentlest heart. But who are you? My curiosity kills me.

Love,

Etsuko.

She walked towards her mirror-self. Usually a broken image with an unsure petite face, wearing a distorted green kimono. She read her letter again and felt her blood rushing to her tear-stained cheeks. For once, she was hopeful. After months of dreadful nights and in the wake of writing the letter, she thought that she could manage one decent rest.

The clock struck 2 am. Etsuko laid on her bed, fiddling in her sleep, grasping on to her linen sheets. She woke up with a jolt, leaving her pillow drenched with icy sweat. It was a different dream this time. Beginning with a rich wooden gate, leading up to a yard of flowers. The bees, the rays, warming. Then it immediately flipped to her being dragged on a stretcher across the hallway. It was completely blue. The people draped in blue too. A bright light blinded her and she felt someone trying to attack her with a needle. That's when she woke up.

Her parents travelled frequently leaving her and her grandmother alone in their humble abode. A few years ago, they came home with an English man. He asked her odd questions, "tested" and proclaimed her sick. The parents' face succumbed to a crate of disappointment. That's how she felt. So, she secluded herself, never going out. Every evening, she dared sitting in the engawa (veranda), overlooking others down the lane. Needy for a new voice but scared. She kept to herself because she presumed that nobody liked her and that was safer.

7 agonizing days and a few blade prints on her hand later, she received what she needed the most. The reply. It said,

My dear Etsuko,

You know me. You know me very well, indeed. Fear not, Etsuko. I'm only here to help you.

Lovingly,

A friend.

Help. Maybe it was that one kind word that made her find solace with the stranger. And with the stranger, blossomed a profound bond. They talked about all kinds of things, only not her head because Etsuko refused to. Just not yet. Every time she asked vivid questions, the friend came up with fascinating answers. Sometimes they were riddles. Sometimes she was sent small drawings of birds or a couple of flower petals.

What do you think lie beyond the stars?

The travelled answer,

Those who are perfectly aligned.

Her mind surprised her still. Although the letters cheered her, the very recent dream didn't leave her alone. The snippets kept replaying as if they were her memory. When she poured her tea, she saw a glimpse of the syringe on the table. With a startle and a spill, the object vanished.

When she stood from her seat, she saw the gloved hand sliding the door open from the other side. When she tried to sleep, an attacker lurked about in her room, making the floor squeak. As each moment passed by, her soul became hollower. Medication made her numb to all receptors except her own thoughts. If they didn't work, how can one expect this 25-year-old to live on when she secretly stashed her pills away? She needed help and she needed it soon. Etsuko didn't want the curse to engulf her. As an opener, she wrote,

Do people feel threatened by their own thoughts?

Etsuko hesitated to send it. She feared that her friend might stop replying and she was in no place to lose another person. In spite of the doubt, as her gut promised, she received a reply which was rather disturbing.

'Minu ga hana'. (Reality can't compete with imagination).

Etsuko sensed an uncomfortable pain in her stomach. For she knew she didn't have the upper hand.

I can't help it.

A month goes by. It's already January with no reply and 'Yuki Matsuri' right around the corner. The Sapporo Snow Festival comes on the island of Hokkaido. Such a happening place. This festival accounts as a cultural event featuring snow and ice sculptures which the people compete in making their own. The local word is that it began two decades ago (around 1950) when a group of high school students-built snow statues in the park, attracting the public. Since then, every year, children, folks, almost everyone from Japan spent a week here, packing the entire field. The time was cherishing to all.

Simple belief of a fragile heart cannot mend mountains. The letters were calming, yes, but they couldn't stand tall before her fears. Etsuko's eyes grew baggier; her face bleak and her movements frail. The family thought a change of scenario might help. So, they prepared to attend the festival. Little did they know that they were close to losing a valuable.

They left for the festival during dusk. It was windy. The place consisted of a plethora of huge ice sculptures. Birds, creatures, buildings, book characters - all magnified and magnificent. People began filling the park. As the sun went low, the lights were lit. One of the floating lights suddenly hit her eyes, pulling her by surprise, causing her to shut her eyes. When she gained her visibility again, she felt ill. Everywhere she turned, the sculptures began to threaten her, like they were the pets of the devil. She tried to walk away but the crowd made her claustrophobic. And among them, she saw that girl again, waiting for her. Her breath became shorter and her legs went weak. She saw the world falling sideways and fell to her feet. People formed a circle around her. Her family soon picked her up and made their way back home. She didn't stir until it was the middle of the night. By that time, everyone else was asleep. She woke up, scared. Held her knees closer to her chest and cried her eyes out. A sudden wave of wind rushed into her room through the window and some papers rustled and made a mess. Among them, she found another letter.

You know where to find me.

Etsuko stared at the paper as perplexity crossed her features and her mind remotely wandered to fix the puzzles. In a flash, the reeking smell of decayed chrysanthemums grabbed her attention. Torn pieces of petals fell on her lap as she upturned the envelope. Chills ran down her spine. The stench that tormented her days and nights now spilled across the whole room.

Despite the weariness that slid through her body, she scrutinized the possibilities of this being the sole clue that would make way to her destination. Uncannily a vague pleasant memory of her childhood dawned on her. A memory of childish giggles as she held hands of a girl, a friend for all she knew whose face she couldn't remember. Yet she could recollect her smile in bits and pieces. She recalled how they spent their days in a garden that was covered by the blooms of various colours. The setting vaguely resembled the kominka (farmhouse) right at the end of the hills where she had been told she was born.

It was a moment of epiphany! Etsuko finally knew where all her answers resided. And so, she set off.

The journey to the farmhouse revolved around a lot of uncertainties. But Etsuko was firmly convinced that this was her only shot at escaping the darkness that had almost deluged her. With anxious anticipation, she hit the road of rugged terrain to the homestead that existed only in the corners of her memory. Finally, after an arduous journey Etsuko arrived at the shadowy and quaint but vast kominka.

She was ushered in by an icy breeze that twirled her hair locks. With soft and careful steps she walked into the garden adorned by the fragile yet wistful florets like she knew. Before she could slide the door open, her gaze fell on an envelope lying on the floor. A fluttering sense of excitement overtook her. It read:

The light has withdrawn into the darkness. As you can see, the clouds are mourning.

We walked here right under the stars chasing the moon and hotaru (fireflies). You were the sunshine and I, the impenetrable umbra. I wished you could taste the black hole I dwelt.

I burn to see you, and not me.

Appalled, she dropped the letter. Walking further she observed a strange affinity towards an ukiyo-e painting right at the center of a wall spread over from top to bottom. It looked like a door, an intriguing one. She picked at what looked like a handle and with all her might pulled it open.

She stood numb, horrified beyond breath.

What Etsuko regarded as the ploys of her mind, now has materialized into reality. She witnessed the exact same cell of her nightmares, with walls painted ink black. Darkness swelled inside as there was just one tiny window that let in light. And there in the corner, right after the trail of withered petals of kiku sat an emaciated figure staring right through her. Trembling, she took a step back. But the frail figure kept moving towards her. Just as Etsuko opened her eyes, what she perceived was her own reflection standing right in front of her. The woman in the faded kimono was her, only weaker.

Befuddled, nothing made sense to her. Her heart sank, her mind cluttered with questions. "Is this it? Is this another illusory attack? Have I finally become a victim of my own miserable mind? Are the letters a lie?" she was on the edge, yelping. These fleeting thoughts dropped when a caressing hand touched her face. "It is real, all of this is real Utsukushī hana (beautiful flower). I look like you, I feel like you and I was born with you," said another voice.

Reluctant, Etsuko lifted her gaze to look at the woman. She had similar features except for the sunken eyes, tattered clothes and severely matted hair.

"Feel at ease for you share my blood," said the woman. "I am Hideko, your estranged sibling." "Es...estranged? How?" stuttered Etsuko.

"We lived here until the deceitful night when I was abandoned, in excruciating pain. They stole you, their golden child, from me. I see that you have a lot going on in your head but would you like to have a cup of macha (Japanese tea) with your only sister? After all, a reunion like this calls for a celebration." Etsuko gathered her senses and agreed.

Etsuko let a sigh of relief. Sipping the lukewarm tea, they looked at the flowers and then the skies. But there was more to be revealed and she vehemently waited for the truth. Both were equally withered, not knowing the right words to choose next.

Hideko began, "We were inseparable, Etsuko. We had our own world, our own secrets. We played, days and nights, braiding each other's hairs, singing songs that mama taught us. Do you remember you were hydrangea and I was chrysanthemum? They were our favorite flowers. Our farm is filled with them. We raced in the evenings to see who could collect the most of flowers. And you'd always win. Oh, how I looked up to you with awe! In the nights, we were so hopeless with papa telling us stories to make us sleep. We wouldn't give in. We were such troublemakers. Do you remember any of this?"

Etsuko replied, "I remember them. But I remember only me in them. Sometimes, I see a tiny part of you but the entirety reminisces to a haze."

Hideko's eyes began welling and she continued, "Of course, how could you. We were so little when it happened." "What happened?" Hideko paused for a moment, thinking how to answer that question. "I made a mistake. I didn't know what I was thinking. You must believe me, Etsuko. They didn't. And they took me away," and she began crying.

Etsuko didn't understand what had exactly happened. So, she asked again to which Hideko replied, "There was an English man. A doctor of sorts. We went to his house one day. He showed me some machines and frightened me, Etsuko. I was scared to death. He convinced mama and papa to disown me. He and his people pulled me in a stretcher away from you. I cried to you for help. They took me to a separate room and he said, "Don't you worry. No one's going to remember you. Even your dear sister will be hypnotized to believe that you never existed. It is all for the best, little girl" and he locked me up. I managed to get "cured" in their terms last year. And ever since then, I've been living here."

"Why didn't you come home, then?" asked Etsuko, feeling sorry. Hideko got up angry and yelled, "This was home! But the time I came back, everyone had already left."

"But you found me. You knew where I was." Hideko didn't reply. She fiddled about the room, trying to contain a tantrum.

Etsuko continued in a graceful voice, "I know how you feel. The English man came home, diagnosed that I'm sick too. Schizophrenia. It's real and I've been in a death-trap for a long time. Maybe we can help each other, Hideko. We are finally together."

Hideko murmured under her breath, walking about, "No no no. It's too simple. It's too easy. I should go."

"Where must you go?" asked Etsuko and before she could manage to hold her sister's arm, Hideko walked past her, locking the door, leaving Etsuko alone in the room.

Through the window, Etsuko fumbled, "What are you doing?!"

"Taking my first step to freedom and last step of vengeance," replied Hideko. "I'll put it straight. Do you remember the mistake I had mentioned earlier? The mistake was that I didn't factor in our parents' intervention. My heart has always been infuriated with the desire to see your death at my hands. I had left you in this dingy cell to die. But our parents, would be more apt to say 'your' parents, stood in my way and left me with this unfinished business. And now, the time has come to execute the plan of seeking revenge on the ones who obstructed me."

Etsuko stood befuddled, heartbroken.

"My poor Etsuko. You must certainly wonder why I am so. Thanks to our long-discarded uncle, I am burdened with the psychosis. Who knew these things can be hereditary. Don't you worry, my little flower. I will return to settle scores with you," said Hideko dauntingly. Turning a blind eye, Hideko left Etsuko wilting in the room, to live her most daunting hallucinations. Before setting off, she soaked in the light that she had resented for 15 years of her life.

The pain, the lunacy of the distraught mind was finally on its way to seek vengeance.

HIS ODE TO JOY

by Tirtha Mutha

Like every morning, Sanam had to hurry up and catch the 8.03 a.m. fast local from Dadar to Lower Parel. She couldn't afford to miss this train. Even though she could easily afford a cab, she liked to travel in the train which gave her a chance to notice people, make deductions and improve her judgments. The next train was at 8.25 a.m., and taking that slow train would mean reaching late to work which she couldn't risk. She worked hard building a reputation at Ekbote and Co., one of the leading law firms in India. She was a petite woman aged 26, her skin tone was caramel, and she wore her long brunette hair in a high bun. She mostly wore business suits to work. She had a dynamic and pragmatic personality and the look on her eye was very powerful.

Sanam Akhtar was born and brought up in a very orthodox household in Allahabad. Even though money wasn't a matter for Akhtars, social prestige was. The social norms in the society dictated them not to educate the girls. Fighting this prejudice, Sanam came to Mumbai to attend the Government Law College. Climbing the ladder in this male dominated world of litigation had been an intricate journey. She worked harder than her colleagues, spent less money than her friends, and was much smarter than her fellow lawyers. She was one of the best defence attorneys at the firm. Sometimes while talking to her mother, she often felt disheartened that instead of celebrating her achievements, she used to tell her to live a more modest life. Her mother often told her to give it all up and come home. Her advice used to be the same, all Muslim girls ought to marry instead of working in cities like Mumbai. She often criticized her for travelling in locals and working late at night. Little did she know that working late was the least dangerous thing she did. Life of criminal lawyers wasn't easy. It involves a lot of danger like getting threats and risking your life to collect valuable evidence. Despite all this, her determination lay stronger than ever.

At 8.45 a.m. she reached work. She would always be amongst the first ones to arrive. She started her day by checking her mail, glancing through the newspaper headlines and completing pending work. She read an article online which was very unconvincing - Karan Goenka, a successful entrepreneur who was one of the youngest self-made billionaires was in police custody for murdering his wife, Trisha Goenka. Karan was known to be an intelligent and hardworking businessman. He was also a philanthropist and sponsored scientists for research projects and provided grants. It was indeed strange that he could be charged for a crime like this.

She continued with her work when her boss, Mr. Ghosh walked in and asked her to visit the head HR's cabin post-lunch hours. She wondered why she was called to see the head HR.

As she entered the HR's cabin, she saw the newsflash on the television; Trisha Goenka murder case. The head HR and Mr. Ghosh were sitting and reading something in a file. They saw her come in and quickly closed it. Ghosh greeted Sanam in his Bengali accent and asked her to take over the Goenka case. She accepted and didn't let Mr. Ghosh spot her excitement. Ghosh told her that the firm held confidence in her due to her 100% victory rate and tackling all cases meticulously. It wasn't normal for a young person to receive responsibility of a high-profile case but she was an exception.

Sanam went back to her desk as she saw her colleagues talking about her with an uncertain look on their faces. She hoped that if she wins this case her parents would finally be proud of her. She received a mail which stated the following:

'Karan Goenka was charged of murder by an accident of Trisha Goenka, the former Miss India. They had been married for almost a year. Karan Goenka was having an affair with Sharon Green, his Australian assistant. On June 25, 2020 at 11 p.m., Trisha confronted Karan about his affair which was followed by a heated argument. Trisha hit him with a vase and pieces of glass had partially entered his abdomen. Trisha then picked up a big wooden showpiece which had a pointed edge. Karan attacked her with a pair of kitchen scissors lying there to defend himself. There was a major blood loss and the forensic department stated that she died on the spot.'

A message from Ghosh chimed in Sanam's phone. She had to meet Karan Goenka later that evening. She glanced at her watch, called for a cab and left.

On the way she read what the media had to say. All the pages said the same thing. Trisha was asking for a divorce from the billionaire and to avoid sharing his half of the resources Karan murdered her.

She was thankful that the media did not know or mention about his affair with Sharon Green.

When she entered the interrogation chamber, Karan sat there lost in thoughts. Murder doesn't come easy for a normal person. Karan had a medium stature and broad shoulders and was in his early 30's. It was well-known that he was successful yet skeptical and carried a no-nonsense attitude. He was wearing a Burberry linen shirt with his head in his hands, obviously regretting his actions. Sanam introduced herself and they started talking. He looked upset, she sensed that the legal procedure upset him, he wasn't sorry for his wife.

Sanam persuaded him to mention each detail.

"I had just gotten home from a long day at work. As I entered the bedroom, Trisha was going through some photos from a file. When she turned around, she was in tears. She just threw those photos on me. The photos were of my recent work trip to Istanbul.

She was acting insane especially about a photo of me and my assistant, Sharon."

"There are talks that you were having an affair with Sharon Green, and that angered Trisha and she threw a vase on you," enquired Sanam.

"That's not true; I never had anything to do with Sharon. We shared a professional relationship. I think it was wrong on Trisha's part to get all possessive and start attacking me without even hearing what I had to say. She stood up, took a vase in her hand and threw it on me. The glass pierced me on my abdomen. After that she picked up a show piece which had a pointed edge and was about to fling it on me when I stopped her by the kitchen scissors that was there near me."

Sanam had to first make sure he was telling the truth so she replied while reaching for the door, "Let me get back to you. I'll visit you tomorrow morning and don't say anything to the police or media."

Sanam knew it wouldn't help the case if she only heard the arguments from one side. She had to meet Sharon. She called her office and within 10 minutes, she had Sharon's address and phone number.

She reached Sharon's apartment later that night. For a normal assistant, she lived in quite a posh flat. She buzzed in but nobody answered. She also tried knocking, when a foul smell reached her. She called for the guard. They went in but couldn't find her. They further went into the bedroom where the smell grew stronger. They went inside the washroom and saw what she feared the most.

There lay Sharon, lifeless. Her body slumped over; half sitting, half lying on the wooden floor. Her bright blonde hair was scattered, stained with dried blood, crimson. Her emerald eyes were wide open; they portrayed a tinge of sadness. She wore a white checkered blouse and a fitted blue skirt. The formal attire meant that she came from work.

A bullet was shot in her head. Blood that was drizzling down had dried. There was a revolver in Sharon's right hand; suicide. Sanam reported this to her office while the guard called the cops.

Sanam looked around. She opened the drawers but couldn't find anything useful. She went through her work files but found nothing peculiar. There wasn't much in her living room except a couch, coffee table, TV set and a few photo frames. She saw the pictures of Sharon and her family. Sanam felt sorry for what her parents were about to go through. Just then she noticed something weird. The wristwatch was in her right hand. In another photo, she was holding a mug that was in her left hand. All this clearly indicated that she was a left hander, then why was she holding the revolver in the right hand? This was puzzling.

She went to examine the corpse again. There was an ink stain on her left hand, it might have had happened when her hand brushed up against wet ink while writing. Also, there was no gun powder on her hand. Gun powder is left as residue after the trigger's pressed, on the shooter's hand. It was clear that she was a lefty and using a revolver with a right hand wouldn't make sense. This all indicated that this was a murder staged as a suicide. To her, the suspect was quite clear; Trisha Goenka. According to Sanam, Trisha could've killed her because she stole her husband from her. She left Sharon's house after the police came and explained to them about how she found the body but did not tell them about the possibility of murder.

She went back to her office and started looking at the evidence and pictures clicked at Trisha's murder scene. She was found in the bedroom and there wasn't any file in the room. According to Karan's verdict, she was in the bedroom with the file. Also, Karan used a pair of kitchen scissors to defend himself. Kitchen scissors lying in the bedroom is quite common in normal house; but in a billionaire's? What were the servants doing?

It hit her then - "why weren't the servants present in the house at the night of the murder?"

It seemed like all of this was pre-planned. Trisha Goenka killed Sharon, and when she confronted her husband, the tables turned round and Trisha was the one who died. This was her first big profile case, if she had come to know about the truth in less than 12 hours, the police will also take no time. Sanam didn't know what to do. Should she tell this to police or try to cover up. But she also couldn't just announce anyone guilty because of some analogies in her head. She was done for the day, she decided to focus on her case and find if Karan had any motive to commit such crime. Sanam went home and tried to sleep but she couldn't. She finally took some sleeping pills that helped.

She woke up next morning and called the police headquarters to make an appointment with Karan. They informed her that he returned to his residence with police security. Sanam decided that she will leave her house at midday. Till then she got ready, brewed a fresh cup of coffee and started to collect information about his past.

By reading his Wikipedia page she found out that Karan was born in a humble family and his father passed away when he was just six. His mother brought him up all alone. He was a bright student with a knack for technology who idolized Steve jobs as a kid. He really looked up to him and wanted to be like him. To fill the void of his father's demise, his mother got him a golden retriever and he named him 'Macintosh', after the first apple computer. He went to study computer engineering at IIT Delhi and produced the first software with an inbuilt video accelerator which significantly reduced buffering times. He sold this software to Microsoft for $50 million. He then setup a company which focuses on building customized algorithm models which leverage data analysis. Forbes awarded him with the 'Businessman of the Year' when he was just 26.

Sanam tried to read about his childhood but there wasn't much information available. She realized that it was late and she had to get ready and reach Karan's house within an hour. She headed for his house after taking a quick shower. In the cab she was reading one of his interviews where he was asked why he didn't use social media, despite of its popularity, to which he replied, "I don't like how people on social media don't express their true self, my social media only broadcasts my true inner self." This struck Sanam because Karan didn't use Twitter or Instagram. She started thinking about other media outlets, when the cab stopped; she had reached her destination. She still couldn't understand whether he had actually murdered her. Maybe after this interrogation she could prove herself wrong. She hoped to get some clarity in Karan's favour because she had to report the case developments to her head every 24 hours and the clock was ticking.

After going in, Sanam carefully examined his house. There were two constables present outside and half a dozen of his bodyguards inside. She went inside and saw there were books everywhere, mostly nonfiction. It was evident that he enjoyed reading mysteries by Agatha Christie and Ian Rankins. His house had a complete black and white theme. But one thing stood out; a large painting. It was a painting of a dog lying on the ground with some radiation that was killing kids around. The dog was painted in different colours but all the kids were painted in completely black oil paint. She didn't understand it, but then it occurred to her; Macintosh. She knew that she had to ask him about the painting.

She saw Karan sitting on his bed, surrounded by the photos of Trisha. He was sorry but it was of no use because Sanam thought she already knew the truth. She sat down and opened the file which contained the photo of Trisha's corpse. Sanam asked him why he particularly attacked her at the neck.

"It was a reflex to defend myself, I had no other option," said Karan trying to sound like he was the victim.

"You are bigger; you could have easily held her."

"I did what I did. I didn't want to kill her, you have to believe me," exclaimed Karan hastily.

"Sir, I have to believe you, that's a part of my job. If you are hiding anything please tell me," said Sanam.

"Look I know what I am saying. I did not kill Trisha and if you don't believe me, you can leave. I can hire other lawyers to prove me innocent," said Karan in a firm voice.

Sanam was slightly shaken by this. She decided to cool down and win his confidence.

"Okay sir, I apologize. You might have heard about Sharon?"

"Yes, I did. I don't understand why she would do that to herself."

"Was she facing any problems that you know about?"

"No."

She lastly asked him about that painting with the dog. Karan did not understand why she was asking such questions. He started getting a little suspicious but not answering would be very weird. He started telling her about his childhood pet Macintosh, a golden retriever who was a gift from his mother when he was seven years old. He had become an indispensable part of his life. Sanam soon realized that Karan and Macintosh had a really amazing relationship, when he mentioned that he regularly tried to finish studies and chores to play catch with his dog. Sanam persuaded him gently to finish the story. Karan replied in anguish that some kids senior to him in school used to bully him and killed Macintosh as a joke. Karan realized that he got carried away by talking about his long-lost dear friend. He immediately got up and left the room.

Sanam looked at that painting again. The kids were dying in it. She called a fellow employee from the office and asked him to dig into Karan's childhood. She instructed him to go through every news clip; his neighbourhood, school, family and friends. She needed to know every piece of information from a kitchen explosion to fires to accidents because of which children would be injured/died.

As she left, she remembered about the social media statement. Karan had stated that he had a social media account where he broadcasted his true self. She recollected reading a research paper in college, that a guilty person usually makes a confession. She linked the dots. Maybe there was somewhere he confessed all his sins. It then occurred to her, maybe writing some keywords on Google could lead to some helpful development. Just when she was about to type, she got a call from her office. Her colleague informed her about a fire in Karan's school when he was thirteen years old, which killed eight high school students. The police ruled out the case as a chemistry lab massacre.

Sanam was shocked to hear this. Karan Goenka killed eight kids to seek revenge; unbelievable. She knew she had to tell this to someone but how was she going to prove this? Internet was her last hope to find some concrete evidence. She realized that she was dealing with a serial killer and that sent chills down her spine.

Karan knew something was wrong when he blabbered to Sanam about Mac. Maybe she had come to know about something. He couldn't risk anything to spoil his goodwill. Defamation meant a substantial loss in business. He had to save himself. He picked up his phone and dialled up a number. "Hello. Sanam Akhtar, lawyer at Ekbote and co., I should have control of all her gadgets."

Meanwhile, Sanam realized that she had to inform her office. Should she tell them about this? This was a very sensitive matter and she had to consciously make correct choices. What if Karan had come to know about her knowing? It was a dilemma. She decided to send a short update, she texted Mr. Ghosh – 'Major breakthrough. Keep a close eye on Karan Goenka. He is guilty, for more than one murder.'

Then, she let the search engine do its job:

Karan+ Goenka+ Trisha+ Sharon=12603 results

She didn't have time to go through so much of information.

Karan+ Goenka+ Murder=3651 results

Most of them were recent with respect to Trisha's and Sharon's death.

Sanam knew she had to something quickly; she had to type something more accurate. Just then it hit her and she yelled, "MACINTOSH!"

She was about type this when Karan Goenka had obtained remote control over Sanam's screen. He could see the words 'Macintosh+ Fire+ Revenge' being searched for. He was jolted. He hurriedly picked up his phone and mumbled something.

Sanam was stunned and horrified. She couldn't believe her eyes. She found a blog where articles were written in the name of Macintosh. Each article was around two to three lines and showed the date of posting it.

The most recent entry was how Macintosh killed his spouse for denying postnuptial agreement, and how emotionally overwhelmed he was. He didn't want to kill his spouse, but she got to know about his dirty side and adultery. So, in the heat of moment, he stabbed her to death. And he also called the police himself to get the benefit of doubt.

Apart from the above entry, there were three other entries.

- Murder of assistant because she was demanding fifteen percent stake in Macintosh's company in lieu of keeping her mouth shut with regards to their affair.

- Poisoning his former roommate in IIT to steal his algorithm which he later capitalized as his own idea. The confession also stated similarities to Steve Jobs being accused of stealing from Xerox. This resemblance filled the writer Macintosh with confidence.

- This entry was posted as a remembrance of seeking revenge of his dog's loss by starting a fire in the school in which eight boys were killed; five out of them were innocent. The writer stated that he was thirteen years old when he realized that by killing the guilty and who could affect him, he experienced some sort of high. Satisfaction which he felt was weird and funny.

By this time, Karan knew his secret was out. He fumbled and accidently moved the computer mouse. Sanam noticed the movement. She abruptly took out her phone, took a picture of her screen and sent a broadcast message to all her contacts.

Sanam got a call from Mr. Ghosh and she quickly, only within a couple of seconds rapidly prompted words like Karan Goenka, online confession blog, dog- Macintosh, serial killer, 11 murders.

Just as she heard her boss squirreling up on the phone, she saw a red dot reflect on the computer screen.

A red laser pointed towards her screen which moved towards her head. She was petrified as she turned around; her whole life flashed before her eyes.

PARADISE

by Khushi Thakare

The soul bounds and the skin crawls.

How can you be so silly Bella? You aren't efficient enough to satisfy your needs alone. I thought you were just blabbering about these things!" No doubt mom was horrified with my text which had definitely made her writhe in today's sunshine.

"Take it easy mom, I've already had a talk about it yesterday morning, not my fault that it was ignored and if you consider my seriousness as 'blabbering' then be it. Watch your blabbering daughter achieving enunciated success. The hostel can provide me with daily necessities, just keep transferring my monthly scholarship."

"What about your dad? You know how much his enraged words sear my heart?"

"He was YOUR CHOICE! And Mr. Steward's dissemblance never mattered to me anyway," I said almost in a single breath. I waited for mom to speak but she remained silent. "Okay, I'm sorry. I won't let you down mom. I've almost reached my school, I must go."

I could hear her sniffling. "Take care Bells."

"I love you mom," I sighed.

The bus stopped and I stepped out into the cold weather. Finally, here I was, at the only High School in Crestview named Crestview High School, Florida. My eyes were glistening. As the cold breeze ran down touching my white pale cheeks and my warm coral lips, unexpectedly I felt a kind of discomfort. Something very strange in the atmosphere, as if something were about to approach me. And that's where my story starts.

Hi, I'm Isabella Jones. A 17-year-old girl with gait walks and fuzzy thoughts. I belong to Miami, Florida with my little family - me and my mom. Well, don't think of the person my mom just mentioned as my 'dad'. Let me make the stream clear, Mr. Steward isn't my dad. I lost my dad 11 years ago when he was at Crestview High School for a survey. He never returned back. My mom and I searched for him with a true-blue hope, yet we didn't find any evidence of his being alive. After waiting for three more years, that was my mom's last straw. She got married again. Mr. Steward was a rich man who got his keys on her. I was shallow, I drank invisible tears and smiled wearing a mask, impossible to assimilate the fact that dad was no more a part of us. My perception said he was still alive, yet every night his fervent face puts on the lump in my throat and then my lachrymal never stops. So, you see, my family is my mom, and her aspiration for me.

To go away from the place you bloomed in is to get bent out of shape. But life is unpredictable, so am I. I became the stubborn pillar of my own life. There I was, standing in front of CHS to catch some fresh air for my mom to breath and live, along my dad's fragrance lingering around me. A hectic day breezing away with swaying strands of my ruffled brown hair began.

Before you start, you should know three things about me.

First, I'm rude.

Second, I'm selfish.

Third, I don't care if you die.

"Knock knock," a soft voice rattled me. I turned around with my thoughts still obscured with the unpleasant haze. The chaos suddenly turned into silence. The almond curves of those blue eyes were oceanic, dark, and furious. Luscious black hair and his skin matching the shades of snow.

"Bella?"

"Huh? I... I'm sorry," I struggled for words.

"Hey, that's fine. Welcome to my frosty city Miss Sunshine!"

"Sunshine?" Thousands of butterflies fluttered in my stomach.

"ALEX! I'm so sorry, you've grown tall and brawny. It was so hard to recognize you."

Alexander Davies, my classmate, neighbour, and the best childhood friend. Alex was an orphan, an old couple adopted him. Eventually they passed away. My previous school helped him to get his admissions done at Crestview. He left Miami when he was ten. Alex was always diligent and decent. I never stepped back for things

I really crave for; thus, Alex was the third reason which attracted me to this bone chilling city. I had already penned down to him about my arrival and was enormously happy having him back, unaware about my breathe, which was slowly being poisoned.

We started walking towards the school compartment discussing the arsenal of memories we had. He told me about the staff at CHS. We reached the office to find out that there was no vacancy for girls available at the hostel. Alex told me to wait outside the office until he tries to manage things. I walked past a bench few steps away from the office. Alone, sitting in the corridors. Something in the surrounding started making me feel nervous again. I checked both sides of the corridors which were totally empty. I breathed out and stood up to check out for Alex.

Thwack!! "What the hell?" I had collided with someone five feet tall, dark and skinny. He was in a navy-blue shirt and trouser. The tag on his shirt read Ben Jenkins. He was a janitor. "Pardon me, mam. I just heard your conversation at the office. I can help you out. There's no vacancy at CHS, but I also work at another hostel located at the base of hills with a cheaper rent." Before I could say anything, I saw Alex returning. "Take this and let me know," Ben handed me a piece of paper with a phone number.

"They said management will take a few days. Shall I book you a room till then?" asked Alex.

"Thanks Alex, but Ben here wants to help," I turned around to point at the empty corridors in front of me. I gulped. "Who are you taking about?"

In a wheezing voice I told Alex what had just happened. "I haven't actually heard of any such hostels around here. But let's see, what do you say?" Of course, the inner Bella was screaming at me, 'DON'T'.

But I could easily relinquish my imaginary fear for those oceanic eyes. "Umm, sure," I held the chit in my hands staring at the numbers written in red ink. As I rewound the incident, I felt as if someone has punched hard in my stomach. The thought that seconds before Ben arrived, the wide corridors were totally empty shook me. My weak nerves assaulted, and I tumbled down the floor.

I could hear a little croon of Alex's voice. My eyelids were heavy. "You okay? Here. Have it, you are hungry." I took the bowl of noodles and poured in hot water. We were sitting at the empty stadium of CHS. Alex told me he had already called Ben who asked us to meet at Marcow's park today at 9pm, which he told was few metres away from the hostel. I shrugged, with no clue if the hostel would allow me to enrol so late. It was 6pm already. In the meantime, Alex introduced me to some of his friends - Joe, Mark, Kristen and Rebecca. Kristen was good at heart. But Rebecca just kept staring at me which made me way uncomfortable, her wile smile was depicting as if she knew me much earlier than others, though she gave me some school notes to complete.

It was nine. We reached Marcow's park. Darkness filled the park, broken swings, cracked slide and rocky soil surrounded it. We waited for a few minutes and Ben arrived. This time in lucid white clothes. "Follow me," he said in a little harsh voice. He took us through the path running into a forest like area. "Crap!" I fell down. Someone had pulled my legs down or maybe it was just a hallucination. As I contoured, boom! I was alone in the thick and tall bushes. "Aleexxx? Beennn?," I screamed out their names. No response. I searched for my phone, but it had already bumped out during my fall. It was completely dark.

My body started shivering with fear. The blood rushing through my veins felt cold. But suddenly.... "Oh rupturing dissembled spirits! Affirm our souls to be gracious for the realm of this spirituality is mystical and mysterious," hoarse voices of hundreds of students fell on my ears. This was a sign; the hostel was few metres away. I started stepping towards the direction of the voice. It felt colder with every step ahead. As the voice became clearer, the bushes went thinner. Near an ancient banyan tree, there was an equally old and dusty building with a half-broken board spelling 'PARADISE'.

I entered in; things were clumsy inside. "Any help?" a lady at the reception said. "I'm new at CHS, no vacancy available there." "We have rooms available. But you get admitted here at some conditions," she handed me a paper; it was mentioned that it is allied that the students must submit their mobiles, documents and ID cards. I thought for a minute but had no other option. Taking my papers, she rendered me the keys.

Thwack!! Ben Jenkins was standing right in front of me. I forgot about Alex the moment I entered there. "Where were you? Where's Alex?" Ben told me that Alex had returned back as one of his friends went through an accident. That was sad, but will Alex go leaving me alone here? "Can I make a call? I've lost my phone already," I asked. "Not allowed," Ben said in an unpleasant tone. He took me to the room. It smelled like a dead rat. "Never cleaned this?" I turned back to ask but Ben had disappeared, again. That made me sick. Lamming inside the room I smashed the door close. The room had spider webs, cockroaches, and oily walls. "Okay, let's fix this up," I changed my clothes, cleaned up the room and arranged my luggage. I decided to take a bath and complete my notes.

It was dark outside the room. The silence felt as if I was the only one in the hostel. Luckily, the bathroom was near to my room. Going in I took of my clothes, it was cold and my body felt weak. I turned on the hot shower closing my eyes and just letting the hot water flow through me, it felt relaxing. Suddenly, a sour smell made its way to the bathroom. I didn't feel like, but I had to open my eyes. What I saw was brutal. No. I didn't scream. Because I had no guts to. I wrapped myself around the towel and ran, and kept running... hardly waiting to breathe. I went down to the banyan tree and checked on myself. Few seconds before dense red blood was flowing through my body, I was bathing under the shower pouring out blood. But now, I was just wet with water droplets on my body. Was this an illusion? Was my schizophrenia back? I loosened my fingers and let the towel slip off me. I screamed and cried there, but no one heard them. I was standing there alone, crying, and naked. The cold winds didn't affect me anymore. I was missing mom. Hours later, I composed myself and ran back to my room. I felt relieved and less afraid now. Maybe because I knew that was just my disease or maybe because I'd accepted that wasn't.

I opened the door and the room was back, back to what it was before. My clothes were scattered everywhere with broken accessories and torn books. I closed the door. Too angry or maybe too afraid to go back. Sitting down I thought about whatever was happening. "This isn't real, it has to be a scaremonger." I got up and searched for my camera lying in the scattered accessories. Climbing on the bed I fixed the camera at one corner of the room. Switching it on, I started to clean the mess again. Underneath the bed, Rebecca's notes caught my eye. It was lying next to the hostel's pamphlet. I stared at them for a while. Immediately, I pushed my hand into the pocket and took out the chit Ben had given me. She was connected, I knew she was. All the three papers were written in the same handwriting with the same red ink. My anxiety got back. Should I wait? Or run? With no stamina left I leaned my head on the bed and shut my eyes close.

My stomach felt contracted with my head hammering down. I stretched out my arms to relax, my body was paining. After whatever had happened last night I could no longer wait there. I swallowed some pills, got my bag pack and ran out for the school. Strange, even today morning I saw no other person than the lady receptionist. I walked to the park and took a taxi. I realized that as I was going away from the hostel, it felt warmer.

As soon as I entered CHS I searched for Alex. We did some lectures together and then I told him about the previous night. He said that was just my anxiety about a new place. I found it fooling to explain it to him. I knew it was something more than that. I decided to go back there and give my fate one more chance.

It was 7pm. I reached the park and started walking through the forest. Though it wasn't dark yet, I couldn't find the hostel. I wandered and wandered. I looked at the watch, it was almost 9. I was tired and hungry. "Oh, rupturing dissembled spirits! Affirm our souls to be gracious...," again the prayer made its way through the forest. Instantly, I ran towards the direction of the sound and within seconds I was there, in front of the 'Paradise'. It was very dark now.

I could still hear the sound of prayer coming from the basement but was too hungry to go for it. I started walking towards the canteen, and on my way I saw a picture hanging over the wall with a garland. Shocked, I went closer. The image became harder for me to move ahead.

Because... it was... him... Dad!!! Suddenly I felt a hand on my shoulder, I jumped off with fear. "Rebecca?"

"You aren't allowed to be so late for dinner Isabella, take a left from there," she pointed at one of the corners. I looked at the wall again, Dad's picture wasn't there anymore. I turned to watch out for Rebecca but she had already vanished. Just like that. I hurried my way towards the canteen, wondering if this place was related to dad or was it my imagination. There was no one in the canteen except a wooden table with some vessels kept on it. I moved towards the table. The moment I opened the vessel, thousands of insects started getting out of that. I threw myself away from the table. I was feeling nauseous.

"ISABELLAA....BELLAA...!" I heard someone screaming my name, as if crying out for help. I hurried upstairs, there was Rebecca, sitting on the staircase and reading a book. But I had no time to stop and figure out things. Someone was screaming in the room next to me. I smashed the door open and the land beneath me escaped. Rebecca's body was hanging to a rope tied to the ceiling fan, cold and dead, but the eyes were staring right at me. I realized I was already crying with fear and sweating even in low temperatures. It was impossible for me to go back and check who was sitting and reading on the stairs.

I entered my room; it was again messed up. Without waiting, I climbed up the bed and took off the camera to check who the scaremonger was. I turned on the recording.

According to what I saw, I had never left the room. It was me who had messed up my room again, sitting, singing songs, and scratching the walls with anger. They say technology never lie. I threw the camera down on the floor and ran out of the hostel as fast as I could. I ran all the way from Marcow's to CHS without stopping. I reached the boy's hostel and called Alex with one of the guard's phone. He told me to enter his room through the window at the backside of the hostel which was on the ground floor. I entered in; my body dripping with sweat. I drank some water and told Alex whatever was happening with me. "We'll go and clear out the things tomorrow morning Bells, don't worry. I've some food. For now, you eat and sleep."

Well, let me tell you guys something. Paradise has a rule, people who know about them have to be a part of them.

I ate some food and slept. In the morning we got ready and went out to figure things out. Alex then realized that he had forgotten his phone in his room. He asked me to wait at the gate. He went to the room, opened the door, and saw me lying on his bed with a deep cut on my neck, dead. He ran towards the window but saw no one standing at the gate. He turned back and saw my dead body smiling at him, and then he heard "Oh rupturing dissembled spirits! Affirm our souls to be gracious....For the realm of this spirituality, is mystical and mysterious."

Yes, I'm selfish, I'm rude and remember...?

I don't care if you die!

Now the next scream you hear might be your own.

ABOUT THE AUTHORS

TANISHK PATIL

An arts student with a knack for things which aren't very normal. You'll find him in the mountains with a bunch of friends or on the ground with a ball beneath his feet. Always ready for philosophical discussions on weirdly heavy topics. On some nights, you  might see him performing for dogs on unknown streets.

△▼

SNIGDHAA GHAI AND BHAVEY WADHWA

 Meet Snigdhaa and Bhavey, two long-lost writer friends from school who came together with an idea for this story back in 2018, and together they wrote this story. They are 20, and aspiring writers, waiting to see what the world holds for them.

KULDEEP CARIAPPA

Kuldeep Cariappa is an independent filmmaker based out of Bengaluru. He has worked in Kannada entertainment for over four years as screenplay and dialogues writer, and director. He has directed political documentary, ad films, and short films. Kuldeep is currently debuting with his feature film directorial.

△▼

MANOJ VAZ

They say, everybody dreams in black and white, some literally. Manoj is an advertising copywriter with three decades of experience handling over 50 blue chip clients. He has published three books; Tinsel - a hard look at Mumbai's Show Biz, The Kidnapping, and the Meth Mystery- both part of the Magic Chest Series for Teenagers.

AKSHARA BRUNO

Akshara Bruno is a CS pursuing student and like many others, she loves to play with words. Dogs are her best friends and she occasionally drinks coffee. Before you go any further, Bruno is her dad's name so please be kind. You can find her recent blog at medium.com/@aksharabruno

△▼

MIDHUN HARILAL

Midhun is a regular guy with a love for doing things he loves. You'll mostly find him devouring on the aftertaste a movie had left him with, otherwise writing at his veranda - inhaling the petrichor of Kanyakumari's soil. He finds music and sketching expressive too. He enjoys his own company.

VISHVAK

Vishvak, a soon to be graduate of Bachelor of Computer Science and Engineering, is an aspiring filmmaker and an earnest storyteller. Vishvak found his interests in storytelling at a young age and began writing in the pursuit of a hobby. In addition to writing, he also enjoys reading books and is an avid film enthusiast.

△▼

SPANDAN NATH

Spandan Nath is a writer and an artist residing in Thane City, near Mumbai. His works have been published in a number of anthologies, so far. He usually writes poetry and short stories. His writings cover a wide range of genres. His works trust the intellect of the reader to decipher them.

SOUMYA SRIVASTAVA

She owns herself as the "Peaceful Warrior" and wields her mighty pen while fighting fierce battles inside with a broad smile. Ready to challenge all non-empirical theories, her innocent heart, rebellious mind, and strong beliefs are always at loggerheads. A keen observer  who speaks less, perceives more and weaves emotions into beautifully intricated literary pieces.

△▼

NENA PATEL

 Nena is a student by day and an avid reader by night. Her ghungroos can make your heart dance while her pen can addict your minds like caffeine to your health. Currently a 16-year-old, experimenting science with metaphors and mystery and trying to kidnap you all from your dreams to cage you in your nightmare.

SACHIN SHANBHAG

Sachin is a Mumbai based Business Analytics professional. A voracious reader and keen observer of life, he brings out its nuances in his writing. His readers vouch for his engaging writing style, be it a humorous take on local trains or the angst felt about life's cruelties. He dreams of writing a book someday.

△▼

KRISHNA ANAP

Socially awkward but secretly amusing, Krishna prefers to explore ideas scrawled by curious minds. Being an ambivert, he believes that silence is as powerful as ink on paper. He loves to quote down thoughts on his Instagram page 'a_freaky_scribbler' as he sets himself into motion to trace his social existence.

RANJITHA RAVINDRAN

Ranjitha Ravindran, author of the story "The Illusion of Life" is a freelance copywriter and a voice-over artist. She has penned several short stories, blogs and poems. She is now working on her eBook, an anthology of poems. She is also a biker and an avid traveller who wants to be a digital nomad.

△▼

GUDURU SAI BHUVAN

Born on 10th January 2002, Guduru Sai Bhuvan was brought up in Jamshedpur "The Steel City." He started writing at the age of 15. He has a keen interest in writing mysterious stories often related to crime. He quotes, "If chasing dreams is an art then putting the same dream into a story is a work of artist."

NAYANIKA CHATTERJEE

Nayanika Chatterjee has been authoring short stories, micro tales, and poems for eight years. Besides business consulting, she provides freelance writing and editing services. With a knack of looking at the world differently, her writings are mostly inspired from real-life events. She believes every person has a story they don't tell.

△▼

VEDDANSH KAPOOR

While graduating in the art of blending the fantasy world with the real one; Veddansh is also pursuing his Computer Engineering degree. He is an avid reader and an MMA practitioner, following his passion in the world of writing.

KARVI GUPTA

Karvi is a textile engineer on weekdays. But on weekends, you can find her painting or sketching. And on every other night she writes anything that comes to her mind. Romancing through poems or terrifying through dark tales or just a philosophy, she can simply write about anything, anyone.

△▼

HARI PUDIPEDDI

Hari is a 24-year-old from Hyderabad, currently working as a trainer in procurement. He loves to create and tell stories; writes short fiction and poetry. He reads anything except romance and is interested in studying philosophy and psychology as a lifelong endeavour.

AASTHA GUPTA

Aastha is a German language editor by profession. Apart from being a writer, she is a sucker for good poetry and theater. When she is not working, she likes to build her Urdu vocabulary and binge on content-driven Hindi movies.

△▼

RANJANA REGHUNATH & AKSHARA BRUNO

Akshara Bruno and Ranjana Reghunath are engineers on the make who find solace in the verses of their imaginations. Both of them are dreamy poets, music addicts and love to maunder over in the world of fiction. They thought it would be a fun idea to write this story together.

TIRTHA MUTHA

Tirtha Mutha is an old soul with a young spirit, who loves family time. She is a national jump rope champion and plays tennis. She will keep you entertained with eccentric news clips and happenings around the world. On a sunny day, you will find her listening

to jazz, reading a book, or playing melodies on her violin.

△▼

KHUSHI THAKARE

Being 17, Khushi is extremely fervent about discovering more of herself with the formative years. She is easily communicative but has always been a withholder. She believes that besides academics, the lanes that you pursue immensely alter your thoughts. Writing makes her reconnect with herself and reading enormously affects her convictions.

OUR STORY

We're all on a Journey, and our "Writers" have made it Beautiful.

A dreamcatcher is an object made with feathers and strings, essentially used as lucky charms in many parts of the world. The same way, Inkfeathers brings together writers, editors, and artists together to form a dreamcatcher that works in favour for the young writers and readers and if you're positive about it, it may bring you luck as well.

We at Inkfeathers are connected to thousands of writers globally, who believe in the magic of telling stories. This stream of connectivity with the writers, the fact that everyone has a unique detail or edge to their story makes Inkfeathers proud to partner with these young literary as well as collaborative minds.

Back in 2013, our founders came together to form an offline group for their love of literature, and this formed collaborative energy with many young literature-wounded minds which eventually led these offline meetings to stand-ups, storytelling events, poetry slams, meet-ups to share experiences and many others. In 2016, Inkfeathers finally launched as the brand project under one Private Limited Company. This expanded opportunity gave a number of possibilities and a new way to expand our support for writers.

This dream of wanting to bring together writers as well as readers has come true beyond measure as writers connect to us from countries like United States, United Kingdom, Canada each day to bring their stories to life.

As of this year, we are extremely delighted to provide you our website (www.inkfeathers.com) where all your queries can be resolved about our self-publishing process and latest anthologies. You can get hold of the latest updates on anthologies, events, offers, new book releases and so much more here. You can go ahead and order a book from our bookstore to get a taste of our mindful curation of stories and poems.

Inkfeathers Publishing family encourages you to really put your feelings out there in words for the world to see, in order to have a common ground to grow mutually. We are a creative platform for all those seeking literary help in terms of having their words published.

Believe us, publishing a book is not easy, but we come to a writer's rescue at each phase of having their book in print in terms of Editing, Designing, Branding, Marketing and all the other work that goes behind until you have a printed copy in your hands for Distribution. Together, it couldn't have been any easier. We will be there for you, to help you turn your manuscript into a freshly bound book that sells off the glass bookshelves.

With Love,
Inkfeathers Publishing

www.ingramcontent.com/pod-product-compliance
Lightning Source LLC
Chambersburg PA
CBHW051140130726
47988CB00005B/1915